ESCAPING THE
ILLUSION

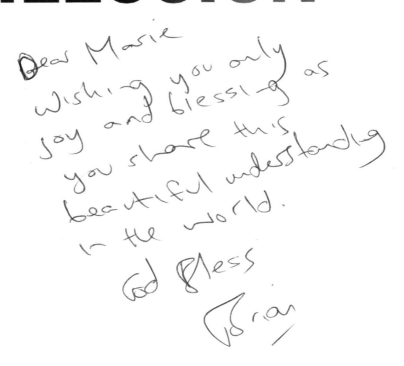

Dear Marie
Wishing you only
joy and blessing as
you share this
beautiful understanding
in the world.
God Bless
Brian

BRIAN RUBENSTEIN
WITH
TERRY RUBENSTEIN

Paperback ISBN 978-1-78705-337-3
ePub ISBN 978-1-78705-338-0
PDF ISBN 978-1-78705-339-7

Published in the UK by MX Publishing
335 Princess Park Manor, Royal Drive,
London, N11 3GX

www.mxpublishing.co.uk

Cover design by Joanna Gilbert and Brian Belanger

To

My Sons

A most remarkable group of young men

ILLUSION (noun):

- a deceptive appearance or impression.
  - a false idea or belief.

1

As is almost always the case, it started with a misunderstanding.

"Hey, time's up. It's our turn now."

The voice belonged to a young male – neither a boy, nor fully a man – in torn blue jeans and a dark hoodie. It was hard to see his whole face, but a long jagged scar, clearly visible under the bright lights of the outdoor basketball court, ran from just below his left eye to halfway down his cheek.

"Get lost. We're in the middle of a game. Go find somewhere else."

Another almost identically dressed young male stepped forward holding a basketball in his hand, his sweat dripping into the snarling fangs of a black cobra tattooed onto his bare chest. Three of his friends stopped running instantly. One, with a shaven head and a tattoo of a different snake peeking out from under his tight-fitting T-shirt, turned to his mate with the ball.

"Mo, who is this ugly dude, telling us to get off our court?" he asked.

"Dunno," answered the one called Mo, the silver stud pressed into his left ear glistening under the bright lights of the court. "But he sure is ugly Jams, I'll give you that."

The one with the jagged scar scowled, his scar becoming more pronounced as he did.

"Ugly maybe, but at least not stupid. We always play here at this time of night. Always. So like I said before, get off *our* court and get outta here."

"You want it, you come take it," said the one called Mo. There was an unmistakable snarling edge to his voice now.

Three more young men stepped out of the shadows and stood next to the one with the jagged scar.

"You serious? We'll beat the hell out of you all."

"I don't think so."

The two groups stood facing each other, only a few feet of dark green concrete and a whole lot of repressed anger between them.

It was quiet – too quiet – on that court. Other than the distant hum of the late-night traffic and the sound of chairs being stacked in the café on the other side of the chain-link fence, there was very little to hear. For a long moment, nothing happened.

Until something did. And then, in a sudden flash of blinding movement, there were limbs everywhere. A furious flurry of punches and kicks. Individual bodies seemed to meld into one seething, swirling mass of violent flesh. Curses and shouts filled the air. Nothing and no-one could be told apart. Just carnage and chaos and misunderstanding.

And then a flash of steel. And a scream. And a boy with a jagged scar lying on the ground. And blood. Lots of it.

Other boys went running, getting away as fast as they could. One ran to the thick bushes behind the court. One in the direction of the street. One into the nearby café.

2

One boy, smaller than the others, came running from the opposite direction. He had been rushing down the alley leading to the court – late, but ready to join the game now – before pulling up sharply as the sounds of violence reached his ears. Hidden in the shadows on the far side of the chain-link fence, nobody saw him frozen to the spot.

A piercing, shrill sound came slicing through the night. And then, the boy in the shadows turned and ran like the others. He had a specific destination in mind, only a hundred metres away. Reaching the underpass that connected the park to the tube station, he retreated into the safety of the darkness, taking in gulps of air. After a moment's rest, curiosity took over. Inching forward, he poked his head just beyond the wall of the tunnel.

More chaos. More running. More shouting. Then, flashing lights and white vans and grown men in uniform. Lots of them, taking the other boys – his boys – away.

Another siren then. He shrunk back into the shadows of the underpass, no longer able to see what was happening. But it was far better than the alternative. Getting caught was not an option.

Finally, after a long time, when everyone had been taken away and it was quiet again, the boy knew he must leave. He edged along the dimly lit tunnel, making his way out its far side. This route took him under the road and directly onto the opposite side of the highway. From there, he made his way the long way round back to his home, moving swiftly through the quiet streets.

But still, even in the quiet, there was misunderstanding. Lots of it.

2

Not for the first time, it was hard to concentrate on what the man in front of me was saying. I recognised some of the words – I'm not stupid you know, even if we both acted like I was: suspension, exclusion, another school ... I got it. I had been in this seat before. We'd had this conversation before, or at least something very similar to it.

This time was different, of course. I couldn't get the image and sounds of last night's carnage out of my head. The chaos, the screams, the flashing lights, the look on the boys' faces as they were being marched into the back of a copper's van in handcuffs ...

"Evan, look at me," demanded the fat, balding man on the other side of an unnecessarily large desk. "Are you hearing a word I'm saying?"

There was a brief moment of awkward silence while I considered my response. Well, maybe awkward for him, but not really for me. It was just a matter of whether I was willing to say what was really on my mind or not. That this was all their fault. The bloody school with its useless teachers, their ridiculous rules and brainless yellow and red card punishment system. I mean, who did they think they were: Premiership referees? And who was responsible for all this stupidity? The pathetic Head sitting on the other side of this bloody desk.

His bulging eyes, big shaggy-dog ears and puffy cheeks were giving me the creeps. (I know that's not very hardcore of me, but it's true – this guy looked like something of a cross between a

4

French bulldog and a porcupine with a serious asthma condition.) So I let my eyes drift around his office, until they settled on a corner of the dusty room, above and to the left of Porcu-dog's head. There was a dirty cobweb up there, and I could just make out a small creature trying to extract itself from its sticky strands. His or her – or maybe it was a trans-creature – situation looked pretty bleak. Its miniature legs were moving frantically, but this little guy – or girl – was going nowhere fast. It was trapped, big-time, and it was surely only a matter of minutes before big hairy, scary spider came back from wherever he'd been hanging out and found his dinner all ready and waiting for him. I winced inwardly at the thought.

Ah, what the hell. At this stage, I didn't have anything to lose. Or so I thought. Time to troll.

"Umm, well Mr. Porcu – I mean Mr. Porterfield, here's the thing. There's quite a big difference between hearing and listening. So yes, I was hearing you. I heard everything you said. No more skipping class. No more throwing stones over the fence onto the road during break. No more smoking on school property. And no more going off to play basketball in the park in the middle of the day."

I paused for a minute, aware that I had just uttered more words in one paragraph to the Headteacher of North West Secondary School – better known as NWSS – than I had in my previous four and a half years of internment here. I was expecting to be told off some more, but it seemed as if Porcu-dog was all puffed out – maybe the asthma was starting to act up? – because he just leaned back in his creaky black armchair, crossed his hands in an exaggerated manner over his fat stomach … and waited.

With perfect hindsight, I would have seen that I was being given just enough rope to hang myself. But hindsight doesn't exist in the now. And anyway, in my defence, I'd been majorly distracted by the trapped creature and the image of him/her/it being served up in a huge bowl of crunchy spider soup. So I ploughed ahead, my eyes still focused on the ensnared insect, oblivious to the fact that I was blindly proceeding to my own funeral even quicker than the poor creature in the web.

"And I even heard you say that I may have gone too far this time. I get it Mr. … Mr. Porterfield. But I think it's important, as I mentioned earlier, to note the difference between hearing and listening. In this instance, hearing means: I am having an audible experience of you. But listening means that I am actually absorbing and considering what you have been saying. And unfortunately, in this instance, I have not been doing that."

I paused again, quite pleased with myself and my highly banterous response. Then I made the mistake of looking, for the first time, directly at Porcu-dog's fleshy, pink face. And I didn't like what I saw. The usual exasperated expression had been replaced by something altogether more disturbing; actually, quite sinister. The Head was smiling. That caught me off-guard; I was confused. What was so funny? And then it hit me: now I *knew* I had gone too far!

"Well Mr. Evan Banksky, it seems as if you've got it all figured out. Which is probably a good thing. Because I haven't. And I – we – are not sure what to do with you. So I'm going to give us here at the school some time to think about it, some time to work out how we may be able to support you further. Or, *if* we are able to support you anymore. The rest of the week to be precise. In the meantime, as of this moment, you are officially suspended until

6

next Monday morning. And when – or should I say, if – you return, you'll be placed on the possible exclusion list for the rest of the month."

Now it was his turn to pause. And to my great disappointment, the King of Banter couldn't come up with anything to interrupt his flow.

"An email informing your mother of the suspension will be sent to her first thing tomorrow morning. And she will be required to attend a re-integration session with you next Monday. At that time, if you do choose to return to NWSS, then there are going to need to be some serious changes. And not just in your behaviour. The changes are going to need to be in you, Evan. Inside you. Because you're a smart kid. And sometimes, though not very often these days to be perfectly honest, you can be quite a likeable young man. But it's getting harder and harder to see that in you."

He paused to catch his breath – I thought for a second he was going to reach into his desk for his inhaler – and I briefly wondered if we were done here. But the big boss was just getting started.

"I know things aren't easy at home. And I know that you think you are wasting your time here. But you're not the only one who gets it, Evan. *I* get it too. I may look like some old, overweight, asthmatic guy whose main job is making the life of a Year 11 student as miserable as possible. But I've been doing this job for almost twenty years. So your troubles and your frustrations are not new to me. I've seen them all before. And I know what we can do to try to help – and what we cannot do. That part is up to you. And that's what I'd encourage you to think about over the next week. Now, just before you go, I've got something for you …"

He reached across his desk and began leafing through a pile of papers. What could he possibly be looking for? A police report of my latest classroom indiscretions? An old unpaid parking ticket he was going to blame on me now also? Free tickets to a Take That reunion gig? (Surely, not even Porcu-dog could be *that* cruel.)

"Ah, here it is," he announced, proudly holding up a crinkled A4 piece of paper. "There's a new external programme which we have just introduced into the school, especially for those students who are, shall we say, struggling a bit. It's called, uh, let me see here ... yes, it's called 'Resilience from the Inside-out.' I don't know much about it, but Mrs. Sedgeman, head of Pastoral Care, says it's all about how you think, how you feel, those kind of issues. So when we see you back here next week, I am going to expect you to attend this programme. Because without it, and I don't mean to be cruel, Evan, just stating the facts as I see them, you're not going to make it here at NWSS. Or probably at any school for that matter. So it's high time we got you some outside help from people who know what they are talking about."

Porcu-dog paused again and glanced at his watch.

"As there is just under two hours left in the school day, I am going to let you leave the premises of your own accord with immediate effect. And I highly encourage you to go straight home, rather than anywhere else where trouble might find you. Now, I've got a staff meeting, starting in a minute, so off you go..."

Just then, the way-too-loud beeping of the school bell reverberated across the room and into the corridor. It felt as if it was going off inside my head. As Porcu-dog swivelled his creaky chair away from me, I grabbed my scruffy school bag from between my feet and stood up. And as I turned away and headed out of the

8

Head's office doorway, my eyes caught a glimpse of the dirty, thin cobweb in the dusty corner. I quickly scanned it, but couldn't see the pathetic creature anywhere. Had he/she/it escaped? Or was that a whiff of big chunky insect soup being cooked that I could smell?

Approaching the rusting black school gates, I caught sight of the big round clock facing inward at the top of the school's perimeter wall. That clock ruled my life, Monday to Friday, 8:30 a.m. to 4 p.m. Though it was just a circle with two pointing hands inside, no more than eighteen inches in diameter, that clock always felt to me like it belonged in a medium-security prison. I often imagined myself looking up at it from my bunk in Wormwood Scrubs jail, knowing that if I could make it to noon, I would receive my statutory daily rations; at 2:15 p.m. I would be permitted my 15 minutes of state-sponsored exercise and at 4 p.m. I would be freed on day release – until the next morning at least. Me and a couple of mates from the school football team had even given that ugly clock a name a couple of years back: Big Alcatraz Ben.

Now it read: 2:19 p.m. Strange, because I was walking out of the premises on my own during prison time. I should have felt free, liberated, a new man. But I didn't – and I wasn't.

"Hey, where are you going?" I heard a familiar voice call out behind me.

I swivelled round to catch sight of my girl friend (please note: two words separated by a space means a girl who is actually a friend; one word means exactly what you think it does), just as she was about to head down the main corridor.

"Hey Tals," I shouted above the clamour of scores of students rushing all over the place like a colony of ants. "Been suspended. And got to attend some stupid resilience programme when I'm back. Anyway, gotta hustle off school property now and not come back for the rest of the week."

Tals turned to the girl next to her, whispered something in her ear, and came running back towards the school gates, a look of worry spreading across her face quicker than tickets sell out for an Eminem gig.

"Does this have anything to do with what went down on the basketball court in the park last night?" she asked, fixing her dark green eyes on mine and poking a loose braid of black hair away from her face.

"What you talking about?" I replied, playing dumb.

But I knew *exactly* what she was talking about. I was meant to meet the boys at the court for a late night game of ball, but had been caught up dealing with Mum and all – again. Rushing to the court, I heard a whole load of shouting and saw everyone running all over the place, so I freaked out and hid in the underpass on the other side of the fence just before the coppers arrived and started rounding everyone up. Including all my boys.

"What? You didn't hear?" asked Tals, a look of relief passing over her face as she uttered the words.

"Hear what?"

"I literally just found out myself, at the end of lunch break. Was looking everywhere to make sure everything was cool with you. Anyhow, it's concerning your gang, your boys, whatever you call them."

"What about them?" I asked, sticking wholeheartedly to the playing dumb thing.

"Seems like they got caught up in some kind of major fight late last night with that lot from the other side of the estate. I heard the police were all over the place. So am real happy to see you here now, Ev. I'm just so glad you didn't get caught up in all that."

I hated lying to Tals. I really did. But there was no choice here. Tals would have gone mental if she knew I was anywhere near that park last night when that fight went down. She'd had her issues with the gang before, and had made her views clear to me. So there was no way I was gonna tell her – *even her* – what I had seen last night by that basketball court.

"I haven't got the foggiest what you talkin 'bout Tals." A shocked expression took up residence on my face. "I ain't heard nuthin about a fight or police. Mum was having one of her downers last night, so I stayed home to keep an eye on her and make sure she didn't pop out for a refill at the off-licence. And this morning it was full-on sorting her out, getting her ready for work and everything. Then I rushed to get over to this prison on time, cause I knew I was on last warnings. Didn't do me any good in the end, though. Cause now I'm suspended and done for."

"Don't joke about this being a prison, Ev. Cause those friends of yours may be in a real jail right now."

"You're right, girl. That's real bad news for the boys. Man, this is all so screwed up."

"Yeah, it is."

Tals was quiet for a long moment as she fixed her gaze on me from a dizzy height. The fact that she was a good three inches taller than me didn't help none. I know this is not how you're meant to use the word "literally" – but I could feel her eyes boring into my head. *Literally.*

"So … suspended. Seriously? How did it get to that?"

"Basically, Porcu-dog told me I'd gone too far this time. Seems like taking Friday afternoon off to play basketball with the lads bombed. So he told me I'm done for the rest of the week. And when I get back, I'm gonna be on the exclusion list for another month."

I paused, trying my best to find a way of shifting the dynamic of this conversation. Moving from a shocked expression to a tough-guy look was a start.

"Anyhow, besides missing football training tomorrow, I don't really care. I just gotta make sure Mum doesn't find out 'bout all this. It may push her over the edge."

A pang of guilt ripped through me. Mum was having enough problems lately – all the more reason to make sure she got kept in the dark about my getting kicked outta school. I'd have to figure out what to do about the integration meeting, or whatever it was called, another time. Shrugging that worrying thought off, I got back on track with Tals.

"Porcu-dog is just a half-wit and so is everyone else around here. This place is a waste of space, know what I mean?"

Now I gave her my most charming/couldn't give a stuff smile, the one I had perfected for hours in front of the bathroom mirror. But I figured she didn't need it anyhow. Atalia Mills – Tals to me – had been by my side for the last ten years, ever since her parents had come from Jamaica to live on our little island on this

12

side of the pond. We were neighbours in the same apartment block just up the street, and in buildings with walls that thin, you got to know each other's lives better than you probably should. In Tals' case, that was cool. She was a good two years older than me, over halfway through upper 6th, but the age, height and skin colour difference had never meant nuthin to our relationship. She was, however corny it sounds, like something of a big sister to me, especially when things had gotten a bit rough with that drug-addict boyfriend of Mum's a few years back. I was only about nine then, and she had just turned eleven, but she was always there looking out for me. And when you're nine years old and feeling pretty alone in the world, that counts for a lot. We'd been real tight ever since.

But recently, Tals had been acting a bit strange. Almost as if the stuff that had always bothered her – her parents' constant fighting, her weight (she was a size 8, so I really didn't get that), the stress of getting through A-levels – didn't seem to get to her so much anymore. Since I had been confused by this change – remember, I *know* this girl – I had casually asked her the other day what the story was.

"Hey Tals, why you acting so chilled lately? You've got that major English exam in a couple of days, and you don't seem stressed out at all. That's not like you. What's going on with you?"

"Yeah, I know," she had replied with a weird kind of look. "It's kinda cool how stress-free I'm feeling. This book I've been reading has really helped. It's about how all the stuff from the outside world can't be responsible for how you feel. Not other people, not other things. Not even English A-level. I'm telling you Ev, this is good stuff. You really need to check it out."

13

"Go easy, girl. You know I'm not into that kinda stuff. And when's the last time I read anything besides the football results? But happy to hear it's helping you with the stress levels. Just don't go all weird on me, K?"

That conversation was a few days ago. But if I thought the new Tals was going to roll over fast, I was about to get a rude awakening. She was taking no prisoners this afternoon, even less so than Porcu-dog himself.

"You know what, I *don't* know what you mean Evan," said my friend, shaking her head in a way that told me that she really wasn't interested in my 'they can go stuff themselves' attitude. "This school's got it problems, I get that. I should know, I've been here for almost six years already. But Porterfield is no half-wit; he's just not a cool guy. And you can't blame him for pulling the plug. That's all on you. How many times can you just skive off and think he's going to let it go?"

I started to open my mouth, another banterous response on the tip of my tongue, but something made me stop. As much as I didn't want to admit it – and for sure, wouldn't in public, not even to Atalia Mills – it was not entirely out of the question that she may have a point. I guess, all things considered, I hadn't exactly given Porcu-dog that many options.

"And listen Ev, one other thing," Tals added, just when I thought we were done here. "You really need to think about hanging out with those boys. They're big trouble – last night sure proves that – and I really wish you'd keep your distance from them.

Cause that kind of trouble gets worse, not better, know what I mean?"

I didn't say anything in response. Tals had touched a nerve – and she knew it. My hanging around with the boys from the estate – Jams, Mo, Jez and D-Von – all mates a couple of years older than me who were long done with school – had been the source of the only proper argument I had ever remembered Tals and I having, just a week or so back. And it had ended with me defending my boys, which Tals was having none of. In other words, it hadn't ended well.

"I've gotta run or I'm gonna be late for English, Ev. Let's speak more about all this later. But you should read this book I've been telling you about. It's been really helping me, especially since my Nan died, and it'll help you too. I'm telling you."

"Ah come on Tals," I moaned. "You know I don't do books."

"Just read it! It's short and it's simple. Even a knucklehead like you can manage it. Anyhow, what else are you going to be doing for the next seven days while you've been kicked outta school? Here, take it."

And with that, just about the only person in the world – besides Mum – who I really trusted, reached into her school bag, pulled the book out and thrust it into my hand. Without saying another word, she turned on her heel and rushed off to English.

I looked down at the title and couldn't suppress a groan: *What If You Already Have Everything You Need Inside of You?*

Man, this girl really was going all weird on me!

3

Shoving the useless book into my backpack, I headed though the gates, pulling my thin winter gloves over my hands as I did. Finally free of the all-powerful gaze of Big Alcatraz Ben and Porcu-dog's ridiculous rules, my legs knew just where to take me. And it wasn't in the direction of home. A mere 200 metres from the school gates was the entrance to the local park. And a further 100 or so steps from there was a little frequented corner of it – at least little frequented by the middle-class moms taking their Cavalier King Charles Spaniels for a mid-morning walk, or the foreign au-pairs taking those same moms' darling little babies out in their strollers, all snuggled up in a forlorn attempt to immunise them from the worst of the vicious London weather.

The truth is that its good news not many people are interested in our corner on the other side of the old basketball court, just before the thick line of bushes that form the outer perimeter of that end of the park. That's where we hang out on the pair of chipped wooden benches which the local authorities had somewhat randomly plonked down on top of some haphazardly laid out concrete a whole lot of years ago. Actually, we – and those who had preceded us – can take a fair amount of credit for the underpopulated usage of this small piece of real estate. It's amazing to see the effect that half a dozen teenagers "from the wrong side of the tracks" can have on the majority of the local population. A plume of cigarette smoke surrounding us, lots of raucous laughing and the occasional wolf-whistling when a pretty girl happens to pass by, is all that we need to ensure that the moms and dogs, the au-pairs and babies, and even the well-built middle-aged male joggers, give us a wide berth. It is our spot – we know it, they know it – and we like it that way.

As the youngest of the gang, I am the only one still in regular school, with all its rules and restrictions. Knowing that the other lads had far fewer limitations, I was pretty sure where I would find them, assuming they had been let out of lock-up by now. Especially as this was exactly where I had found them at the same time on Friday, when I decided to take off from school a couple of hours early and create a slightly longer weekend for myself. It was just my luck that Miss Mara, the Year 11 Head of Science, happened to be walking through that part of the park on her way to the tube station at exactly that moment. Hence, how I landed up in Porcu-dog's office staring at spider webs by Monday afternoon.

But as I approached from the Queens Road side, I was struck by the empty benches ahead of me. *Not serious. Maybe they scored some weed and gone for a quick smoke*, I figured as I ambled ahead.

I knew exactly where they would go. There's a path right behind the bench, which leads into the thicker bushes. After about a dozen steps or so, you hit a massive fallen tree that brings the path to an abrupt end. At that point, it looks as if there is nowhere else to go. But if you scramble over the old tree and are prepared to tolerate loads of unruly brambles and overgrown thorn branches scraping against your legs, you can slog right into the densest part of the scrub. Another few steps and you come to a little clearing where a cluster of dead logs are strewn across the ground. A long time ago, the logs had been arranged into a rough circle, creating an instant mini-amphitheatre. Once, while we were passing around a bottle of Smirnoff and heatedly debating the merits of UFC v WWE, someone – I think it may have been Jez – aptly christened our secret, semi-round spot, *The Ring*. The name stuck. It even ended up becoming the name for the WhatsApp group the five of us shared: da Ring Gang.

It was the perfect place to hang out, smoke stolen cigarettes and mess about. No one could see us from outside the clearing and anyone approaching would always be heard blundering through the thick undergrowth long before they reached us. And if we *were* unexpectedly disturbed, there was a great little hiding place inside the smallest of the logs at the back of The Ring, where you could quickly stash your contraband if you had to. The old piece of mossy wood was thin and hollow in the middle, and its opening was almost invisible to the eye, unless you bent down on your knees and knew exactly where to look.

But when I reached The Ring, there was no sign of them. Maybe it was going to take longer than I thought for them to get springed from jail.

So I did a quick 180 and was about to head back the way I'd come, when something glinted in the shadows. I knew straight away where it was coming from. Taking three short steps towards the smallest log, I bent down and plunged my hand into the entrance of our secret spot. My fingertips touched something hard. Even with my gloves on, I could tell it was cold and made of steel. Had one of the boys accidentally left a lighter behind? My hand moved down the object, seeking purchase. It was definitely not a lighter. I felt a broadening, into some kind of handle. And when I pulled the object out, a thick black handle gave way to a gleaming, razor-sharp blade, about six inches long. I was holding a knife. And worse, faint smudges of dark red were clearly visible on the blade, even in the shadows of the bushes.

18

For a long moment, I just sat there on my haunches, a host of questions flooding through my head. What was a knife doing in our secret spot in The Ring? How had it got there? Who had put it there? And most disturbingly, what were those faint streaks of red on its blade? No good answers came to mind.

And then, another question, the big one perfect for this precise moment: what do I do with this knife now? It didn't take long to answer that one. Thrusting my arm as far into the log as far as I could, I pushed the blade right up against the far interior wall of the hollowed out piece of wood. Then I backed up and tried looking into the log from a few different angles. I couldn't see the knife from any of them, not even the flash of glinting steel that had attracted my attention in the first place. It was safely stored away inside our secret spot, and wouldn't be discovered by anyone, anytime soon.

I stood up then, looked round The Ring one more time, and began trekking back through the thick bushes. Emerging into the sunlight, I made a beeline for the park exit, pulling my hoodie tight and lengthening my stride – not that easy for a short guy – as I did. It had suddenly occurred to me that I needed to intercept Mum on her way home from work and get hold of her phone. There was no way she could find out about my suspension in the state she was in, so a quick deleting of any emails from NWSS was an immediate priority. Then I could get on with the task of finding my boys – even if it meant a visit to jail.

My route took me past the local park café – or the caf – as we called it.

"Hey, Evan," I heard a high-pitched, familiar voice call out. Just my luck. "You got a second, mate?"

19

I looked up to see the friendly smile and enormous fame of Monroe, the 6 foot 4 chef, standing in the entrance to the caf, a small checked dishtowel hanging out of one giant paw, a big black dustbin bag suspended from the other. I glanced behind him into the caf's brightly lit interior. The small place was empty, save for an old lady with grey hair tied back in a long ponytail and a black walking stick resting against the table she was eating at. She was sitting in the corner booth enjoying what seemed to be a steaming plate of bubbling shakshuka. (Keith, the café's owner, always maintains that his shakshuka is the best anywhere west of Cairo. The rest of us figure it's maybe the best anywhere west of Edgware Road.)

I have to say, I'm not a huge fan of restaurants or their employees. They always seem to regard people of my age – and look – as something of an inconvenience at best, and a major nuisance at worst. On a good day, they barely look at you while taking your order and serve your food more or less cooked. On a bad day, knowing there is no chance of a tip and a big chance of some kind of hassle in their establishment, they'll chuck you out and tell you that if you come back anytime soon, they'll call the coppers.

But Monroe is different. And not just because he comes from the Philippines, has a huge curly brown moustache straight outta the 1970's, and always wears a way too tiny white apron that doesn't have a chance in hell of covering even a small percentage of a frame that is well larger than that of the average Premiership centre back. Monroe is a gentle giant; the real deal. One bear-hug and he could crush half a dozen of my ribs in double-quick time with those two huge hammy arms of his. But I've never seen him angry or heard him raise his voice, not even the time we were horsing around in the caf with a basketball and one of us – I genuinely can't remember if it was intentional or an accident – hurled it straight through the large, all glass drinks dispenser on the near side of the counter. After what seemed like a full 45-minute half, plus injury time of complete silence, Monroe simply pulled one of those old-fashioned looking wooden brooms out from the cupboard behind him and wordlessly began to sweep the jagged shards into large piles, spaced at regular intervals. Three of the boys had done a runner by then, bolting out the door without even a glance behind them, but me and Jez stayed rooted to the spot, transfixed by the wide arc of Monroe's broom as it brushed across the restaurant floor. After a few moments, the big Filipino finally looked up and stared straight at us.

"Go on now," he said, his voice level, though clearly a pitch lower than usual. "You better get out of here before Keith gets back," motioning towards the caf's door with the broom.

In a flash, we were out the door, streaking across the park's muddy pitches in pursuit of our mates.

But now wasn't the time to shoot the breeze with Monroe. Finding out where the boys were at meant that I had some urgent business to attend to, so I wasn't about to respond to his "you got a second, mate?" request by joining him inside for a casual cup of coffee.

"Under a bit of time pressure here, Monroe. Can I catch you later?"

Monroe's tone suddenly turned serious, "Didn't you hear what happened?"

"Hear what?" I asked, playing dumb again. This was becoming a habit.

"There was a big fight down here last night, just over by the basketball court," answered Monroe, pointing towards the fenced-in concrete rectangle on the far side of the caf. I looked up to see our court and its surrounding chain-link fence completely enclosed in yellow police tape. It looked just like one of those crime scenes you see in the movies. Then it hit me: it *was* a crime scene – and this wasn't a movie.

"It was while we were closing up; I was the last one here," continued Monroe in a strained voice. "Your boys were right in the middle of it and so were some other ones I didn't much recognise. It didn't sound too serious to start with – some shouting and swearing, but that was all. But then someone must have pulled a knife. Cause there was an almighty scream and when I stuck my head out the door, some kid I didn't recognise was bleeding all over the ground right inside the gates to the court. Boys were running and yelling all over the place. The next thing you know, a whole load of police showed up in one of those huge white vans."

Monroe paused for a moment, a look of relief spreading across his face. It reminded me of the same one I had just seen on Tals' face, not twenty minutes earlier.

"I'm not sure where you were at last night, Evan, but I'm really glad it wasn't here. Thank God you didn't get caught up in that whole thing, mate."

"Yeah, me too," I mumbled. "So … d'ya know what happened to the boys?" I managed to ask, doing my best to keep the slight tremble I felt in my chest out of my voice.

"Not sure exactly. I saw one of them – it was too dark to tell who – running in the direction of them bushes, where you all hang out the whole time. Someone else ran towards the street. And Jez came running straight in here. He was white as a ghost, shouting at me that someone was dying and we had to call an ambulance real quick. So I took out my phone, called 999 and told them what happened. The police arrived first; the paramedics a few minutes later. And the coppers rounded everyone up pretty quick, including Jez. It turned out one of the boys – I think it was the one you call D-Von – was just standing and staring in the middle of the basketball court, like he was paralysed or something. It took them a bit longer to find that big one with the tattoo on his neck, but they caught him trying to climb over the other side of the park, past the benches where you …"

Monroe stopped abruptly, mid-sentence.

"You know what Evan, I've already said too much. It was really confusing in the dark anyways. And the police asked me not to discuss the details of what I saw with anyone. But all I can tell you, is that last I saw, they were bundling all the boys into the back of that big white van. I bet they took them off to jail, or juvenile detention or whatever you call those places these days. Anyhow, my guess is that they are in some serious trouble this time and you may not be hearing from them for a while. Knife crime is a big deal in this city – you know that. But that doesn't mean I'm not worried about them."

"Yeah, me too," I mumbled again. "But one question: do you know how the lad who was bladed is doing?" I asked.

"I dunno mate. But it looked serious. The paramedics came and were stuffing bandages all over him, trying to stop the blood.

It was everywhere. And then they put him in the back of the ambulance and took off. I ended up being busy with the police for a long time because they wanted to take a witness statement. But the truth is – besides all the running and yelling and panic – I didn't really see anything."

Yeah, me too. This time though, I didn't even mumble it. Just kept that thought all to myself.

It hit me then that this was massively more serious than I had thought. Tals hadn't mentioned anything about a lad being seriously hurt. I guess she hadn't heard that part of the story yet – or it wasn't known beyond Monroe and the coppers. I had just figured that my mates were in a fight that I had gotten a little out of hand, which explained all the coppers getting on top of things so fast. But a stabbing? In the park? That *was* a big deal.

And then my own blood went cold. *The stashed knife in The Ring.* With streaks of red on it. Was there any chance that was just a wild coincidence? Unlikely, mate. Because right then, I had a recollection of something that happened while goofing around on the benches down by The Corner a month or so ago. We were shooting the breeze about what we would do if we ever got in a serious fight. It had become a more common topic lately, as there had already been some run-ins with those yobs who lived on the other side of the estate, led by the big ugly one with the massive scar running down his face. And Mo had said something like how he had got himself a little protection down at the high street hardware store a short while ago for just that reason. When one of the other boys had asked him what kind of protection, he just smiled an evil smile and replied, "A knife. A sharp one." Jams cracked a crude joke just then, and the conversation changed direction. And we didn't talk about it again.

"Listen Evan," said Monroe, interrupting my private thoughts. "I can see this is tough for you. I know you think they are your friends. But these boys aren't good for you, mate. Never mind that they've all dropped out of school and hang around this empty park all day doing nothing but playing basketball, making fun of people and throwing stones at squirrels. They were looking for trouble – especially those two big lads with the snake tattoos – and it was just a matter of time before it found them. I just hope that boy who got hurt will be OK. And I'm so glad you weren't here when it all went down last night. You're a good kid, and you're better off staying away from that lot."

A sharp gust of wind brought a scattering of dead leaves blowing in through the open doorway just then. Monroe took a step towards me, the checked dishtowel resting in his giant hand like a miniature serviette.

"You know what, it doesn't take a rocket scientist to see that it's really quiet in here this afternoon. So why don't you take a seat and I'll I fry you up a plate of those chilli-fries I know you like," he offered. "An early dinner, on the house."

I hesitated for a moment, unaccustomed to anybody offering me something for nothing. And just then, the old woman with the grey ponytail huddled in the corner called out in Monroe's direction, "Excuse me young man, but have you got any Tabasco sauce I can sprinkle over this shakshuka here?"

"Coming right up," answered Monroe. He spun away from me to grab a small brown bottle off the shelf behind him, which was when I took my chance. I was in such a hurry, I didn't even glance behind me.

"Hey Evan," I heard Monroe calling from the open doorway, "Come on, it'll just take me a couple of minutes to get those fries …"

But I didn't hear the rest. Or maybe I didn't listen. Either way, I was already off, racing across the rolling fields of the park. There was no time to waste. Because once I had made the detour to take care of Mum's emails, I needed to go find my mates something urgent.

4

The man in the loose-fitting dark blue uniform stared at the list of names in front of him. Was it possible? Could it really be him?

He picked up the thin file and turned it over slowly, carefully examining its contents as if there was more to be discovered than the single piece of paper contained within. There wasn't. Just the list of five names. He scanned them again, his eyes resting on the final one.

What were the chances ...?

He leaned back into his chair, closed his eyes and pinched the bridge of his nose, just above the top of his old school wire-framed glasses.

The memories came flooding back to him instantly. A vicious argument. Children crying. Bright lights. An earth-shattering explosion. Groaning and shrieking and screaming filling the night air. Glass and debris and blood. Carnage and chaos. Death and devastation. And then ... darkness. For a long time.

Opening his eyes, the man in the uniform considered what to do next. He was too close to this, he realised. It was a decision that required broader shoulders than his own. With renewed conviction, he picked up his phone and quickly found the number he was looking for. Though his mind was spinning, his hands were steady as he typed.

I think I found him. He may be in real trouble. High risk. Permission requested to breach conventional protocols and employ special contingencies. Advise how to proceed ASAP.

Though it was already extremely late, the reply came immediately.

Permission granted. Proceed with caution. But proceed nonetheless. Let us not lose another.

He nodded as he read. It was the response he had expected; he had hoped for. And then he read the final words, and a thin smile came to his lips.

And remember. It's an illusion. All of it. Always.

5

"Get out of here! Go on, get out!"

I was about to turn into the alley leading up to our apartment building when I heard the commotion on the other side of Hendon Road.

"Please, just one more." I winced at the unmistakeable desperation in the woman's shrill voice. "Last flutter. I promise. This will be the big one."

"Hey, Ann. Or Annabel. Or whatever your name is. I'm not going to tell you again. Sod off! And don't come back until you've got the twenty g's you owe me."

I could see a short, stocky, mean-looking man in a sharp navy suit starting to close the shopfront door in the woman's face. But sticking out a foot, she jammed it into the door and wouldn't move despite the obvious pressure of the hard metal frame on her frail body.

"Vic, I'm begging you. Don't kick me out. Please …."

Dodging a speeding black van and completely ignoring the flashing red on the pedestrian crossing, I sprinted across the street, coming to a halt in front of the neon 'Money Back as a Free Bet on All Losers' flashing sign.

Grabbing her slender shoulders, I turned the woman towards me, causing her to stumble slightly and relinquish her position in the doorway. She was about to object – her mouth opened and closed without saying anything – before she registered who I was.

"Evan, what you doing here?" she finally asked in surprise, her short bob of blonde hair swinging back and forth as she tried to make sense of the situation. "Why aren't you in school?"

Before I could answer, the plonker in the suit, taking advantage of the distraction, flung open the door and jabbed a fat finger in my direction. "Listen mate, you need to get her outta here. And she needs to give me my twenty grand. I'm getting tired of waiting. I'll give her till the end of the month, and that's it. Otherwise things are gonna get a whole lot more ugly for her. You know what I mean?"

But he didn't wait for my response. The door slammed shut with a thud, while the two of us were left standing on the exposed pavement, a huge picture of a pitch black racehorse streaking across the turf staring back at us. A flood of thoughts – confused, angry, desperate –filled my head. But when she suddenly started to weep, my heart felt like it was going to shatter into a thousand tiny pieces.

"What am I going to do? What I am going to do? What am I going to do?" she repeated, over and over between her wretched sobs. The tears were causing the cheap mascara to run down the sides of her cheeks, creating messy streaks of black on her pale face, but she was oblivious to the pedestrians staring at her – at us both – as they hurried on past. The matching brown top and trousers uniform she wearing offered little protection from the cold wind that was blowing through us both.

"Come on," I said, finally breaking my gaze off from the racehorse and gently taking her by the hand. A quick change of plan formed in my mind. I'd have to first take care of this situation before getting on with the main job at hand – finding out what was up with my boys.

"Let's get you home and fix you a nice cup of hot tea. How does that sound, Mum?"

Fortunately – or maybe unfortunately – our flat is only a cigarette butt flick away from the high street betting shop. Even so, given the state she was in, it wasn't easy to get Mum across the road and up the little alley that leads to the back of our eleven storey council flat building. Her loud sobbing had now given way to a dull moaning, but the words she kept repeating hadn't changed:

"What am I going to do? What am I going to do?"

"We'll figure it out, Mum," I said without much conviction, more to myself than to her.

What were we going to do? She owed the bookie twenty big ones. And I knew that meant that minus what we had right now in our current account in the bank, we were exactly £19,752 short.

Well, at least Mum still had the new job at the coffee shop next to the tube station run by her distant cousin Jamie. *Or did she?*

"Mum," I asked tentatively, as we arrived at the back entrance of our ludicrously named 1960s looking building, Sweet Orchard Place. "Why aren't you at work? Are you on a break? We gotta get you back there quick. Come on, I'll walk you over there now. It's only a few minutes if we cut through the alley."

I was holding Mum by the arm, but now I felt her full weight against me. This close, I could smell the gin on her breath from last night's session, not to mention the ever-present odour of

31

stale cigarettes. Not a great combination under any circumstances. Still, I had done my best to get her cleaned up and in some kind of shape for work before I left for school this morning. But now I was beginning to doubt whether that operation had been met with any success.

"Forget it Ev," Mom sighed, as she fished around in her jeans pocket for a smoke. "I'm not going back there."

"What do you mean not going back Mum?"

I kept pushing the UP button repeatedly, but though it was lit, the lift was taking an eternity to come down. Most likely jammed again somewhere between the 7th and 8th floors. No surprise there.

"Damm, no more fags," said Mum, ignoring my question. "Evvy, be a doll and nip round to the off-licence to buy me a new pack."

"I will Mum, later. But first tell me what happened at work this morning."

"OK," she said wearily, "There was this guy in a pin-striped suit who ordered a skinny latte. I know him; he comes in most mornings about that time with a posh briefcase and orders the same drink. So I made him the latte. Then, when it comes to pay, he tells me he actually ordered a cappuccino. 'Sorry but I think there's a mistake here. Would you mind making me a cappuccino instead?' he says. *Would I mind?* 'Of course I mind,' I told him. 'You asked for a latte, like you always do, so that's what I gave you.' Then I heard Jamie pipe up from behind me, 'No problem sir, we'll get you a cappuccino straight away. I'll bring it to where you're sitting. Would you like chocolate sprinkles on that?'

32

"And then Jamie whispers to me, 'Just remember, the customer is *always* right.'

"Can you believe the nerve of that guy? I mean, if you ask for a latte, you get a latte! So I told Jamie if he can't support his employees like a manager should, then I can't work in a place like this. Don't matter that he's family and all. So I quit – right there and then. Didn't even wait for my shift wages. Just chucked off my apron, grabbed my coat and walked right out the door. The business guy hadn't even got his damn drink yet."

Mum had finished her story. I sighed. This lift wasn't coming any quicker than that poor man was getting a skinny cappuccino from my mother, the now ex-barista. Ergo, it wasn't coming at all. We were going to have to climb eleven storeys – just what I needed with my mother in her hungover, smokeless, outraged, unemployed, massively in debt state.

"Come on Mum, let's get you upstairs and get that kettle on."

Just under an hour later, I collapsed onto our single worn couch. It was plonked in the middle of what would – in a parallel universe – be called a living room. I'd changed out of my school uniform and chucked it in the back of my battered wardrobe. Wouldn't be needing that for a while, if at all, I figured. And I had finally settled Mum down, though not until I had ran down to the off-licence and decreased our disposable income by a further £9.91 spent on twenty Marlboro Golds. Still, it had taken more than just a cup of English breakfast tea and fresh smokes to do the job. Fortunately, after a brief search, I was able to locate an old box of anti-anxiety tablets in the medicine cabinet that the GP had prescribed some while back when Mum was going through a rough spell after she had broken up with that weird Gothic guy. So between the meds and the after-effects of her hangover, Mum didn't need much convincing to get back into bed and write off the rest of the day.

That gave me the perfect the opportunity to get hold of Mum's phone. Applying my high-tech skills to a delicate situation, I got real clever and figured out how to block all incoming emails from the school. Falling back onto the threadbare sofa cushions, I breathed a sigh of relief. Now I just had to play it cool for the rest of the week, giving Mum the impression that it was business as usual down at NWSS. It would also give me loads of time to think up a killer lie to explain to Porcu-dog why Mum would be unable to attend Monday morning's meeting. Maybe an elderly aunt up in Scotland who had just suffered a stroke or something ….

Next, I fed and watered Brock, named after the legendary UFC Heavyweight Champion and multiple times WWE World Champ, the Beast Incarnate, Brock Lesnar. The Beast is the world's coolest dog, hands down. Admittedly, he ain't much to look at: at least four different breeds of canine appear to have been involved in his creation. The result is a somewhat unseemly blend of brown, black and grey colouring across a long, skinny torso, culminating in a scrunched up neck, two sharply pointed ears and a short black snout that never seems to quite fit the rest of his body. But it is the eyes that set super-dog apart: deep black pools that can cause a man to quiver in his boots if you don't turn your gaze away fast enough. Those eyes are the key: they transform Brock from a nervous-looking rescue dog with a tough past, to a Beast with a confident present and a dominant future. Or at least that is our story, and we are sticking to it! Now, while I waited for the familiar sound of Mum's snoring to emerge from her bedroom, and with the Beast-dog happily splayed out on his stomach by my side, I could finally relax and think.

Just about the only thing I remember ever having learned in a PSHE lesson – that stands for Personal, Social and Health Education or something like that – was the idea of writing a list of what was going on in your life. The informal education guy who was teaching the class had said it was a good way of compartmentalising things or something like that. Not having much else to do, and figuring I had nothing to lose, I ripped a piece of paper out of a very little used school notebook and drew a line down the middle dividing the page into two columns. The list didn't take long to write – here is what I came up with in less than ten minutes:

What I knew about my life before this morning	What I found out since this morning
I am an only child and have never known who my father is	I'm suspended from school for the rest of the week
Mum drinks way too much and hasn't had a proper boyfriend for years	Mum doesn't have a job anymore
We have £248 in our bank account; £12.55 in my money belt and no credit card	Mum owes a mean bookie 20 grand and has till the end of the month to pay it back
We live in a run-down council flat and don't own a car or basically anything of value	My 4 mates are in jail and there is a knife with red streaks on it lying in a log in The Ring

I have never met my only living grandparent who has been living in Australia for the last 20 years	Tals, my only other proper friend, is real annoyed with me for getting kicked out of school

I stared at my list for a long moment, and then I wrote the following across the bottom of the page in big capital letters:

CONCLUSION: MY LIFE IS A COMPLETE MESS!

After another moment, I added one last sentence:

AND THERE IS NOTHING I CAN DO ABOUT IT!!!

6

The man in the loose-fitting dark blue uniform banged on the glass table in front of him, demanding attention. An image of a teenage boy appeared on the small plasma screen just to the right of his head.

"Settle down. One final item," he announced in a deep, gravelly voice. "Local lad; known by the name, Evan Banksky. Fifteen-years-old. Attends a local secondary school. Lives with his single mother. Whereabouts of father unknown. No siblings. Approx 5 foot 5, dark hair, blue eyes, medium build. Proceeds almost nowhere without his dog, which goes by the name of Brock; species unknown... looks like a rescue one."

The man in the uniform – the only person present wearing one – glanced round the dimly lit room. He waited, while the rest took a long look at the subject in the photo.

"We have concerns about him," the speaker continued after a while, the sheen of his freshly shaven head shining underneath the sole fluorescent light hanging from the ceiling. "So he's going to need extra surveillance. Those of you operating in the NW4 area, keep a close eye. Specially you lot," he said, pointedly jabbing a bony finger in the direction of five different individuals spread out across the room.

"That's it. Any questions?"

A hand shot up from one of the rows near the back. It belonged to a tall man in dreadlocks with eyes glowing a very deep kind of green.

"What kind of concerns?"

"Significant concerns." Another long, pause. Only the humming of the fluorescent light could be heard. "With implications."

A different voice came out of the shadows to the right. The face it belonged to was almost entirely obscured by an enormous, wild grey beard.

"Since when do we single out individuals for additional scrutiny? What's so special about this kid?"

Tension flooded the room. The man in the dark uniform stared straight ahead, his deep brown eyes boring into the questioner like daggers. When he finally answered, his voice was even more gravelly than before.

"Orders from above. No more details necessary. This one's on a need-to-know basis. We done here?"

Another hand went up, this one near the front.

"What about our policy of non-interference? Why the sudden shift in strategy?" asked an older woman with a Mediterranean sounding accent. She was wearing a dishevelled woolly hat and there were five or six bags strewn around her chair.

"Which part of need-to-know do you not understand? He's important to us. Engage without interfering. That is the instruction. Clear?"

He fixed the woman in the woolly hat with a hard stare from behind his old school, wire-framed glasses.

"Clear," she finally responded.

After a while, the man in uniform spoke again.

"This is coming directly from the Chair herself. So no more questions. We got a job to do; now let's go do it."

Chair-legs scraped against the hard wooden floor. The room began clearing out.

"And remember," came the gravelly voice from the front, rising above the noise. The scraping stopped. He always finished the meeting this way, but even so, what he was about to say never failed to send chills down the spine of even the most hardened operators.

"It's an illusion. All of it. Always."

7

The noise coming from Mum's bedroom told me she wasn't going anywhere fast. The Xanax or whatever that pill was called, was doing its job. That gave me the opening to go find cuz Jamie and ask him to give Mum her job back before he went and hired someone else. Meanwhile, Brock had jumped off the couch and begun clawing at my leg, the genius signal we had worked out when he needed to tell me he had to do his thing. So I grabbed his black nylon lead, snatched my house key and threw my grey hoodie on. Passing the full length mirror with the big crack running through it next to the front door, I stopped for a minute and decided to do what very few male teenagers have done throughout the course of human history: I looked at myself in the mirror.

And I wasn't quite sure I liked what I saw. On the one hand, starting from the top, I thought my light blue eyes were pretty cool – at least that's what Mum always said – especially when set against my dark, wavy hair. (I had so far resisted the temptation to have one of those 'special cuts'; Jez had one some time back which we all still ribbed him about months later.) On the negative side, my nose was way too big for my regular-sized face; and, to my eternal dismay, just a few weeks before my sixteenth birthday, a ridiculous amount of blotchy spots had recently taken up residence on the rest of it. I needed to do something about that – fast.

Casting my eye further downwards revealed similarly mixed results. I had worked pretty hard to get my upper body into decent shape: my pecs were solid, their form well-defined underneath my loose-fitting hoodie. Ditto for my bis, tris and abs. Mum had bought me a £14 a month under 16s membership for my last birthday at the discount gym on the far side of the estate and the results were starting to show. But I couldn't do much about being – and, how can I say this in a way that doesn't offend approximately 30% of the male population of the world? – vertically challenged. And the bad news was that I hadn't made much progress in recent months. Actually, I was starting to fear that my growth spurt had ended not long after it had started.

My baggy blue jeans were ripped just above the left knee, the tear running almost all the way down to my sharp looking green and black Nikes – £17.99 Boxing Day sale at Sports Direct. This brought me to the bottom of the mirror. That was it, nowhere else to go.

Deciding it was time for a quick rating, I gave myself a 6/10. Not great, but at least not a fail. Only problem was that it was hard to see much room for improvement, at least not until they made radiation a legal means to kill those damn acne spots. I flexed a quick bicep (hey, if a teenager can't pose for a minute in the privacy of his own company, then when can he?) but then Brock lunged at the lead, reminding me that he had business to get on with.

"OK, OK, I know. We gotta get going. Let's hit the road, cool dog."

And with a final glance towards Mum's bedroom, I pulled the door closed and headed straight down those eleven flights of stairs; there was no way Brock was going to be able to wait for that pathetic excuse for a lift.

Once downstairs with Brock, I decided to first walk back to The Corner before heading over to the coffee shop to talk to cuz Jamie.

Maybe the boys had lucked out and got an early release or something. Anyhow, since chasing terrified little squirrels all round The Corner – actually the whole freakin park – was Brock's Number One favourite thing to do, I figured I'd kill two birds with one rock, or whatever that old expression was.

No such luck. I could see from a hundred yards out that the benches were still empty. I called out just in case they were hanging out in The Ring. "Hey, boys! You in there?" But there was no sign – or sound – of them anywhere.

That didn't stop super-dog from staking his manliness all over the decaying wood of the bench with what looked to me like an overly dramatic leg-lift. I smiled: that's *my* dog, learning from the master poser himself. And then, suddenly spotting some poor little creature with a bushy tail and a serious nut obsession, Brock was off, tearing across the fields and bringing light to the world as only a dog can.

I did a full 360, scanning the whole park to make sure I hadn't missed the boys anywhere. But the place was pretty desolate, not unusual on a late afternoon winter's day. So I sat down on the bench and pulled out my smartphone, hoping that would bring better news. Any news.

I was just scrolling through the local news feed when a commotion on the far side of the tree-line caught my attention. Next thing I knew, Brock came tearing out of the bushes, with a jet black Staffordshire Bull Terrier hard on his tail. I whistled – my high pitched dog whistle puts any of those fancy dog-walkers in Hampstead Heath to shame – and Brock instantly cut a major change in direction and headed straight for me at super-dog pace. The Staff came too, and I have to admit, I was seriously impressed with how she was able to keep up with The Beast. A very tall dude in dreadlocks emerged from the trees and came ambling after them.

When the dogs reached the bench, I put my hand out to pet the Staff and establish from the outset that we were friends, not foes. She dug that, and jumping up for a closer look, sprayed a good dose of dog-slobber on my jeans leg. Laughing, I pushed her down gently, telling her to be cool. She was good with that, and seconds later, was off again, her and Brock having spotted another poor squirrel trying to make a run for the nearest oak tree.

"Hey, Maddie, come here girl," shouted Dreadlocks Dude. But his dog had squirrel-meal on her mind, and she wasn't going to change it in a hurry. Certainly not while Brock was her prospective lunch companion!

"Sorry about that man," he said as he approached the bench. "Mads can be pretty excitable sometimes. You OK?"

"Yeah, sure, no problem," I replied.

"Mind if I sit down for a bit? Looks like them two may be out hunting for a while," he said, gesturing with his head towards the two dark specks galloping with abandon across the grass, while seating his large frame down on the bench.

"Uh … sure," I said, which was a pretty brainless thing to say, considering he was sitting already.

The dogs were almost on the other side of the park now, but we could hear their excited barking and yelping. We both sat there for a while, listening to the joyous sound of two happy hounds having the time of their lives.

"Amazing creations," he said. "Dogs, that is. See how quickly they connect to each other. No judgment. No insecurity. No pre-conditioned thinking. Just two animals free in the present moment, in the now, experiencing this beautiful world. They got nothing on it. Just having a feeling, an experience, nothing more."

"Uh, yeah, I guess so," I mumbled, only cause I didn't know what else to say. *Who was this guy? The Dalai Lama?*

Another minute or so passed. The dogs were still yelping around the base of a huge oak tree, their quarry far above, safe in the canopy of its branches. Dreadlocks Dude hadn't moved a muscle since he'd sat down.

"Us humans, we get it all confused," he announced suddenly. "We don't get how the system works. But they get it. We got a lot to learn from them mutts."

There was something strange about his accent, familiar and yet foreign sounding at the same time. And he had this strange lilt in his voice, as if he was reciting one of those posh poems Mrs. Dicken was always making us read in her English class.

"Here's the thing," he said, as if we were already having a conversation, which definitely wasn't my take on things. "We live in a world of thought. And I mean Thought with a capital 'T'. From the cradle to the grave, all we are ever living in is the world of Thought. Always have been. Always will be."

He turned to look at me. And the first thing I noticed – you couldn't miss it – were his eyes. They were a kind of green you almost never see. Against his dark skin, they almost glowed. He fixed those glowing green eyes on me and held my gaze. I didn't know what to say, or where to look. But I was getting pretty freaked out.

"Uh, listen mate, I don't really know what you're going on about. I'm just hanging out on this bench, watching my dog, trying to figure some stuff out."

"Nah, I get that man. Sorry, didn't mean to bother you. It's just that when Mads does that slobbering thing, I know straight away she's made a friend. And I could see straight away that you could do with a friend. Figuring out stuff on your own ain't that easy. Believe you me, I know it."

He bent down to pick at something on his shoe. And then he lifted his head and swivelled it to look me dead in the eyes.

"You see, the problem with trying to figure stuff out is that we are coming from the wrong paradigm. And by paradigm, I don't mean that nightclub in Brighton I used to hang out in. I'm talking about the whole way we think about something. Like the earth being round. That's a paradigm. But for a long time, most of human history in fact, people were living in the wrong paradigm. Cause they thought the world was flat. Sounds crazy to us now, but it's true. They were so convinced it was flat that they wouldn't sail their ships very far, because they were terrified they'd fall off the edge of the world. Hard to believe, but that's how it was back then, round the time of Columbus and that lot."

I nodded, only because the alternative was to get up and walk away from this nutter. But for some reason, I couldn't. Don't ask me why, but what he was saying made a fair bit of sense, Brighton nightclubs and all.

"So," he continued, his gaze never wavering, "When you uncover the truthful paradigm, then you're good to go. Everything changes. You can sail to the edge … and beyond. You can discover new continents and explore new worlds. And you can see clearly how the way you thought things always were – like the earth being flat – just ain't so."

Suddenly, he was up and off the bench, letting out a long, high-pitched whistle that carried across the rolling grass. It was a sound so loud, so clear, like I'd never heard before. It made my whistle sound like a mouse with a serious self-esteem problem, suffering from laryngitis. In seconds, the two dogs were bounding back towards us, a blinding blur of black, brown and grey.

"This is deep stuff, my friend," he said, his eyes fixed on the onrushing animals. "And it's true. So remember it when you're doing all this figuring stuff out thing. Cause it's gonna make all the difference. Trust me."

His back was towards me now. And the sun was starting to set. So I couldn't be certain in the poor light, but I'm pretty sure those eyes were glowing even greener now.

"Good girl Mads," he said as his dog came to heel by his side. "And nice to meet you, Brock and Evan," he added, as he walked slowly back towards the treeline from which he had first come.

The Beast and I watched the two of them go. And then, just as they reached the giant oaks and disappeared amongst them in the fading light, it hit me: Dreadlocks Dude had never asked our names … and we'd never offered them.

8

I sat on the cold, hard bench for a long while afterwards, until the whole park was enveloped in darkness. Brock lay panting heavily at my feet. Snippets of the conversation – could you really call it a "conversation"? – kept replaying themselves in my head.

How the system works ... a world of thought ... truthful paradigm ... flat earth ...

I didn't know what to make of it all. On the one hand, Dreadlocks Dude – who somehow knew our names but never told us his – had said some pretty way-out stuff. Especially with those posh words, strange accent and weirdo eyes. On the other hand, there was something in what he was saying that felt real to me. True to me. I couldn't put my finger on exactly what it was, but something inside of me told me that this guy was talking sense.

And then I caught myself. *What was I doing?* The boys weren't here, and from what I could see, weren't going to be here anytime soon. I was just sitting on this freezing bench watching my dog slobber all over the grass, my mind flipping out because some mysterious guy with weird-looking eyes had just wasted ten minutes of my life acting like he was some famous YouTuber with a deep message. He was probably seriously stoned and back in the bushes now, smoking another joint and thinking up some more crazy stuff.

Get a grip on yourself, Banksky, I told myself. *You got more important stuff to worry about. Like getting Mum her job back.*

Pulling my hoodie over my head, I jumped off the creaking bench and together Brock and I headed for the park exit. Five minutes later, I was tying The Beast's lead in a double sailor knot around the iron railings outside the station, next to a couple of aging bikes that had most likely been left there by some pretty optimistic commuters. Now that it was dark, didn't they realise that there was a good chance there would be nothing left but a frame and the handlebars by the time they got back? Nothing lasted long around here if it wasn't bolted down with reinforced concrete.

Brock let out a low-pitched groan, but he knew we didn't have a choice. Mom had told me before that there was no way I could bring The Beast into the coffee shop, no matter how many times I promised that he'd be as well-behaved as a snooty Maltese Poodle who had been to St. Margaret's Finishing School for Snobby Canines. (Man, I really don't like Maltese Poodles. I mean, sometimes you just have to tell a dog that it just isn't a dog, four legs and all!)

Bending down, I cupped his face in my hands. "I won't be long, super-dog," I reassured him. "Just gotta ask cuz Jamie to give Mum another chance. Otherwise, we got ourselves a major problem, know what I mean. So stay here and make sure nobody takes anything off them bikes, K? Wish me luck."

And before Brock could give me one of his *are-you-seriously-leaving-me-all-alone-outside-in-the-freezing-cold* looks, I ducked under the big red awning and into the shop.

The smell of coffee and burning ham and cheese toasties made my stomach growl. *Stay focused, Banksky, I reminded myself. You got a job to do here.*

The place was busy, filled with commuters grabbing a final coffee of the day and a bite to eat as they exited the station, as well as a bunch of other people who for some strange reason enjoyed hanging out for long periods of time in a cramped coffee shop. I just didn't get that. Were they like addicted to the smell of roasted coffee beans or something? Or just completely desperate for free Wi-Fi? Proving my point, there were at least half a dozen people waiting in line for their caffeine fix when I walked in. But as queues aren't my thing – they cramp my style – I ignored the waiting customers and their dirty looks and went straight to the till.

"Hey Sandra," I greeted the blonde-haired lady standing by the barista machine. She was kitted out in the same boring brown coffee shop uniform Mum had been wearing earlier. "Is Jamie around?"

Sandra turned to face me, expertly keeping the silver half-pint jug of hot milk frothing away under one of the spouts that protruded like an octopus's tentacle from the big black machine.

"Hey Evan, nice to see you too. I'm fine, thanks for asking," she said, a trace of an Eastern European accent accompanying just a hint of a smile.

"Ah, sorry Sandra. My bad. It's just that I need to speak to Jamie something urgent. How's it going? How was your weekend? How are the twins doing?"

"No worries. They're all good. Kept me up half the night, but hey, that's what they're meant to do at this age, no? Anyhow, not too much longer before their father makes it over from Romania, I hope. Just waiting to sort the visa out. Then I'll get some more sleep hopefully."

"Sure," I said. "I bet they miss him a lot."

"Yah," she replied sadly. "And me too. But that's not what you're here to talk about … hold on one sec …"

"One medium semi-dry cappuccino and a slice of millionaire shortbread. That'll be £4.25 please ma'am," Sandra said to the lady standing next to me.

Sandra held out the terminal so that the woman could simply tap her card on the contactless point, and then, in one quick movement, turned to the next person in the line, a short, squat man in a way too bright green suit.

"What can I get you, sir?"

"A flat white and cheese toastie," he answered, casting an annoyed glance at me. I guess he wasn't the hoodie type.

As Sandra began busying herself with the order, she called over her shoulder.

"Listen Evan, I'm pretty sure I know why you want to talk to Jamie. But he's just taken a fifteen-minute break. So why don't you head downstairs, grab a chair, and I'll tell him you're here to talk to him as soon as he comes back. In the meantime, I'll make you one of those frothy hot chocolates you like. You look like you could do with a bit of warming up."

I hesitated, reluctant to give up my post at the counter and be distracted from the purpose for which I had come. But the image of a steaming hot chocolate was hard to get out of mind.

"And I'll throw in some extra cream and a warm blueberry muffin as well," she added with a smile. That sealed things. "Go on, head on down and I'll bring them to you in a few minutes, just as soon as things settle down here a bit. And Jamie will be back soon, I'm sure."

"OK," I said and began making my way down the stairs to the seating area that was positioned directly underneath the main storefront. On my way, I glanced out the window to check on Brock. He was lying flat on his stomach with his head between his paws, glaring directly at the door of the coffee shop. I was almost tempted to ask Sandra to make a second hot chocolate and send it out in a mug that had *World's Coolest Dog* sprawled across it. But I quickly assessed that might be pushing things a bit far. So I resolved to save half my blueberry muffin for The Beast as a kind of compensation instead. A champ needs to eat, you know.

There weren't many available seats when I got downstairs, but I managed to find one against the padded sofa bench which had a small, round wooden table in front of it and an empty armchair covered in cheap grey fabric opposite. I was squeezed in on both sides. On the one, two 6th form looking types – a lanky boy in a colourful jumper that could only have come from a NEXT Boxing Day sale and a heavily made-up girl with freakishly long purple fingernails – were taking turns asking each other questions from a thick chemistry textbook sitting between them on the table. It was nauseating. On the other side of me, I vaguely recognised the local homeless-looking lady I had seen around before, outside the station sitting on a low wicker box as well as in and around the park; and even here, in the coffee shop, when visiting Mum the other day. She had at least four or five battered-looking plastic bags scattered around her on the sofa bench, plus another couple at her feet. And she had on this funny looking woolly hat that I had always seen her wearing. That's how I recognised her, actually. It was always the same hat, a bit dishevelled, sitting at a weird angle on her head. It reminded me why I had always given her a wide berth. Not because I have anything against homeless people or anything, but just because ... well, I'm not sure, but she made me nervous somehow.

Taking out my phone, I did a quick google search: *Knife Fight, Hendon*. But then I remembered that you could almost never get reception down here in the bowels of the shop. Which was another reason to avoid this place like the plague. Glancing up from the empty screen, I sensed somebody staring at me. It was the homeless lady, sitting not two feet to my left. I looked down again, but as O2 had not suddenly installed an extra receiving tower down here in the last six seconds, my screen was still blank. That being the case, I figured it was a good tactical move nonetheless. Except when I looked up after a minute or so, she was still looking full-on at me. So I tried a different approach: I stared back. Bad move.

"Hey, I know you. You're one of the boys who hangs out on the benches down in the corner of the park, aren't you?" she asked.

Before I had a chance to answer, she continued with another question. "What you doing messing around with those other lads? They are up to no good, that lot. Just the other day, one of them – that one with the shaved head and the big tattoo on his neck – grabbed one of my bags and wouldn't give it back. He ended up throwing it into the dustbin by the playground. It took me at least a half an hour to find it, and then another long while trying get all the rubbish and dirt off the bag. That was a nasty thing to do."

I didn't know what to say. A quick glance at the stairway showed no sign of Sandra. Where was a man's hot chocolate when you needed it?

"But don't worry sonny, I know you aren't like them. You see, I spend my whole day just sitting and watching people. They

52

pass me on the street, in the underpass, in the park, even here in this lovely warm little coffee shop. None of them notice me. And they think I don't notice them. But I do. All of them. And I mean *all* of them."

She sat back on the bench, and took a long sip from the paper cup she had been cradling the whole time between her mitted hands. I just sat there like a silent plonker, wishing Sandra would appear and make the save. No such luck.

Then, without warning, homeless lady hopped out of her seat with surprising speed and pulled up the empty chair in front of me.

"Mind if I sit here? That stiff bench is no good for my old back."

She sat down in it before I even had a chance to answer. What was with all these strange people asking if I minded them sitting down by me – and not waiting for an answer? This day was getting weirder by the minute.

"Enough about me," she declared, placing her elbows on the table and focusing her gaze on me. "Let's talk about you, young man. I'm going to be blunt here. Do you mind me being blunt? Well, here's what I see going on: you think those boys can put a feeling in you. Don't worry, that's a simple mistake. We all make it, thinking someone or something can put a feeling in you; make you feel better – or worse. But it's just not possible, cause it just doesn't work that way, you know."

No, I don't know, I was desperate to respond. But for the second time that day, the King of Banter had been reduced to a quivering, silent stooge. So I just sat there like a total moron, my mouth shut, my ears open, my mind completely confused. I guess she took that as a sign to continue.

"I can see this is news to you. So let me explain. You see, us human beings, we've been given the most incredible gift. And do you know what that gift is?"

Now she paused, taking another long sip of her drink. I wasn't sure if it was for effect or not, but I kept quiet, and, remembering a line I'd heard in a movie once, I let the lady talk.

"The gift is the incredible, miraculous mind that each and every one of us has been born with. It's a real superpower, it is. Because our minds make it possible for us to experience life in all its brilliance. There are no exceptions: everything we are aware of, everything we know, understand, see, hear, feel – everything!"

The homeless lady was clearly really excited about this gift she was going on about. I glanced around, concerned that we were attracting the kind of attention I definitely didn't want to attract. But it was clear that the two Einsteins to my right were so engrossed in their textbook that even if an asteroid landed directly on the coffee shop in that moment, they would have kept asking each other multiple-choice chemistry questions while being transported by ambulance to the nearest medical facility. And no-one else in the shop seemed to notice our existence. So I decided that the best tactic was to wait for her to tire herself out.

"Now, here's the thing which most people forget," she continued in her excitable way. "We forget this gift and we forget how it works. We forget we have this amazing power of thought. Which means – and if you haven't been listening properly until this moment, now's the time to start – we forget that thought is what creates our reality. Nothing else. Isn't that just marvellous?"

Until now, I had tried to keep it together. I'd let this crazy old nutter with the battered shopping bags and wonky woolly hat speak her mind. But we all have a limit. And I had just hit my mine. I mean come on ... *enough already!*

"Listen, I don't know you at all," I said, the agitation rising in my voice. "And you don't know me. I'm just sittin here waiting to speak to someone. But you're way out of line with what you're going on about."

This was the moment to stop, to shut my big mouth, to just let it go. But that – as you may have realised from my earlier "discussion" with Porcu-dog – ain't my style.

"I've just had the worst day ever. Everything's a total shambles: I got suspended from school; my mates are in major-league trouble; my mother lost her job. And I just found out she owes a ton of money to a seriously dangerous guy. So please don't go tellin me that this thing called thought is creating my reality. That just ain't right. If it wasn't for that fat old Head, if it wasn't for that idiot at the betting shop, if it wasn't for the blind coppers who nicked my mates, if it wasn't for my own mother who can't stop drinking and ..."

I tried to catch myself, but it was too late. The words were tumbling out, and now, like an overflowing dam that couldn't hold the water back any longer, there was no stopping them.

"... Drinking and gambling. If it wasn't for all those people, I'd be doing just fine. It's because of them. All of them! *They* are making me feel like a total loser. *Not* my mind. *Not* this crazy power of thought thing you keep going on about. It's *them*, not me. Don't you see ...?"

And then I felt them, just starting to form at the back of my eyes. But there was no way I was going to start crying in front of this nutter bag-lady. No way. So I closed my eyes and held my breath. I had learned that if I waited for just long enough, if I kept my eyes closed for just the right amount of time, the moment would pass.

And when I finally opened them, Sandra was standing in front of the table, holding a round plastic tray with yellow flowers painted all over its base.

"One hot chocolate with extra cream; one warmed up blueberry muffin, just liked you ordered sir," she smiled.

"Where'd she go?" I asked.

"Where'd who go?" Sandra asked back, as she set the tray down in front of me.

"The homeless lady with a million shopping bags and the wonky hat."

"Ah, Elsie, the sweet old lady with the Spanish-sounding accent who hangs around these parts. Yes, I know who you're talking about. I'm not sure, hon. Sometimes she pops in to get out of the cold for a bit and have a hot cup of tea when she has some spare change. But I haven't seen her in here today at all. Anyhow, that's a bit strange to be asking about her. Why do you want to know?"

"Because I was just talking ..." my voice trailed off, my sentence left hanging in mid-air.

Sandra took a good long look at me, her fingers twirling the edge of her barista's apron into a tight little knot.

"Are you OK, Evan? You look like you've been ... you look like you're having a rough day."

I turned away, knowing that if I tried to speak now, I would forever be ashamed. That stinging feeling at the back of my eyes was as strong as ever.

I took a big gulp of my hot drink and wolfed down half the muffin, grateful for the distraction. After a long moment, still unable to look directly at Sandra, I glanced up at the stairway and motioned with my head.

"So what's the story? Is Jamie back yet?"

"Yeah, he just walked in" she replied. "He'll be down in a minute to speak to you. But just remember, Evan: he didn't tell your Mum to leave this morning. She quit. So even if he *is* family, just be nice, be respectful, and use that clever brain you've been blessed with to convince him to give your Mum another chance. Now, I gotta get back to my customers. You take care, hon."

So, for a change, I did what I was told. Once Jamie had finally made his way downstairs, a huge cheese and tomato panini poking out of his hand, I played nice, respectful and did my best to come across as at least half-intelligent.

"I'm sorry that Mum kinda lost it this morning," I began, as he parked his ample frame on the chair that the homeless lady had been sitting on a few minutes previously. "But you know how she gets sometimes. She was just having one of them days when she's feelin real down and lonely. And I sure I haven't been making things easier for her, cause she knows things haven't been going too well for me lately at school."

I hesitated for a moment, not sure if I should reveal how serious my problems at school were. But then I decided to go for broke and play the sympathy card like a real pro.

"Actually, I just got suspended for the rest of the week. Please don't say anything to her cause she'll just flip out and it'll make things worse. So I guess she's just a bit stressed by everything, ya know. Anyhow, I found her some psycho-drugs that have calmed her down and I ain't got no doubt she'll be good to go in the morning, if you're just able to give her another chance. Please … cuz."

"Listen here," Jamie said, taking a big bite out of his panini and wiping some dangling cheese from his double-chin, "I'm not blind; I could see your Mum was having a tough day. And to be honest, that business guy in the suit is a bit of a plonker anyhow. So as long as she promises to keep her head down and just make coffee and heat up toasted sandwiches, then she can come back to work tomorrow morning. After all, she's family – sort of. And anyhow, I don't have time to go train a replacement and Sandra and I can't manage on our own. So yeah, I'll give your Mum another chance."

"That's great. Thanks so much Jamie. I'll go tell her straight away and make sure she's here first thing in the morning to open up. You won't regret it, I promise you."

I got up to go, stuffing the rest of the muffin into my jeans pocket, my mission accomplished. But Jamie held out a fat hand and stopped me.

"Wait a minute, son. There's just one condition."

I sat down slowly. This was an unexpected deviation from my plan.

"I know things look a bit rough for you right now. Sure, I may not be this most tuned-in guy in the world, but I'm no fool either. So I've got a deal for you: you make sure you don't get yourself kicked out of school again – ever – and your Mum will have a job here as long as she shows up sober every day and keeps making coffee for people however they want it. Deal?"

What was I going to say? "No, you can take your deal and shove it. We don't need your job, your judgement or your charity. Cause me and Mum are catching a plane to a private Caribbean island first thing tomorrow morning for a two-week sun-drenched holiday in a 5-star luxury resort. So thanks, but no thanks, Mister fat coffee shop manager and useless cousin."

Jamie's hand was hanging in mind-air, suspended halfway across the round wooden table.

"Deal," I said, and reached out my hand to meet his.

9

When I finally got out of that damn coffee shop, the wind was up and the street had gone real quiet. I found my poor dog talking to a complete stranger, practically begging to be re-homed now that his owner had clearly run off with another four-legged canine; probably, in his mind, a younger and better-looking version. OK, maybe that's a bit of an exaggeration, but I could see by the look on Brock's face that he wasn't a happy camper.

"Hey super-dog. Really sorry I was so long, but The Banksky had some important business to take care of that took longer than I planned. But you know I'd never leave you, right? You're the only dog for me."

The Beast gave me his deadpan look. Deep black pools staring back unblinkingly, informing me in no uncertain terms he was going to make me suffer. I needed to come up with something better. Fortunately, I had a plan.

"Ah right, big guy. Here, take this and just cut me some slack, OK?"

I pulled a lukewarm, half-eaten blueberry muffin out of my pocket and held it in front of his jaws. One sniff, and it was gone before you could say "Hat-trick Harry Kane." All forgiven. That kind of forward planning is why they pay me the big bucks.

Untying the world's best sailor knot, I grabbed the lead and me and my dog headed home. We made a sharp left as we came out the station concourse, jogged through Queens Alley (though considering the variety of four letter words scribbled along its walls, I'm not too sure how keen Her Majesty would be with having this portion of London real estate named after her), and then raced the last hundred yards or so, right up to the mini-parking lot at the back of our building. It wasn't much of a contest: The Beast beat me hands down – for the 473rd time in a row.

"That's my dog," I wheezed. Man, I needed to do some more fitness work. "Now, come on, let's get you back upstairs and go see if Mum is awake so we can tell her the good news."

But as I opened the front door, it was clear that those psycho-drugs were still doing their thing, because the unmistakable sound of Mum's heavy snoring came floating through the open door of her bedroom. I sure wasn't going to wake her now, so I'd have to wait before telling her she had her job back. Which wasn't necessarily a bad thing, because even though I was completely knackered, there was still one final place I had to be before I could call it a day. The whole business with Mum and sorting out her job had ended up being a major distraction. I needed to get back on mission, which meant heading over to Colindale Police Station. It was our local and the most likely place I would find my boys – or at least some info about them.

First though, I needed to break the news to The Beast that I'd be riding solo on this one. I figured Brock might not be welcomed by all them mean-looking German Shepherds who work down at the police station, though I was pretty sure he could take down those vicious police dogs if he had to. None of them had ever lived rough on the streets like he had.

"Sorry, super-dog," I told him, as I slipped the collar off his thick neck. "You're gonna need to stay here. Read a book or watch

Spot or something. Keep Mum company while she sleeps it off. And a whole packet of chicken nuggets when I get back, K?"

Deadpan eyes; The Beast wasn't happy. I couldn't blame him. But a man's gotta do what a man's gotta do. So I quickly stuffed a few old power bars I found in my drawer in my school bag, figuring that if I did manage to find any of the boys, at least I could offer them something to eat. You don't get Domino's in jail, you know. And without risking a look back at those deadly eyes, I closed the door behind me and raced down the stairs.

My journey got off to a flyer. The 183 stop is less than a five minute walk from our building and a big red double-decker came speeding past just as I hit the main road. After a quick sprint – who needs Usain Bolt? – I found myself a seat on the upper deck. Leaning my head against the window, I fought the urge to close my eyes and get lulled to sleep by the mechanical movement of the bus. After such a hectic day, the sudden shift in pace suddenly left me realising how tired I actually was.

I knew the bus would drop me right outside the police station in about a quarter of an hour. So in order to stay awake, I decided to spend some time with my main man, Dr. Dre. I whipped out my phone and started feeling round my bag for my headphones. No go. Only power bars, a half-finished bottle of Red Bull, my old gym gloves and some book I must have forgotten to get rid of when I cleared out my bag earlier once I knew I wouldn't be going back to school for the rest of the week. It took me a sec to figure out how it had got there. Then I remembered Tals shoving it into my hands, just before I got chucked off school property.

Well, music without headphones doesn't work too good. And though reading ain't really my thing, especially if I don't got to do it for school, the alternatives were either a second storey night-time view of North West London (not exactly appealing) or a really stiff neck from falling asleep against the bus window. Limited options. So I pulled the book out of the bag and turned it over in my hands. *What If You Already Have Everything You Need Inside of You?* Weird title. And way too long. But for some reason, the simple black and white image on the front of some kid about my age, looking straight up at the sky, got my attention under the dim overhead lights of the bus. I opened it to a random chapter and something caught my eye ...

"Life" is a short film telling the true story of a boy named Owen. Owen was a talkative and outgoing child until he was diagnosed with severe autism and withdrew suddenly into his own silent world. For the next four years, he did not utter a single comprehensible word. Then, shortly before he turned seven, Owen said out of the blue to his older brother who was feeling sad on his birthday, "My brother Walter doesn't want to grow up, just like Mowgli or Peter Pan."

And so began a new way for Owen to communicate with the world and the people in his life. Walt Disney movies became the source of Owen's hope and the characters in them his greatest friends. These characters leave nothing to the imagination and are full of emotions such as love, loss, joy, rejection, fear and hope, all expressed in an over-the-top way. This helped Owen understand these emotions far better than trying to read human facial expressions and emotional nuances. The Disney characters also helped Owen to understand that when we momentarily lose our way, we can get scared, we can feel lost and we can feel hopeless...

The bus came to a sudden stop. I banged my head against the top of the seat in front of me and the book went skidding out of my hands. Glancing out the window at the darkened streets, I saw we were already on Aerodrome Road, directly outside the RAF Museum and not fifty feet from the police station. I had been so absorbed in what I was reading that I'd almost missed the stop. Jamming the book into my bag, I flew down the winding steps of the double-decker, exiting the big red machine just as the back doors slammed shut behind me.

I pulled my hoodie tight and began crossing the road, rubbing my forehead as I went. As I approached the automatic doors of the station's public entrance, they slid open – a little too welcoming for my liking. A few uncomfortable-looking plastic chairs were scattered in a sort of a small waiting room on either side of me. On them were two random people who didn't seem to be doing much besides waiting. Which is how I deduced it was a waiting room. Thank you, Sherlock.

I walked up to the single counter at the far end of the room, separating the coppers from the rest of the world by means of a solid glass partition – bulletproof no doubt. A woman in a stiff blue uniform stood behind the counter, staring intently at a screen while manoeuvring a wireless mouse with her right hand. A solid silver name tag just below her left shoulder read: *PC Judy Patel*. I stood there like a very lonely moron for a while, not quite sure how to start the conversation with the first police constable I had ever voluntarily spoken to. How about something like …

Good evening, I am a local citizen named Evan Banksky and I have four close acquaintances incarcerated somewhere in your penal system. My understanding is that they became involved in a major altercation in a local park which involved both physical violence and some form of dangerous weaponry. My apologies for arriving in torn trousers and a hooded jumper, but I came straight from my employment as an actor in a West End production and did not have time to change prior to this engagement. Would you be kind enough to inform me if my colleagues are present here and provide an update please regarding their general wellbeing?

Fortunately, despite what Porcu-dog and others may think, I have been blessed with at least a partly functioning internal filter and some serious street smarts. So instead, I said:

"Uh, s'cuse me. I'm looking for my mates who got nicked last night for getting in a massive fight."

With considerable effort, Constable Patel managed to remove her eyes from the screen and looked at me from behind the see-through 2018 edition of the Berlin Wall. Her emotionless stare caused an involuntary shiver to run through my body. On reflection, perhaps the first approach would have been more effective.

"Can you repeat that … please?"

"Um, OK. You see, I have four friends who got into some trouble down in Hendon Park yesterday and the police arrested them. I'm trying to find them, and as you're my local police station, I thought this would be a good place to start."

The good constable gave me a long, hard look. Did I mention long? And hard? Her dark brown – almost black – eyes, reminded me of Brock's. Actually, The Beast's stare had nothing on hers. We were going to need to toughen him up.

"Why don't you go take a seat over there," she suggested/ordered, motioning with her head towards the only unoccupied plastic chair behind me. "I'm busy with something here, but when I'm done, I'll have a look on the system and see if we can locate your acquaintances. Can you write down your name and contact details plus their names on this piece of paper in the meantime?"

She slid a blank piece of white paper and a slightly gnawed pen underneath the glass shelf of the partition. I quickly jotted down the boys' names and pushed the paper back in her direction. Then I turned around, leaving her to do whatever constables behind glass partitions do, and headed for my designated seat, glancing at my neighbours on either side as I did. On my left was a woman who looked just a few years older than me. She had two large green hearts tattooed on her right wrist, a silver stud pressed into her nose and was chewing gum furiously. Her face was buried in her extra-large, pink-plated iPhone while her fingers typed away at almost blinding speed. I don't think she noticed my existence. On my right, some old man with a massive grey beard, all straggly and wild, was fast asleep on the hard chair. Well, the good news was that

Constable Judy Patel aside, my visit to the police station was likely to remain a pretty anonymous event.

A torn copy of the *Evening Standard* was hanging off the edge of the empty chair. I was just about to sweep it onto the floor, when a headline at the top of an open page caught my eye:

North London Stabbing
Teenager Fighting for Life in Hospital

My blood went cold. Doing my best not to attract anyone's attention (though assessing the current occupants of the waiting room, it was hard to imagine whose attention I could possibly have attracted), I picked up the paper as noiselessly as I could, sat down on the chair, and began reading the single paragraph stretching down the right hand side of page 5.

London experienced another act of senseless violence last night when a seventeen-year-old male was critically injured after being stabbed in the neck during an altercation in Hendon Park, North London. The incident, which occurred at approximately 10 p.m., took place on the park's lone basketball court, just outside the entrance to the park's café. One local resident said the court is often used late at night by youths who live on the nearby council estate. It is not clear what precipitated the altercation in the first place, though it has been suggested that trouble had been brewing between informal gangs of local youths,

67

and it was only a matter of time before this spilled over into something more serious. Another resident expressed her dismay that knife crime had found its way to a part of the capital, which, until now, had seemed relatively immune to violence of this nature. The Evening Standard *understands that a large number of policemen arrived on the scene rapidly, in part thanks to the quick-thinking 999 phone call of a local retailer. As a result, all those presumed to be involved in the incident were apprehended shortly afterwards. Detective Sergeant Robin Manning, the lead officer on the case, said: "A number of youths aged seventeen and eighteen have been taken into custody for questioning. As this is a serious violent crime, the police will be enforcing our right to hold these individuals for a still-to-be determined period of time before terms are set for their release." He refused to comment further, other than to request any members of the public who may have information about this incident to come forward immediately. It is understood that the police are still searching for the weapon used during the struggle. Meanwhile, the exact condition of the stabbed youth is unknown but is presumed to be critical. Police investigations are ongoing.*

Suddenly feeling as if I had a big round target painted on my forehead, I looked around to see if anyone was watching me. No worries there: the woman on the iPhone still didn't know I existed; the old guy with the wild beard was still sleeping; and PC Patel still hadn't taken her eyes off the screen in front of her. I briefly considered bolting out the automatic doors and up Aerodrome Road, but then I remembered I had given my details to the good constable not five minutes earlier. Genius!

So I was stuck on this freakin plastic chair in this freakin police station while a freakin newspaper article about my freakin friends who got in a freakin fight was sitting on my freakin lap. And to make matters worse, I was sure that the freakin knife which the freakin police were searching for, was lying in a freakin dead log in some freakin bushes and I was the only freakin person not in freakin jail who knew where it freakin was!

10

I needed a distraction – fast! Except I had no way of listening to any music. No headphones, no Dr. Dre. So the only stupid idea I could come up with was to eat a power bar. Feeling around the inside of my bag for a stray bar, my hands grasped something else – that useless book again. What a shambles! But now that it was in my hand, I guess I had nothing better to do than pull it out and find the page I had been reading earlier …

> … *With the unexpected support of the Walt Disney characters and his own fantastic family, Owen did brilliantly. He showed great awareness about his own emotional world and came to recognise the limitations of how he appears in the eyes of others. Owen reacted exactly like any other person would to the challenges of his life. He got scared when "caught" in the belief that the unknown is scary; he was devastated when he thought love could only be experienced within a particular relationship; and he became anxious when he did not know what others wanted from him.*

> *Over time, Owen came to see that it's normal to mistakenly feel that other people or circumstances have power over us. And through the range of Disney characters, he discovered a way to connect to the outside world, creating a journey through life that is so different – and yet so familiar. For Owen is no different from the rest of us. Just as we can all figure*

out our way through the situations of our life, so does Owen find his way again and ...

"Hey, what's that you're reading there, son?"

I half jumped out of my seat. It was the old guy with the huge, grey beard. He was wide awake now and was leaning right over my shoulder, staring at my book, bits of his wild facial hair brushing against my hoodie.

"Nuthin," I replied, though what I really wanted to say – should have said – is: *Back off old geezer and get out of my space! And I got nuthin to do with that freakin knife!*

But I was in a police station. And Constable Patel and her more-deadly-than-The Beast's-stare were just the other side of a bullet-proof partition. And I'm a chicken. So I didn't.

"Doesn't look like nothing to me," he said. "You look pretty absorbed in that book. That's a good thing, because I don't see young people reading anymore nowadays. At least not if it isn't a device they can't hold in the palm of their hands."

He motioned to the iPhone addict on my left. His meaning was clear.

"All this WhatsApp and Snapshot nonsense. Whatever happened to ...?"

"It's Snapchat."

"What?"

"It's Snapchat, not Snapshot."

"You say tomato, I say tomata. Big deal."

"What?"

"Never mind. Anyhow, you don't look so much like the reading type, if you don't mind me saying. So where'd you get it? Amazon? WH Smith?"

"Nah. A friend."

"Hey, that's what friends are for, know what I mean?"

"Uh, not really."

"Oh, OK. Well anyway, as I was saying, kids don't seem to read anymore. So it's really nice to see you reading a real book, with paper pages and everything. I'm proud of you, son. Good on yer."

"Uh, OK."

"So, like I was asking, why don't you tell me something interesting from that book? My eyes are so bad these days that I find it hard to even watch the telly for a half hour. So do an old man a favour and just tell me what you've been reading."

His hand disappeared inside that massive mane on the front of his face, identifying some hidden spot to scratch at. But he kept his eyes on mine the whole time, clearly expecting an answer. And like I said, once you get past the Mr. Porcu-dog jokes and the tough guy look, I'm a bit of a chicken deep down. Especially when The Beast is back home, chewing the furniture. And to be fair, I was actually a bit scared that any moment, this guy could pull a concealed weapon out of his beard and use it to hold me hostage, right there in the middle of the police station, until I met his unconditional demands. It wasn't a pretty thought.

"Well, umm, I guess it's kinda talkin 'bout hope and stuff like that..."

"Hope? What you mean by hope?"

"I'm not really sure. It's just that there's this kid – his name's Owen – who's got all these special-needs problems and all. And he doesn't talk to anyone for like years and years. And then he watches all these Disney movies – you know like the *Jungle Book* and all that kids' stuff – and learns how to speak and figure things out. And he really …"

"You're telling me that some Disney movie helped this kid with all that?"

It would really help if old Wild-Beard stopped interrupting. Couldn't he see I was trying to build some serious momentum here?

"Yeah, cause he couldn't figure people out so good. Like read their faces and emotions and stuff. So he got all in his head, know what I mean? But then he found a way to make sense of it all. And he starts to chill and be cool. Get it?"

"Well, sort of. But I'm still not too clear why this boy Owen started to do better. Where did the hope come from?"

Good question. I needed to think about that one for a minute.

"I guess its cause he figured out that he was all sorted. Like, he kinda knew that even if he was a bit different, with all his special-needs stuff, that he was actually cool inside."

Wild-Beard wasn't convinced.

"No, sorry mate, but I don't get that. If he's got problems with relating to people and communicating and all, why would he suddenly feel fine? Surely, the opposite? He'd just feel worse and worse, because he'd see more and more that people don't get him and he doesn't get people."

"Nah, you're missing the point," I said straight away. "You're not seeing what he saw."

"So what did he see? Go on, tell me, because I don't get it, and I've been around a fair while, as you probably guessed already."

"He saw that nobody had any power over him. Ya know why? Cause it ain't possible, man. It ain't possible for someone to put a feelin in you. You may think it's possible, but it just ain't. Simple as that."

I crossed my arms and leaned back in my chair, the cheap plastic creaking as I did. That should keep him quiet for a while. Now, could he just leave me alone so I could get back to my stupid book?

But Wild-Beard was in no hurry. It was obvious he wasn't going anywhere fast.

"What do you mean that no one can put a feeling in you? Come on, that's ridiculous! Look at PC Patel over there."

We both glanced up at the constable behind the glass partition – did I mention bullet-proof?

"It's been over a half hour since she told me that someone would come by soon and record my formal complaint about my neighbour's dog. But no one has come yet. So I'm getting all frustrated waiting here. I got things to do, you know."

Yeah. Like get a shave, mate.

74

"So don't go telling me that no one can put a feeling in me. I'm annoyed right now, and getting more annoyed by the minute. And it's her fault. Or at least someone else back there who isn't doing their job."

"Hey man, haven't you been hearing anything I've been saying? It doesn't work that way. Listen, you're not getting peed off cause of her. You're getting peed off cause of your own mind. So if you're thinkin that she's the problem, then she's gonna be the problem. Cause like someone was just tellin me earlier today, thought is the only real power. That's what I mean by sayin no one's got power over you. Got it?"

Wild-Beard didn't answer straight away. While I was waiting for him to say something, I glanced at the ice-lady behind the nuclear bomb-proof partition. Was it just me, or did a faint smile just pass across her face?

"OK, I think I get all that, mate," said Wild-Beard finally. "But what's that all got to do with this Owen kid?"

"That's the whole point, man. Owen got it. He got that it all comes from the inside, not the outside. He got that even if he's a bit different or strange, it don't matter none. Cause it ain't about them. It's about his mind and his heart and no-one else's. So that's why it's a story of hope. You see now?"

The little waiting room was all quiet. Even the iPhone addict with the nose ring on had stopped attacking her screen and was staring straight ahead. (I briefly worried that she might be going into a cold turkey withdrawal but she seemed to be holding up OK.) PC Patel was standing on the other side of the transparent demilitarised zone, a big smile now clearly evident on her face.

Suddenly, Wild-Beard got off his seat, walked up to the counter, and addressed the constable. "Don't worry about that complaint, Luv. It's not really such a big issue anymore."

Turning directly to me, he said, "Yes. I see now."

And then, without another word, he walked through the automatic sliding doors of the station and headed off down Aerodrome Road, picking at his wild beard as he went.

I watched him go for a bit, wondering who – and what – that was. But when I turned round to face the counter, PC Patel's broad smile had been replaced by a worrying frown. Something on her screen had reignited her attention and now she was speaking in a low voice into her desk phone. Moments later, a tall, stern-looking guy appeared next to Patel behind the partition. He was wearing a cheap-looking grey suit and had a shaved head and goatee that had been trimmed to perfection. From a short distance, it gave the guy a bit of a menacing look; this looked like one copper not worth messing with. Then he seemed to ask a question and Patel responded by pointing to something on the screen and then pointing at … me!

I couldn't hear what the two policemen (police-people just doesn't sound right) were saying, but their urgent-looking exchange and a couple of suspicious glances in my direction were starting to make me nervous. Meanwhile, iPhone addict's detox efforts had proven to be unsuccessful; she was back typing at 72,000 characters a minute. Her addictive texting indicated that she would most likely have been oblivious to a nuclear missile test being conducted by that North Korean crazy guy against the see-through glass right here in this very waiting room.

And as for me? I may not be the sharpest pencil in the box, but all their talking and pointing was telling me that something clearly didn't feel right here. So I started shuffling casually towards the automatic doors in preparation for a stealthy escape. I would deal with the coppers having my name and address another time. But just as I was about to calmly stroll through those inviting doors and attain my freedom, PC Patel's voice came booming through the intercom from the other side of the demilitarised zone.

"Mr. Banksky. Have you a moment ... please?"

It's highly unlikely, in the course of human history, that the word *please* had ever sounded more like a battlefield order.

Seconds later, a heavy door swung open, revealing the interior of the small partitioned room from where PC Patel had been speaking. The Wall had fallen.

Big-shot officer was standing on the other side. "Hello. I'm Detective Sergeant Robin Manning, the senior officer in charge of this investigation," he said stiffly. "Some important information has just come to our attention and we would like to ask you a few questions in this regard. Can you come this way ... please?"

He motioned with his suited arm behind him. I caught a glimpse of a door on the other side of PC Patel's lair, leading to a long corridor. As I followed the officer, it occurred to me that his name sounded very familiar. And then I remembered: wasn't it a DS Manning who had been quoted in the *Evening Standard* article I had just read in the waiting room? A knot started to form in the pit of my stomach. *Did they know something about the knife? That freakin knife.* But before I had a chance to think about it any further, he ushered me into a small, windowless room with two identical plastic chairs, like those out in the waiting room (did they get some kind of bulk discount from Argos?), on either side of a small rectangular table.

"Would you mind taking a seat … please?" Another order poorly dressed up as a request. "Thank you for speaking to me, Mr. Banksky. Now, do you mind if I ask you a few questions?"

"Uh, sure."

Manning thrust a plastic file across the table in my direction. It looked a bit like the ones we use for our reading assignments at school, and for the briefest of moments, I wondered if I was about to get interrogated for suggesting, in my most recent essay, that Shakespeare may have been racist, communist, fascist and anti-Semitic – all at the same time. But then, Mister big-shot copper opened the file to the first page, where four rectangular photos stared directly back at me. I almost fell off my chair.

"Do you know any of these young men?" he asked.

"Of course," I replied instantly. "Them's my boys. Where are they? Are they here? They cool?"

"Evan. May I call you Evan?"

"Uh, yeah, sure."

"Let's be clear here. From now on, I ask the questions. Not you. Got it?"

"Uh, OK. Sorry."

"So, can you identify the people in these in these photos?" he asked, ignoring my apology.

I pointed at each of the pictures in turn. "Jams. Mo. Jez. And D-Von."

DS Manning didn't look impressed. "Their real names …
please."

That *please* again.

"Jamal. Maurice. Jeremy. And … actually, I'm not too sure
what his proper name is. Maybe Darryl or Desmond or something."

"Right. And could you tell us, exactly, how you know Jamal
and Maurice?"

"Why, did something happen to them in lock-up?"

The Detective Sergeant glared at me. Whoops, forgot about
the asking questions thing.

"Sorry, didn't mean to ask that. Yeah, well Jams and Mo are
two of my best friends. We're like bros, you know. Hang out all the
time together and stuff. I've known 'em ever since they came to
live on the estate, about five years ago."

"OK. Thank you. Now, let me ask you about an incident that
occurred last night in Hendon Park at approximately 10 p.m."

"Yeah, the fight. What's the deal with that?"

This time, Manning decided to let my question go, instead
choosing to respond with one of his own.

"Evan, could you tell me where you were last night around
the time of that incident?"

I hesitated for the briefest of moments as it occurred to me
that I was about to cross a serious line – lying to the coppers. But
my mind quickly refocused and the lie followed smoothly.

"Sure. I was at home with my Mum. She'd just had a long, rough session with the bottle, ya know what I mean? So I was trying to get her sorted and into bed, so she could be up in time for her morning shift at the coffee shop. But that didn't go too good, cause even though she made it to work this morning, she messed up with this douche-bag with his posh briefcase and decided not to give him the skinny cappuccino he ordered, insisting that it was a skinny ..."

The door to the small room opened, interrupting me mid-flow. A very serious looking lady in uniform whispered something in the Sergeant's ear. He nodded, a frustrated look briefly crossing his face, before turning to me.

"Evan, as you are a minor, we are going to have to terminate our discussion at this point unless you agree to it being a voluntary conversation. So..." said Manning, fixing me with a stare that reminded me of a psycho-nutcase killer I had once seen in a seriously scary horror movie. "... Do you agree to this being a voluntary conversation?"

"Well, um ... well ... seeing I don't know nuthin about no fight or anything, I think I'll just be on my way. And my Mum is probably sick with worry by now, so I really gotta go fast."

The lies were coming easier and easier.

"OK," Manning said, though from the tone of his voice, it was obvious that any one of a hundred words would have been more fitting to come out of his mouth at that moment than *OK.* "However, we are most likely going to want to speak to you again in the near future, when we will require either your mother or father to accompany you to the station for a formal interview. Is that clear?"

"Ain't got no father!" I blurted out. Instantly, I regretted my words.

"That's fine," Manning replied, completely disregarding my outburst. "We can always just speak to your mother. Now, Sergeant Neill here is going to escort you out. But don't go too far, because we'll be needing to speak to you again real soon."

A sudden wave of relief washed over me. I could feel the knot in my stomach unclenching instantly. I stood up to leave – a little too quickly perhaps.

"Oh, and one other thing, Evan," the Sergeant added. "There is a young man lying in a hospital bed fighting for his life as we speak. We believe we know exactly who was involved in the altercation that put him there. They are all in our custody. But we have yet to recover the weapon that was used to wound him so severely in the first place. So if there is any information you have – anything at all – that will be helpful in locating this weapon and bringing the perpetrators of this crime to justice, I highly recommend you bring that to our attention when we next speak."

Manning fixed me another stare so long and psychotic that I almost expected to be charged admission for that horror film right then and there. Then he motioned towards the officer standing by the doorway.

"Sergeant, please show Mr. Banksky out."

I followed my escort back through the inner sanctum of the station, making our way via PC Patel's impenetrable bunker into the waiting room. The automatic doors slid open as we approached, at which point my uniformed attendant bid me farewell.

"We'll be in touch," she said nonchalantly. And then, perhaps reading the anxiety that I am sure was written all over my face in bold red letters, Sergeant Neill added, "Don't worry about a thing."

But she clearly hadn't read me right. My problem was not worrying about *one* thing. My problem was trying not to worry about *everything*.

When I walked back into the flat, Mum was lying peacefully on the couch, an unlit smoke between her lips. She was giving Brock a proper cuddle while reading some old celebrity magazine. Realising that there wouldn't be a better time to get her head around the idea of going back to work at the coffee shop, I made Mum another cup of sweet tea, placed it carefully in her hand, and sat down on the floor facing her. It didn't take long before The Beast and I managed to convince her to give it another go. To be honest, considering the alternatives facing us right now, Mum didn't have a choice. And she knew it.

So the good news, when I woke up the next morning and glanced at the cracked clock next to my bed, was that Mum had got herself up and out the house in time for her early morning shift.

There was no school to get up for. Which was cool with me, because the events of the day before had left me so tired that I stayed in bed until lunch time. Probably would have slept even longer had Brock not started clawing the hell out of the side of the chipped bedframe, breaking the important news: *The Beast has to go, you know*.

I took top dog down to do his thing, came back up for a quick bowl at our wobbly kitchen table of the greatest cereal ever invented – Crunchy Nut Cornflakes, hands down – threw on my sweats, grabbed my kit and headed for the gym. My abs and pecs had work to do. I trained hard, working through some of the newest stuff from Kanye West as I did. It was good, for a short while at least, to take my mind off the boys and their situation. And that freakin knife. Then I took The Beast for a run in the park followed by a short detour to check in on Mum at the shop. She seemed to be doing fine, if a little quiet behind the coffee machine.

Walking with Brock back to the flat, I noticed a sleek black Mercedes E-class parked in the middle of the lot. You couldn't miss it – not because there weren't other cars there – but because a Merc E-class had never sat in the Sweet Orchard Place parking lot before. At least, never in my time.

"Nice wheels," I said to Brock as we approached the car. "Wonder what it's doing in a nice place like this?"

Intrigued, I tried to look into the interior of the vehicle, but the blacked-out, one way windows made that impossible. So we kept going, headed for the stairwell.

As we walked past, the rear passenger door swung silently open. A short, slightly overweight, middle-aged white guy with curly grey hair, thick eyebrows and wearing some seriously expensive threads, stepped out of the car. Curious, I glanced in his direction.

"Evan?" he asked. "Evan Banksky?"

I turned round fully. Something about the guy looked vaguely familiar.

"Yeah, who's asking?"

"I am," he replied, taking a step towards me. Brock gave a soft, low growl. I placed my hand on The Beast's head, shooing him instantly.

"It's all right, boy," I muttered under my breath. "Let's just see what this guy wants."

"And who are *you*?" I asked boldly, though I could feel my stomach muscles tightening even as I uttered the words.

The guy in the flash suit didn't answer for a long time. You could hear nothing but Brock's heavy panting and the faint sound of the passing cars on the main road just behind the estate. Then, finally, he cleared his throat and answered.

"I'm your father."

11

I was seven years old the first time I ever went to The Lane. (For those who don't know – and you *should* know – I'm talking about White Hart Lane, the legendary former ground of the greatest football team ever, Tottenham Hotspur.) For the big games, it was almost impossible to get tickets to the stadium due to its relatively small 36,000 capacity. Had been for years. And this was a BIG game. Spurs v Inter Milan, the Italian giants, in the first knockout round of the Champions League. It doesn't get much bigger – or better – than that.

Old David Chipman – known to us boys on the estate simply as DC – was a second-hand car salesman who had been living in a one-bedroom flat three floors below us for as long as I could remember. He and Mum used to spend the long summer evenings on our apartment's little balcony drinking G & T's and rollin rizlas together, shooting the breeze about Spurs in a way that meant that the almost 45 year age gap between them didn't matter one jot. DC was just about the biggest Yid Army supporter you could ever meet. Over the years, he had seen all the greats play: starting with Blanchflower and Greaves; then Ardiles and Archibald; Hoddle, Gazza, Ginola and King; right up to Harry and Deli Ali. Back when we were a bit younger, he would keep us kids spellbound for hours, telling magical tales about the great glory nights at The Lane.

Out of the blue one early November afternoon, about eight years or so ago, DC comes up to me while I'm kicking a ball to myself around the parking lot, imagining that I was Peter Crouch making Jens Lehman look silly.

"Hey, little man. Do you know where your Mum is? I wanted to know if you've any plans for tomorrow night?" he asks me.

What was seven-year-old me going to answer? *Well, actually, I'm quite busy tomorrow evening, Mr. Chipman. First, I have that piano recital I've been preparing for; then I have a lesson with my English tutor; and finally, as a treat, my grandparents are taking me out for dinner to that posh new Chinese restaurant in St. John's Wood.*

"Dunno," I replied, kicking the ball against the chipped fence in our lot.

"Well, what would you say if I told you I just bought a nice big car from a Mr. Kelley, a rich man down in Maida Vale, who happens to be the proud owner of two season tickets at The Lane? But as he's going to be in Geneva for some last-minute big business meeting or something, he can't use them this week – so he gave 'em to me as an extra somethin special for buying that big 'ole car of his. And he says to me, 'Have you got someone you can take with you to the match?' And I reply, 'Yes Guv, I sure do. He's my little neighbour man who's never been to the Lane before, but sure would love to.' So what you say we go find your Mummy and ask her if 'ole DC can treat you to see the Yid Army, just this once?"

And that's how I landed up watching my team thrash Inter 3-1 in one of the truly epic nights the Lane has ever known. There was one player who stood head and shoulders above the rest that night. You may have heard of him: that's right, Gareth Bale. Until that moment, Bale had been considered a somewhat flaky Welsh player with a fair bit of promise and not much to show for it. Man U had turned down the chance to sign him for about five million quid not long before, and it was looking like pretty good business

86

on their part. And then …. then there was the Inter game. Bale destroyed them; he was like a one-man wrecking crew on super-fast rollerblades. That was the night that a 21-year-old converted fullback tore apart a defence reputed to be amongst the best in Europe, treating some of the world's leading professionals like schoolboys on the playground.

After the match, as we were making our way home on the tube amongst the swarm of delirious fans, DC turned to me and, if memory serves me correct, said:

"Every now and again, it works out that you happen to be somewhere, at a moment in time, when something big goes down. When things change in a way such that they won't be the same, ever again. Like when Armstrong walked on the moon all those years ago. Know what I'm talkin' about?"

I didn't, to be totally honest. Wasn't Armstrong an Irish guy who had played up front for Arsenal even before I was born? But I still remember, with crystal clarity, what old DC said next:

"Tonight was one of those nights. This will go down as one of the great nights in the history of the Lane. For a certain Gareth Bale. And for a certain Evan Banksky as well. You'll remember this night for the rest of your life, little Evan, because it ain't ever gonna be the same around here again."

I gave the geezer in the expensive suit a hard look and declared: "I ain't got no father. So I don't know who you are, or what game you're playing at, but just leave me alone, man."

It felt good to get the words out, to lay the smack down to this dude with the smooth wheels. For the past couple of days, I'd been feeling all discombobulated and stuff. But now I was finally getting my mojo back. Look out fans – here comes The Banksky!

"I tell you what," Suit-Man said. "Seeing as you don't believe me – and I don't blame you for that – why don't you ask me something? Actually, any questions you want about your mother that would have been true fifteen or so years ago. Then you can make a call on whether I'm legit or not. OK?"

Well … there goes The Banksky. I was expecting him to jump back into his smooth car and crawl back to whatever slimy mansion he had climbed out of. Now he wanted me to ask him questions about Mum. What the …?

"Go on," he said. "Just ask. Anything."

Fine. I could play this thing out.

"What does she prefer – bath or shower?"

"Bath."

Fifty-fifty chance. Stupid question.

"What's Mum's favourite colour?"

"Green."

Lucky guess.

"Who's her favourite Arsenal player of all time: Adams, Bergkamp or Brady?"

"That's not a fair question, and you know it, Evan. Your mother wouldn't dream of having a favourite Arsenal player. No self-respecting member of the Yid Army would."

I ignored him.

"Her favourite snack?"

"Cottage cheese and crisps, all mixed up with ketchup. Always has been."

I could feel myself starting to sweat. Suit-Man was becoming a problem. Who was this guy? And how did he know so much about Mum? My mind began swirling, distracting me from the task at hand.

Focus Banksky, I told myself. *You need to catch this geezer out.* So I thought for a long moment, and then it came to me. It was a killer question, one he would never get, could never get. No one knew; just me and The Beast and Mum. This would settle things.

"What is her 'weird' habit when she's lying in bed?" I asked, making double quotations marks with my fingers, half-smirking as I did.

He didn't answer straight away, his thick eyebrows furrowing in confusion. My half-smirk became a full one. I knew I had him. The Banksky was about to reveal this guy as a Premier League fraud, once and for all. Then, just as I was about to lift my arms, declare victory and maybe release Brock for a short moment to make sure Suit-Man really did get back into his E-class and not come back again, he spoke up.

"Good one. You almost had me there for a minute. But then it came to me; I mean, how can you forget a habit as ridiculous as twirling your big toe round and round a pillow cover for hours on end? It's just about the weirdest thing I ever saw someone do – and I've seen some pretty weird things."

I just stood there, looking at him. My mouth opened and closed a couple of times, but nothing came out. Finally, my mind clicked back into gear, and my mouth followed suit.

"OK. I get it. You were some old boyfriend of Mum's; I guess one who hung around longer than most of the others, otherwise you wouldn't know all this stuff about her. Now... what do you want, all these years later? We ain't got any money, you know."

Suit-Man gave me a funny look.

"Evan, you got it all wrong, son. I know you don't have any money. And I wasn't just some 'old boyfriend'. I know it's tough to take in, but like I said, I'm your father. Really. We can do a paternity test if you like – just to prove it. But in the meantime, I can see you're not going to believe me, whatever I say, so why don't you go upstairs and ask your mother a question? A question only she will know the answer to. And then come back down and ask me if I have the same answer. Because that will prove whether I'm lying – or telling the truth. "

Before I had a chance to reply, he asked the question. "Where were you conceived Evan? It sure as hell wasn't here on a housing estate, so where was it? Ask her, and then come down and ask me, and then let's see where we stand. How does that sound?"

But I didn't need to ask her. Cause Mum had told me herself. Once, way back when I was about ten-years-old, I had asked Mum for the millionth time who my father was. And for the millionth time, Mum had answered in the same way, with a firm shake of her head.

"It was so long ago," she said with her sad, lopsided smile and a shake of her head. "That man was a mistake – but what came out of that mistake was the best gift a mother could ever wish for: *You*. That man isn't in our lives – and never will be. He's not right for us. So what good does it do to know who he is? It's just you and me and Brock. We're good together. We don't need anyone else."

Pulling me close and wrapping her thin arms around me, I still remember how tight Mum had squeezed me then. But if you haven't noticed, I don't give up so quickly. Even when I was ten-years-old and Mum was squeezing a whole lotta luv into me. So I asked again. For the millionth and one time. And, finally, she relented – a little.

"OK, I'm not going to tell you *who* he is, no matter how many times you ask, but I *am* prepared to tell you how it all started. But only if you swear that there will be no more questions after this. Promise?"

"Promise," I replied.

And so Mum started pretty much near the beginning. She told me how her father had walked out on her and grandma when she was just seven-years-old. Grandma's way of handling that was to spend the next ten years running from one bad relationship to another until she finally found a man who seemed half-normal. The catch: he insisted Grandma join him back where he had come from – on his farm in the middle of the Australian outback. But Mum wasn't having any of that. So while Grandma headed off to the other side of the world, Mum stayed behind and tried to figure life out. Her first big call was to drop out of school. She soon picked up a part-time job working weekends and most evenings in a bar down in Camden, right by the Lock. Which is when a smooth-talking, dude with attitude arrived on the scene.

"He was a real cool customer, that one," Mum recalled with a weird kind of faraway look in her eyes. "I was taking a smoke-break outside the bar and he started flirting with me, just like that, even though he was at least fifteen years older than me. Full of silky, smooth words and flash clothes. Can you believe he picked me up on our first date in one of those cool blue Porsches? I was a girl of eighteen who got completely swept off my feet. What chance did I have?"

Mum paused for a minute. She was looking at me, but it was clear she was really looking someplace else, sometime else.

"After a couple of weeks, he pitches up early one Saturday morning at my little West Hendon flat-share. And you know what he's got in his hand? Two plane tickets and one of those fancy colour brochures telling me all about the most romantic holiday ever. He says, 'You've got an hour to pack, Gorgeous, because I'm taking you on a holiday you'll never forget.'"

Mum never did forget it. Because exactly three weeks after she got back from Miami Beach, Florida, exactly three weeks after she told that man she never wanted to see or hear from him again, she first found out about me. Although it would take another nine months for definitive proof, Mum said she knew from that very first moment, that I was a boy.

"My special, precious boy," Mum said with that same sad, lopsided smile. "And I know exactly when and where it all started. Where *you* started, Evvy."

"I don't need to ask Mum," I said, the words tumbling out of me while the man in the posh suit listened impassively. "I know already. So why don't you go ahead and tell me, *Mister Thinks He Knows Everything About Our Lives.*"

He didn't hesitate, not even for a split second.

"The Fontainebleau Hotel, Miami Beach."

The man who was calling himself my father took another step towards me. Brock bristled by my side. And standing there in that decrepit, run-down parking lot, the same one I'd kicked a ball around in all those years ago, I knew, from somewhere deep inside, that the words of old DC Chipman had come true in more ways than one.

It wasn't ever gonna be the same around here again.

12

"Listen, Evan," said Suit-Man after a long while when neither of us had said anything. "I know this is a big shock to you. And I'm sorry for just coming up to you like this, out of the blue. I've actually been sitting in this parking lot for over an hour, waiting for you to come home. But it would be really great to speak properly. So why don't you hop in the car, and we can just sit and talk? Or we take a little drive if you prefer? It's a lot warmer here. What do you say?"

Not so fast, smooth guy.

"What about Brock?" I said, gesturing with my head towards The Beast, still bristling at my side. "Where I go, he goes."

"Um, well … let me think about that for a second."

For the first time since we had started speaking, Suit-Man looked uncertain. He glanced towards the open car door, which had exposed the plush interior and its leather upholstered seats. I could tell I had the dude rattled. That was cool with me. I figured that any moment, he'd step back into his E-class and zoom off, leaving me and super-dog alone for good.

"Right," he said finally. "If that's the way it's got to be, then that's the way it's got to be. Come on Brock, jump in."

And with that, he held the passenger door of the car an inch or so wider with one arm, while making a welcoming gesture with his other in the direction of my dog. It was a move I wasn't expecting. I couldn't help but feel that I'd been outmanoeuvred – again. But he'd called my bluff, so now I had to play the hand I'd been dealt.

94

"Let's go, Beast," I said reluctantly, tugging gently on the lead. Brock didn't budge.

"Look," I said quietly, bending down on my haunches so that me and my dog were at eye level. "I don't like this anymore than you do. But this guy just made me look pretty stupid. So let's just go with it for a bit. You can slobber and shed hair all over his expensive leather seats for all I care. But we need to find out what he wants; who he really is? OK?"

Brock gave me the deadpan black eyes look – again. He wasn't cutting me much slack lately. But I held his gaze, reminding him that even though he was my absolute top dog, there could still only be one boss around here.

A moment later, we were settled in the back of the E-class, Brock sniffing and shedding all over the upholstery. That's my boy! Suit-Man came round the other side, joining us on the spacious, cushioned back seat. He glanced at Brock, a frown passing across his face for the briefest of moments, and then leaned forward and said something I didn't quite catch to a man in the driver's seat.

"So, who's this in the driver's seat? Your chauffeur?" I joked.

"Ah, yes, he is my driver, actually. Evan meet George."

Smooth move, Einstein! What stupid thing was I going to say next: nice threads mate; where'd you get them – Primark or Matalan?

Having proven myself to be a complete idiot from the moment I had first spoken to this guy, I changed tactics. Going forward, I'd play it cool – like The Beast. *Silent, but deadly.*

So we sat there saying nothing for a good minute or so. Pressed up against me, Brock started gnawing at my jeans pocket. He could smell blueberry muffin crumbs. I gently but firmly pushed his face away. "Chill, Beast," I whispered.

Finally, Suit-Man cleared his throat.

"So, I guess you're wondering what I'm doing here, showing up out of nowhere after all this time?"

I didn't reply. *Remember the new tactic: silent but deadly.*

My muteness didn't seem to bother him.

"Let me start near the beginning. I grew up not far from here with almost nothing. Got a job on the Stock Exchange floor and made a bit of money. Then I decided to go out on my own, into property. Which is when things started happening. Buy, do it up, sell. That was the plan. And it worked, time after time. But I knew it wouldn't last forever – nothing does. So I got out just in time. When the GFC hit in 'oh seven, I wasn't exposed like most of the others. So I could sit tight, and wait it out. Which I did. And while everyone was getting killed by the market, I was back on the field again. I did good, real good. Made some serious money. The rest is history."

He stopped and looked straight at me. I barely knew what he was talking about. GFC? What did that stand for: Great Football Clubs? And what did that have to do with 'oh seven'? I didn't remember any English clubs winning the Champions League that year.

"But listen to me go on, rambling about stuff you probably don't care about. Sorry 'bout that; I just wanted to give you some background so you'd know where I stand."

I said nothing. *Stick to the game plan, Banksky.*

"Anyhow, what you probably really want to know is some context. What am I doing here? What do I want? Well, let me be straight with you – just like I am in business – and come out with it."

Yeah, come out with it Suit-Man. Like where you been the last sixteen years while we've been duckin and divin all over the show?

Then he did a strange thing. He turned his head away from me and looked out the tinted window.

"I'm about to turn fifty next month, Evan. I've got a wife and two beautiful little girls aged seven and five. Marla's just turned forty and she's done with nappies and all that. But I want a son. Always have done. And especially now. You see, I'm getting tired of the game. Been playing it for over thirty years. But now I'm ready to hand it over. To someone younger, fresher, hungrier. Someone who can take everything I've built ... and build more. Sure, I could sell the business – don't think I haven't had huge offers. But why would I want to sell something that I built with my own hands, day after day, year after year? I don't need to work another day for the rest of my life; for at least two more lives. So what's the point in selling? I don't need more money. What I need is ..."

He was silent for a long moment. George, the driver up front, stifled a cough. Suit-Man turned his face towards me; the redness around his eyes catching me by surprise.

"... What I need is my own son to give it to. And that's you ... Evan."

We sat in the back of that E-class in total silence for a long time, two absolute strangers, our legs almost touching. All this talk of family and money was filling my mind with confused thoughts. Playing it cool had suddenly become a lot harder. And then, the first crack in my plan appeared.

"How did you even know I existed? Mum said she never told the man who was my father that I'd ever been born."

"Good question," he replied effortlessly. "Here's the thing: I'd always had a hunch that maybe your Mum had gotten pregnant during that trip to Miami, especially because she refused to see me every time I tried make contact for months afterwards. So I just had this feeling that something was up. But there was nothing I could do, so I got on with my life and my business."

Well, why don't you mind your own business now, and just leave us the hell alone!

"So why are you making contact now, after all these years?"

Not exactly silent. Nor deadly. Moron!

"Well, I could have just left things as they were, Evan. But that isn't my style. So when I decided it was time to settle down and retire, I started thinking back on my life and who had been part of it. And thinking about your mother, I decided it was time to find out once and for all what happened with her. Like had my hunch about her being pregnant been correct?"

Yeah, it was correct airhead. Here I am!

"So, how did you find us?"

Suit-Man took his time before answering that one.

"I learned a long time ago that there is very little that money can't buy. And one of those things is information. So I hired a private investigator, and, to be completely honest, it was pretty easy after that. Once we established that your mother hadn't married or changed her name, it didn't take long. And then there's Facebook of course, where you can find just about anyone these days. So it was easy to find out about you. And it was easy to find out about her life. I know about the drinking. I know about the gambling. I know she owes some bad people a serious amount of money she doesn't have. I know she starts and loses jobs more often than Chelsea football club changes managers. I know that she says and does outrageous things all the time. I know she can spend days on end stuck up there in that little flat, not going anywhere or doing anything. And I know that her life, which I guess means your life too, is – to be frank – a complete shambles."

It was time to smack the stuffing out of this guy! Who the hell does he think he is, having a go at Mum like that? Spying on us and pretending to know everything about our lives?

But that's not what I said. Not at all. My plan was in tatters. Silent and deadly had completed its transformation to meek and mild. Which explained my next stupid question.

"Does Mum know you are here, talking to me?"

"No, she doesn't. And I know she wouldn't want us to be having this conversation. We both know that. But you're almost sixteen-years-old, Evan. So I think it's time you started making your own decisions. And that's why I'm going to give you something to think about; an offer for you to consider."

"Offer? What kind of offer?" I croaked.

Suit-Man opened his mouth to respond, but then he seemed to change his mind. "Well … actually, I can see how this is a lot to take in in one go. And we've just met. So how about you join us at home for dinner tomorrow night and then I'll explain what I have in mind? We live not too far from here on The Bishops Avenue. And Mrs. Dennis makes a brilliant beef wellington on Wednesday nights. You can meet the girls and Marla. You can even bring your dog," he added, motioning – cautiously – towards The Beast.

That's right, we've just met. And you've just told me you're the father I've never known. So that makes perfect sense: dinner, meet the family and have a little chat. Maybe over port and cigars in the study afterwards. What kind of a pushover does this guy think I am?

"Uh, well, ya know, I'm not sure 'bout that … then again, I got no football training tomorrow night … did you say beef wellington?"

"Absolutely. One of Mrs. Dennis' best dishes."

"Uh … guess no harm in coming for a bit of a graze. So yeah, I guess I'll come."

A Premier League wuss of a pushover, that's who!

"Great. 6 pm. Can I send George here to come and pick you up then?"

No, don't worry mate. I've got my own E-Class parked around the back side of the building so I'll drive over in that.

"Yeah, sure."

"Perfect, see you then," he said, flashing a smile that I bet had already sealed a whole lot of big West End property deals over the last twenty or so years. "Oh, Evan. One other thing: Probably best not to mention anything to your mother at this stage. What's the point in possibly upsetting her while we are just getting to know each other? That cool with you?"

No, it's not cool with me, douche-bag. Why would I keep this from Mum? She's the one who – her problems and all – has always been there for me. So why would I go betray her now?

But I was way too far gone for that response.

"Yeah, that's cool."

"Brilliant." Then he slipped his hand into his jacket pocket and pulled out a small piece of rectangular cardboard.

"Here's my contact details. Just message me if any change of plans."

He handed me his thick business card. On the front of it, embossed in gold letters against an all-black background, were printed the following words:

William J. Woodford,
Founder & CEO, Total Construction Ltd.

I stared at the card for a long while, not sure what to do next. Fortunately, The Beast did. He started scratching at my leg. Time to go. I opened the car door and Brock leapt right out, heading straight for the single lamppost in the lot, his back right leg already half-suspended before he got there.

"K, see ya tomorrow," I mumbled, as I closed the car door and watched my dog do his thing.

George, the driver, put the E-class into reverse and kicking up the gravel stones of the Sweet Orchard Place parking lot, the car sped off in the direction of a life I had never known. I stayed staring at the place where the luxury vehicle containing my alleged father – William J. Woodford – had been parked. Then I called Brock to my side. But super-dog was having none of that, instead uttering a high pitched bark and giving me a strange look.

"Sorry Beast, not sure what to make of all this yet. We'll get a better picture tomorrow night. Now … let's go inside – and not a word to Mum, K? I just need a hot shower and some peace and quiet to think things over."

My dog, once a ferocious beast who could put fear into the eyes of the most hardened gangsters, responded by putting his tail between his legs and following me obediently up the eleven flights of stairs.

Brilliant, I thought. *I've even managed to turn a Beast into a world class pushover.*

Just as I was stepping out the shower, Mum arrived back from work. She had picked up a Domino's on the corner opposite the tube station on the way home. We ate it wordlessly on the couch, while an old guy on the TV was going on the whole time about some war in Africa that meant lots of poor people had to go find another country to live in real fast. I felt sorry for them. But I had my own stuff to worry about right now. Mum was in her post-drinking/post-gambling mood – all quiet and upset and sad and embarrassed at the same time. There was nothing to do but sit it out and wait for her to come back to herself in her own time. We'd been here before.

Of course, I didn't mention anything to Mum about William J. Woodford, his E-class and all his perfectly correct answers to my questions. Or his invitation to dinner and Mrs. Dennis' beef wellington or any of that crazy stuff. And I for sure didn't say anything about the boys in prison, the knife I'd found, or the likelihood of her accompanying me to the police station for an interview. Now was definitely not the time.

But I couldn't stop turning the events of the last 48 hours over and over in my mind. Assuming William J. Woodford really was my father, what was I going to do? What was I to make of his wild story about not knowing he had a son until recently, becoming a gizillionaire and wanting to share all his dosh with me? Which got me to thinking about all the other mad stuff happening in my life. The boys in lock-up and that lad in hospital. The coppers and that tall big-shot guy in uniform with the psycho stare. And that freakin knife with streaks of red hidden in The Ring. Was I just gonna leave it there forever and tell no one?

The questions went round and round, like one of those big old washing machines in the laundromat on the other side of the estate. My head was on a super-fast spin cycle – and I couldn't get it to stop.

I needed to get relief. Without the boys and the basketball court to go to, watching *Game of Thrones* was the next best option. But even then, I couldn't focus properly. My mind kept drifting to a whole bunch of questions for which there seemed to be no good answers. Eventually, I gave up. So having scraped the last bit of cheese off the inside of the cardboard box, I scrunched it up real small so it could squeeze into our way-too-narrow kitchen bin and took Brock down one last time. Then I said good night to Mum and collapsed on my bed.

But sleep didn't come easy. Wild visions assaulted my dreams: dozens of uniformed policemen marching through the park carrying giant pink iPhones; a grey-bearded Brock hunting squirrels in the bushes while a Staffordshire Bull Terrier in dreadlocks bit at his heels; a battered shopping bag filled with fifty pound notes abandoned inside a hollowed out log; an assortment of Disney cartoon characters chasing each other with enormous steak knives; and all the while, a huge old washing machine going round and round, spilling streams of dark red liquid all over an empty basketball court.

13

I was woken up late the next morning by Brock's clearly illegal high-tackle – definite red card! We wrestled on the cold floor for a good few minutes before jointly deciding to call it a draw. The flat was dead quiet, meaning Mum had got herself off to work again. Definitely a sign of progress. Had she turned a corner, perhaps?

Padding to the kitchen, I encountered some seriously bad news: the Crunchy Nut box was empty. There was nothing in the lone cupboard that could even remotely qualify for breakfast other than a stale box of Rice Krispies, whose packaging looked like it hadn't changed since the 1950's. (Actually, I'm sure it hasn't. Fortunately, Snap, Crackle and Pop really haven't aged a bit!) I decided to pass.

I reckoned the day would best be spent by some uninterrupted *Games of Thrones* catch-up time. But after three full episodes, Brock was starting to climb the walls. Even Ghost, the great Direwolf, lost his appeal after a while. So once I finally got myself out of my boxers and vest, the problem was what to do. No mates, no Tals – she was taking these A-levels *way* too seriously, no football training, no gym (I had just received a text that read: *The gym will be closed for essential maintenance until Friday morning.* Seriously? It's not as if the place had a sauna, a hot tub, an Olympic size swimming pool and a Pilates studio full of women over the age of 55 trying to rebuild their core. So what kind of "essential maintenance" were they on about?).

"How 'bout a squirrel hunt?" I finally offered The Beast.

His over-the-top response – yelping, barking and an embarrassing amount of slobbering – was roughly the equivalent of my own reaction that time Jez scored us tickets on the half-way line for a Spurs-Chelsea home game. Moments later, not bothered by the foul weather, Brock and I found ourselves making the short walk to The Corner. That's just the way we roll, if ya know what I mean. I reached the benches and plonked myself down, pulling my jacket tight to keep out the cold wind. Meanwhile, The Beast got busy with what he was put on this earth to do: sending the entire bushytailed population of the park into full-blown panic mode.

Left alone, I had the time – way too much of it actually – to think about everything that had gone down last night in the Sweet Orchard Place parking lot. *Had that really happened?* Had someone claiming to be my father just appeared out of nowhere in a Mercedes E-class with his own driver and invited me to his home and into his life? A life that – although less than three miles down the road – might as well be on the other side of the world when you took into account the difference between The Bishops Avenue and the council estate we lived on. (To give you a better picture: the entire estate consisting of a few hundred flats could probably fit on the property of *one* of those huge Hampstead homes!)

A thickening in my back pocket reminded of the business card handed to me last night. I reached back and pulled it out. *William J. Woodford.* My father. Head of a massive construction firm. And wanting to give it to his just-discovered son. Me. *How wild is that?* I guess I was going to find out over dinner at six o'clock tonight.

But in the meantime, I needed to keep my mind busy or I was gonna go crazy. Easier said than done when sitting by yourself on a freezing park bench watching your dog running in circles.

106

Especially as I'd run out of data and couldn't get Wi-Fi connection in the middle of the park. I groaned. No *Game of Thrones*. Or even old episodes of *Line of Duty*. Things were getting so severe that I almost wished that the tall dude with dreadlocks and the cool Staffie would appear, just so that I could have someone to talk to. But the park was so empty that a full-on game of Hogwarts Quidditch could be taking place without anyone noticing. Which got me to thinking about the time a few months back when the whole gang was skiving off on the benches – even Tals was there that day. For some stupid reason, we began handing out Harry Potter character names to everyone. Jams was Snape. Mo claimed Voldemort, with an evil kind of laugh. Somebody decided that I should be Neville Longbottom. I can't remember who Jez and D-von were – maybe the Weasley boys? And then Jams told Tals she was Hermione.

"Why Hermione?"

I immediately regretting asking that. But it was too late now. Fool.

"Cause she's all prissy and stuck up, just like that Hermione bird. Won't let any of the boys near her, ya know what I mean?"

As he said the final words, Jams flicked his used rollie in Tals' direction and winked at us boys. (Tals couldn't see cause Jams was sitting with his back to her.) Then he turned to face her directly and said,

"Hey Hermione. How 'bout you and me go on a little date some time. Screw this crew. Just the two of us. I'll show you a real good time, girl, I promise you that. Know what I mean?"

You'd have to be blind and deaf not to get his meaning.

"I don't think so," Tals responded quietly.

"What's the matter?" asked Jams with a sneer. "Big Jammo not good enough for a posh 6th former like you?"

"Not at all," Tals replied smoothly. "It's just that I don't think we'd have too much to talk about. Like once we had finished discussing what you'd had for breakfast and how cool your tats are, what would be left to speak about? Your views on global warming? Your thoughts on the mental health crisis facing young people in this country? Your career plans for the future?"

She paused then and fixed Jams with a look that – from my vantage point – didn't look too good.

"I don't think so, *Big Jammo*. So thanks, but no thanks."

There was a long moment of silence that enveloped everyone on the bench. I'd never heard anyone speak to Jams like that. In turn, he glared at Tals in a way that made me real nervous. I didn't know what to do. So I looked down. As did everyone else. Except Mo, who had this stupid grin on his face. And except Tals. She wasn't having any of it. She returned his stare with interest.

After what seemed way too long a period of time, Jams finally said in a low voice, bordering on a growl, "You watch your mouth, girl."

"Or what?"

"Or I'll have to do something to keep it from being so disrespectful."

Another long silence. I sensed Tals looking at me – I was sitting right next to her – waiting for me to say something. Anything. But I didn't. I just kept looking down at a crack in the bench that was the most fascinating crack I had ever discovered. Wuss. Chicken. Coward. You choose the word.

Suddenly, Jams let out a laugh. A laugh that was rough and coarse and loud all at the same time. And then the rest of us joined in, laughing along with Jams like we were all hanging out at a Michael McIntyre gig together. Everyone except for Tals. She hopped off the bench and without another word, began walking swiftly across the park in the direction of the exit. As she went, I was pretty sure I saw a single tear drop from her eye to the ground. But that didn't stop me from laughing with the rest of the boys while we watched her go. And just then, two thoughts occurred to me. One: I felt like a complete mug; and two: I doubted we would be seeing Tals round by the benches for a while. Come to think of it, it was the last time I ever saw Tals down by The Corner. After that, it was just us boys.

The memory of that whole ugly episode made me wince. To make matters worse, the wind was up now and the thick, black clouds were rolling in fast. Seconds later, the rain began lashing down. There was only one place I knew of to get relief from the rain at such short notice.

"Come on Beast," I called, "We gotta get to dry ground."

Brock came bounding over and together we made a mad dash for the caf's front door. I came crashing through it at such pace that I was almost in the middle of its little seating area before I came skidding to a very wet halt. That old lady with the long grey ponytail and the walking stick was sitting in the corner booth again, while Monroe was standing next to her table. They seemed to be in the middle of a serious discussion, but the chef broke it off as soon as he saw me.

"Evan, Brock, how you both doing? Haven't seen you around for a few days, and was starting to get a bit worried, especially after all that trouble around here at the beginning of the week." Then he looked down at the puddle we were both making on the floor. "Now, don't stand in the middle of my café making a flood all over my floor or I'll need to build an ark any minute. Come on in and let's get something warm inside of you. How about a hot bowl of mushroom soup? I just made a huge pot of it."

I wasn't sure about that, being broke and all. But as I'd skipped breakfast and my stomach was growling something bad, the smell of that soup already had me hooked.

"Uh, yeah. OK. Thanks."

"No worries, mate. Go take a seat over there," he said, pointing one of his arms in the direction of a booth near where the old lady was sitting. "I'll bring it round in a sec."

I plonked down on a padded bench and tried to wring some of the water out of my hoodie while Brock collapsed at my feet, all squirrelled out. Glancing over to where the old lady was sat, I noticed that she was looking very intently at a photo on her phone. Actually, very intently would be an understatement. More like staring as if she had seen a ghost. I was just starting to wonder what that was all about when Monroe arrived with a massive steaming bowl of soup, sprinkled with onion croutons. Just what The Banksy ordered! I grabbed the gleaming spoon already resting on the table and fished out a perfect size mushroom.

"You the man. Thanks Monroe."

"Sure thing, Evan." He hovered above the table, like a giant dinosaur checking on her unhatched eggs, while casting occasional

110

glances at the old lady as he did. "So ... what's up with you? Walking around getting all drenched in the middle of the day?"

"You don't want to know."

"Try me," he said. "It's not like I got a whole lot else going on right now."

I really didn't feel like telling Monroe about the sudden arrival of my alleged father, his multi-million pound business and this mysterious offer that he wanted to speak to me about over dinner, all of which were taking up some major space in my head. But I guess there was some other stuff that I didn't mind talkin about.

"Well, things are just a bit rough right now," I began, already feeling the warm glow of the soup as it settled in my empty stomach. "Got suspended from school for a week and then you know the story with the boys in lock-up. Plus some other stuff that's all a bit much."

"Sorry to hear that man," said the big Filipino with a gentle shake of his huge head. "I guess you've got a lot on your mind right now?"

"You got no idea. I'm having so many crazy thoughts that I'm even dreaming about them now. And they leave me feeling all messed up."

I shook my head, as if that would help get rid of the confusing feelings. It didn't.

Monroe looked at me thoughtfully. "I get that, mate. So ... would you mind if I share something with you that I recently figured out about all this feelings stuff?"

111

"Hey, it's your caf. Go ahead."

"Actually, it's Keith's place. I just work here. But I know what you mean. Anyhow, here's the thing about feelings: Most people don't realise that thought and feelings are always connected. It's kinda like they are married for life."

"Yeah ... So?"

I was already finding this conversation less exciting than watching paint dry.

"So whatever you are feeling – like fear or worry or whatever – is always coming from thought."

In spite of myself, I considered that for a moment. "OK," I said cautiously as I shovelled another spoon of hot soup into my mouth, my body temperature rising at least another three degrees as a result. "Maybe that's true. But I just wish some of these thoughts would leave me alone, cause the feelings they are bringing is all getting a bit much, ya know?"

"Yep, I know Evan. I feel the same way sometimes," said the chef. "You see, because thought is invisible, we kind of end up acting as if it's not actually happening. And then we make the mistake of thinking that the connection to feelings is no longer there. Which creates a problem for us."

"What problem?" I asked. Was it the mushroom soup or was I actually warming to what the big guy was saying?

"Well, when we don't see that the power supply of feelings is thought, we try to look for some other reason that explains why we feel the way we do," answered Monroe.

It hit me in that moment that the old expression, *never judge a book by its* cover, was a real good one. This was one clever chef.

"I'm not sure I get you."

"OK, so let's make this whole idea more practical. Why don't you tell me one thing that you've been thinking a lot about lately?"

I hesitated for a second. There was no way I was going to say anything about that freakin knife. But Mum's issues with Vic, the threatening bookie? That was cool.

"My Mum has gotten herself into a hole. She owes a ton of money to someone who isn't going to take 'no' for an answer."

"Oh, man, that sounds tough," said Monroe in a genuinely caring tone. "How you feeling about it all?"

"Awful. It's driving me crazy. I'm really worried. This isn't the kind of guy you mess around with."

"Yeah, sounds about right. So let me ask you something. What is causing you to feel so worried?"

I didn't want to be rude, but that sounded like a stupid question.

"Isn't it obvious? This guy is dangerous. He could hurt Mum. Or worse."

Monroe ignored the frustration in my voice. "Fair enough. But let me ask you something else. Has there been any time over the last few days when you felt differently about this situation with your Mum?"

Good question. I took a big gulp of mushroom soup as I considered my response.

"Yeah, there has been," I said after a while. "The other day, when I was reading about this kid named Owen who'd had a tough time of it with autism and everything. It got me thinking that maybe some of my problems weren't as bad as I had thought."

"Nice one," said Monroe. "So how did you feel about your Mum's problems after reading about that Owen boy?"

"I felt better, more relaxed."

"Well, there you go," said Monroe matter-of-factly. "When you had a different thought, you had a different feeling. Simple as that."

I thought about that for a moment. "Yeah, makes sense. Actually, what you're saying is pretty cool," I said as I dropped the spoon on the table, pulled the soup bowl towards me, and grabbing it by its sides, drained the last bit of liquid. When I looked up from my bowl, my eyes caught those of the old lady. For some weird reason – and it's definitely not cause I'm some kind of magnet for significantly older women or anything – she smiled at me. And as much as it ain't my style to admit it, I gotta say: it was a really nice, warm smile.

"Hey, thanks Monroe," I said, refocussing quickly. "That was real good." I looked up at the big man a little anxiously. "Listen, I'm a bit tight at the moment. Can I sort you out next week?"

"No worries, Evan. It's on the house, mate." He glanced around the near empty café. "With the weather like it is today, there isn't going to be many customers coming our way. So that big pot on the stove was going to go to waste anyway."

"Nice one, Monroe. Appreciate that."

I looked out the window and saw the rain had slowed to a steady drizzle. "Well, gotta get Brock back on the hunt. But thanks for the chat, the soup and the dry roof when I needed it. Catch you later."

I made my way out the door thinking about what Monroe had just said and how it sounded a lot like some of the other strange conversations I'd been having over the past couple of days since I'd been kicked out of school. The bag lady at the coffee shop, the man with the wild beard and now the chef at the caf. They had all been saying pretty much the same thing: *Thought creates feeling. Nothing else.* Weird.

"Hey, Ev, wait up, Bro," a familiar voice called out.

I looked up to see the tall, loping figure of Jez jogging across the park in my direction. While we both shared the hoodie and torn jeans thing, that was where our physical similarities ended. Jez was already well over six foot. His whole long and lanky look didn't quite go with, well, my *not* long and lanky look. Now that he wasn't in school no more, he had also allowed a permanent patch of stubble to rent space on his thin face while growing out his stringy black hair on the back side of his head. The whole vibe made him appear to be like a seventeen-year-old who didn't go to school anymore, didn't have much else to do, and didn't seem to care either way. Which I guess was kinda true.

"Jez!" I shouted. "They let you out! Welcome back, Bro."

We did the fist-bump thing and threw in a man-hug for good measure. "Where's the rest of the gang?"

"I think they still stuck in lock-up, Bro."

"So how come you got out?"

"Think they knew I was sweet, ya know. Cause when it all went down, I ran straight into the caf over there and told that massive chef guy to call 999. So I think he kinda stood for me and told 'em coppers I was cool."

"That's sick, mate. Really."

"Yeah, it is."

Neither of us said anything for a moment. But then my big mouth kicked into gear.

"I got kinda lucky being late for the game that night. Had to sort Mum and all. Otherwise, I reckon would have landed up in lock-up like the rest of you."

"Yeah, I guess that was lucky," Jez said, a funny look on his face. *"For you."*

I didn't know what to say to that. So we just stood there getting soaked by the soft rain, looking at each other. It was, well – considering I was talking to one of my best mates – weirdly kind of awkward. So I decided to try another direction.

"Things got a fair bit wild with the gang the last while, don't ya think? Especially with them other boys who wanted the court. Even if they are a bunch of losers." I added quickly.

"Yeah, guess so," Jez answered, looking away as he did.

I decided to plough ahead, big mouth and all. "Reckon Mo and Jams have been acting a bit aggro lately, taking all that booze and weed and stuff. Guess that didn't help none."

"Dunno. Guess not."

I'm no psychologist, but it was pretty easy to see that this wasn't a talk Jez wanted to have. Then again, when I thought about it, neither did I.

"Hey, it's freezing out here man," Jez announced suddenly. "Ya wanna come over and play some Fortnite. Nobody's home so we can nick a few beers from my old man's bar fridge and just do our own thing."

"Sorry mate. Would be sick but gotta go see someone over in Hampstead."

"Hampstead? You serious? Isn't that where all the rich geezers live? What ya going there for?"

"Long story." I glanced at Brock. "Listen, we gotta go get ourselves suited and booted. Let's game later, K?"

"Sure."

We did another quick fist-bump and were about to head off in opposite directions when my big mouth decided to have one more go.

"Hey, Jez … when d'ya think the other boys will get out?"

"Dunno. I reckon that D-Von may get let out soon. Not so sure 'bout Mo and Jams. Seems like there's more heat on 'em. But here's the thing, Ev: they ain't got nuthin on them. And as long as they don't find no weapon, then the boys will be cool. Cause it's like the main evidence, ya know. So without it, then there ain't no crime, know what I mean?"

"Yeah, I know it exactly, Bro," I said.

117

But what I really wanted to say was: *Mate, we are standing not fifty feet away from the very evidence you're talking about. The knife, the freakin knife! It's right over there, in the flippin Ring!*

For once, I managed to keep my mouth shut.

14

As arranged, George picked us up at six o'clock, sharp. Less than ten minutes later, having made our way up the long, winding driveway of the biggest home I had seen since our school trip to Blenheim Palace back in Year 7, The Beast and I were climbing out of the back of the E-class. WJW – that's what I had taken to calling him in my mind (what were my other options: Dad? Come on!) – was waiting for me in front of an enormous oak door as we arrived. He had gone for the casual look: a button down grey jumper, blue trousers that definitely didn't come from Primark, and a pair of brown leather shoes that looked like they were worth significantly more than the average monthly apartment rental at Sweet Orchard Place. This caused me to look down and experience a brief moment of panic. I had swapped my hoodie for a New York Yankees baseball cap that I wore in reverse, and a tight-fitting black T-shirt that was poking out from under my jacket. But besides that, my wardrobe had not experienced a significant functional upgrade for my first-ever dinner on The Bishops Avenue. Actually, in retrospect, a strong argument could be made for experiencing a significant wardrobe malfunction by *not* upgrading.

But if he was bothered by the back-to-front cap, tight shirt and torn jeans, WJW didn't let on. He ushered us into the entrance hall with a firm handshake and a big smile. He even got down on his haunches to ruffle the top of Brock's head. The last person who had done that outside The Hollywood Bowl had almost lost a finger. But somehow The Beast sensed that a more muted response would be more appropriate in this environment, so he settled for a low growl while I wondered if WJW had any clue how close he had come to sustaining serious injury.

"Great to see you, Evan. And Brock. Thanks for coming. Now, come in and meet Marla and the girls."

He escorted us into an open-plan room so large that 50 Cent may not have been able to sell the place out if he was playing there. WJW steered us towards one corner of the room where the rest of the family was seated.

"Evan, this is my gorgeous wife, Marla, and my darling daughters, Aimee and Eleanor."

"Uh, hi," I said. I've always been real smooth at introductions. Brock stayed silent, clearly overawed by the occasion.

"Hi Evan," the two girls said in perfect unison. Had they practised that?

Then: "Do you want to see our bunny wabbit?" asked the younger one – was that Aimee?

Bunny wabbit? Seriously? Fortunately, Marla came to my rescue.

"Maybe later, sweetheart. Let Evan take off his jacket and settle down, first."

Then Mrs. Woodford lifted herself elegantly off the sofa and stood up. She was tall and slim, her heavily made-up face surrounded by wisps of long brown hair that arranged themselves into a strange kind of curl at the end. Her high heels clicked on the wooden floor as she stepped towards me. For a second, I thought she was going to welcome me with a kiss on either cheek, like I had once seen a couple of French folk do on a TV show. But then she just clasped her hands in front of her and said,

"Welcome to our home, Evan." She completely ignored Brock.

We all stood there not saying or doing anything besides welcoming each other and making bunny invitations. I guess it was even getting a bit weird for them, cause Marla suddenly coughed and announced:

"Well, the girls have got an important ballet recital tomorrow after school and I don't want them to have a late night. So let's make our way straight to the dining room."

She led us to a table approximately the size of Wimbledon Centre Court. WJW eased himself into a chair at the head of the table and motioned for me to sit directly to his right. Fortunately, I'd had the smarts to feed Brock before we came, so he lay down calmly at my feet. Good super-dog. In front of me was a place-setting consisting of what appeared to be a china plate, a crystal glass and more cutlery than Mum and I had in our entire kitchen drawer.

I wasn't sure how to break the ice, but fortunately, Marla was clearly an experienced hostess who knew how to take charge of this kind of situation. Unfortunately, she chose the wrong subject for conversation.

"So, Evan," she began politely. "How is school going?"

"Uh, not too good."

"I understand. Doing your GCSE's can be quite stressful."

"Nah, it's not that. I couldn't give a rats about my GCSE's. It's because I got myself suspended."

"Ooh, I hate rats," cried out seven-year-old Eleanor. "Mommy, are there rats in Evan's school?"

An awkward silence.

"No darling, there are no rats in Evan's school," explained Marla quickly, stroking her daughter's back as she did. "I'm sorry to hear about the suspension," she added.

"Don't matter none. The whole thing's like one big wind-up. Even though Tals says that I didn't give that old nutter Porcu-dog much choice cause I bunked off during school time and kept getting caught smoking, we can all agree that's way harsh. But I don't care. The whole place is a waste of space anyhow."

Another long silence. During this period, it occurred to me that I would benefit from establishing a relationship – any relationship – between my brain and my mouth.

"Girls," Marla said eventually. "Come and help me with the first course, please."

That left WJW and I alone on Centre Court. I was starting to feel real uncomfortable, but then WJW found a way to my heart.

"So ... Just over two months to go and Spurs are still properly in it at the business end of the season. Do you think this is the year they can finally go all the way?"

I wanted to say: *They. Who is "they"? Don't you mean "we"?* But I let that one go. After all, I was a guest here and beef wellington was about to be fed to me.

Except it wasn't. Marla and the girls reappeared moments later carrying small plates of some oily, slimy orange thing sitting on top of some gross, mushy green thing, while bits of tree leaves lay randomly scattered on top of each one of the orange-green things.

"Smoked salmon and avocado stacks," announced Marla. "A little appetizer to get us started."

I had never eaten smoked salmon before, so this was gonna be a problem. And what about the beef wellington? Wasn't that the Mrs. Dennis dinner deal on Wednesday nights?

Marla must have sensed something was up. "Is everything OK, Evan?"

I needed a lie. Fast.

"Uh, yeah, fine. It's just that I'm allergic to fish, ya know."

"Oh, I didn't know that," she said. I wasn't sure if it was a look of sympathy or annoyance she offered me. Either way, my lie was gathering momentum all on its own accord.

"Yeah, well, when I was about five or something, Mum took me out for fish 'n' chips down by the Thames somewhere, but I had like a major reaction and they ended up having to call the ambulance and take me to the hospital and give me all injections and stuff. I almost died, ya know."

The only part of the story that was true was Mum taking me out for fish 'n' chips – once. The rest I had seen in a movie a couple of weeks ago. But the Woodfords didn't need to know that.

Marla turned to her husband and gave him a withering look. "William, next time, please ask our guests if they have any food allergies ahead of time so we can plan accordingly."

"Of course, my darling," WJW responded.

I sensed a bit of tension. Perhaps I could help here.

"But the good news is that Brock is *not* allergic to fish. So, would you like me to give my portion to him so it doesn't go to waste?"

Silence. The girls looked at me as if I had just told them that Peppa Pig was actually a goat. Marla looked at me as if I had just asked Brock to lift his leg and do his thing on her appetizer. And WJW didn't look at me at all. He just looked down, suddenly fascinated by the random leaves on his salmon stack thing. Only The Beast looked at me normally. Actually, having heard his name, he began scratching the side of my chair furiously.

By now, Marla had recovered her composure sufficiently to suggest, "Evan, perhaps it would be best if your dog remains outside while we eat our dinner."

Outside. Did she just propose that The Beast, super-dog, the world's undisputed coolest canine, relocate to the garden for the duration of the meal. This could be a deal-breaker. But then, Aimee (or was it Eleanor? – I was already getting confused), piped up,

"Hurray! We're gonna take the doggy into the garden. He'll love the grassy bits. And maybe we'll see the sqwirrel that's been eating all the bunny food."

I swear Brock's ears perked up when he heard the S-word. The girls ran to open the massive sliding door that led onto a patio that led onto a deck that led onto a set of stairs that led onto a garden bigger than Wembley pitch. Brock flew out the door at pace, already in full-blown hunting mode. The girls went squealing with delight after him. Meanwhile, Marla disappeared into the kitchen, which left WJW and I alone in the dining room. It was time to talk – man to man.

"So," he began, placing his elbows on the table and fixing his gaze on me. "You've probably been wondering about that offer which I mentioned last night."

"Uh, yeah." *Focus Banksky and play this cool*, I told myself.

"Right then. Well, I expect this will come as a bit of shock to you, Evan, but I want you to come and live with our family. As you can see, we've got a beautiful big house here with tons of space. You can have your own en-suite room in the loft, kitted out with a laptop, plasma screen, sound system, FIFA 2018 and PS 4 or XBOX 1 – whatever you prefer. I'll send you to a private college, where you can get a proper education and some decent A-levels – it's not too late for that, you know. You'll eat dinner with us every night. No more fish; Mrs. Dennis will make you whatever you like. You'll join us on the awesome holiday to Florida we have planned for this summer – Miami, Orlando, Disney World – the whole shebang. And though Marla isn't exactly a fan of dogs, you can bring Brock to live here too. You've seen the huge garden already and Hampstead Heath is only five minutes walk away – he'll love it. And then, when you finish school, you can come and work for me. No, not for me – *with* me. Unless you want to go to Uni first, of course – that's your call. But sooner or later, I'll teach you all about the business. I'll introduce you to everyone you need to know, and then, when the time's right, I'll hand it all over to you. Because like I said the other night, I've built something really special with my own sweat and blood, and now that I'm ready to step away, I want to give it *to* my blood. Which is you, Evan."

He finally finished and I sensed that I should say something in response. But because I didn't know what, when I did, I sounded like a ten-year-old kid who'd just been offered a free year's supply of Ben & Jerry's ice cream.

"That all sounds awesome. Thanks Mr. Woodford."

"I don't expect you to call me Dad, but please, Evan, call me William. Or Will, if you prefer."

"Uh, OK ... Will."

"Now, one more thing," he continued. "I know you're worried about your mother. I would be. So here's what I'm going to do: I'll pay off this debt she's got. Straight out, in one go, so that she'll be completely free of that whole burden. Well ... that's the offer, Evan. Your mother's problem goes away, you come and live with us, spend time with a real family, and – when the time is right – inherit a huge business portfolio. What do you say, Evan? Are you ready to start a new life?"

My mind was whirling at the speed of a Spurs' counter-attack; I could barely keep up with what he was saying. So, like a good manager, I changed tactics.

"I may not be the sharpest tool in the shed, but it feels like there is something missing here. Are you giving me the full picture ... Will?"

He paused and took a deep breath, glancing towards the kitchen and suddenly looking extremely uncomfortable in his head-of-the-table chair.

"You're a perceptive young man, Evan," he said. Then, leaning forward and lowering his voice slightly, WJW (I'm sorry, but Will just wasn't going to work), surprised me. "I know I look like a successful guy who has got his stuff together. But it's been a much rockier road than the skinny version I gave you last night. There's been a lot of ups and downs along the way. And some of those downs were more like black holes at times."

"Black holes? Whaddaya mean?"

Then WJW surprised me again. "Have you heard of the 12-Step Programme?"

It sounded vaguely familiar. "Hasn't that got something to do with druggies and boozers?"

"Um, yes, sort of. The programme helps people get past their addictions and move forward with their lives. And one of the ways in which this is achieved – one of the key steps – is to make amends."

I had absolutely no idea what WJW was going on about. The confusion on my face clearly gave that away.

"I don't think it's necessary to go into the whole story right now, Evan, but suffice to say, I battled a serious cocaine addiction for a number of years. Things got so bad that Marla threatened to leave me and take the girls. Which is when I joined the programme and started getting help. And I've been doing real good the last while – haven't touched the stuff for almost two years now…"

We were interrupted by a loud noise coming from the garden, followed by lots of excited girl-like shrieking. I knew that sound: Brock had found his quarry, high up in a tree. A moment later, Marla came rushing past with two fleecy-lined matching coats.

"Need to get these on the girls before they catch a cold," she explained.

… "Anyhow," continued WJW, clearly focused now on sharing his story, "Making amends means apologising to the people you've hurt and doing right by them. So that's what I'm doing now. Doing my best to make amends for the damage I've caused your mother and you."

"K. I get that. But it's Mum you should be sorting things out with me, not me."

"You don't think I've tried?" he exclaimed. I couldn't help but notice the frustration – was it desperation? – in his voice. "Once I had tracked your mother down, I asked her loads of times to meet with me, so that I could make good. I called, texted, private messaged her … I even pitched up at the flat one morning soon after you'd left for school. But she wouldn't even open the door to let me in. She's completely shut me out, Evan."

I was totally shocked by what WJW was telling me. Not the shutting out part. That sounded exactly like Mum, especially once she had made her mind up about someone. And Mum had a very long memory. *But not telling me?* We had always shared everything – or so I thought. Now I had just discovered that I hadn't known a thing about any of WJW's attempts to reconnect with her.

"Look, it's ultimately your mother's call. I can't force her to speak to me or meet with me. And I certainly can't force her to accept my apology and my best effort to make things right by her."

WJW was right. He couldn't force Mum. Nobody could. But I still had a real big question which was sat right on the tip of my tongue. Yet just then, a small lady carrying an enormous silver tray entered the dining room from the direction of the kitchen.

"Ah, the beef wellington," declared WJW, "This looks absolutely delicious. Thank you, Mrs. Dennis. And would you be good enough to call Marla and the girls in, please?"

The rest of the evening flew by. After the disappointment of the salmon stack appetizer thing, the main course made a brilliant comeback. The beef wellington was completely sick. Which was kinda what I expected. But what I hadn't expected was the weird kind of feeling that spending time with WJW and his family seemed to give me. In the end, though I didn't have much to say to them about ballet and bunnies, the girls turned out to be quite sweet; WJW seemed to visibly relax once he had put his "offer" out in the open; and even Marla appeared be warming towards Brock by evening's end, conclusively proven when she asked Mrs. Dennis to prepare a little "doggie bag" of leftover beef wellington for The Beast. A bit old school, but definitely a corner turned.

Soon after, Marla took Aimee and Eleanor upstairs for a bedtime story. Seriously. I don't think Mum had ever read anything to me other than the lotto results and the football scores. Which reminded me to check my phone to see if Mum had left any messages. None. But looking at the clock on my mobile, I was shocked to see that it was almost nine. I wasn't bothered that Mum would be worried about me – I often stayed out far later with the boys – but I just wasn't in the mood for any questions she may start asking about where I'd been.

"Listen, I need to get going. Uh, thanks a lot for dinner. And please tell Marla and the girls I said goodbye."

"Will do, Evan," said WJW in response. "George is waiting in the drive to take you home. I'll walk you out."

As we made our way through the massive front door and down the front steps toward his E-class, WJW turned to me and asked, "Have you got any more questions about what we were discussing earlier, Evan?"

"Yeah, one big one," I answered. "I get everything you said about wanting to make things right and say sorry and all that. But as you said, Mum obviously doesn't want your amends. So ... why don't you just move on? Why bother with all this?"

A sad look crossed the man's face. And then it was replaced by a more determined one.

"My lawyer asked me the same question when we were first discussing possible custody rights," he began.

Custody rights? Where did that come from?

Before I had a chance to follow that line of questioning, WJW steamrolled ahead with his answer.

"And what I told him, as I'm telling you now, is this: Because you're still my son, Evan. And I still have a responsibility to sort things out with you. So while I may not be able to make amends with your mother, that doesn't mean I can't make amends with you."

I pulled my thin jacket tight around my shoulders. The temperature had dropped since I had arrived.

"So that's what this whole offer is all about, then?"

130

WJW nodded slowly. "Yep, that's *exactly* what it's all about."

"But here's what I don't get: why not just give Mum and I some money – enough to sort her debt and help get us on our feet? Surely that's the best way to make things right?"

WJW took a long time before answering that one.

"Of course I thought about that, Evan. I even consulted my sponsor – that's like a kind of mentor who keeps an eye out for you all the time you're in the programme – and we both agreed that would not be a good idea. If I just gave you the money, what good would that do in the long run? We both know your mother would just drink or gamble it away. And how would that help you? You'd still be stuck with all your problems – your challenging social and home environment, your below par education. You'd still be looking at things from the bottom up. But my proposal gives you options, Evan. It gives you a chance. It offers you a new life. The life you always deserved. And the life that I can give you. That, son, is what I believe making amends truly means."

My mind was spinning out of control. The day before, when I'd first found out WJW was my father, I'd felt like a Conference team whacked out of the FA Cup by a Premiership side. Now, the extent of his whole offer laid bare, it was much worse than that. I felt like one of Anthony Joshua's early opponents when he was making his way through the heavyweight ranks. In other words, I'd just been knocked flat on my back.

"Look, this is all a bit hectic, know what I mean? Like you said yesterday, you've just appeared out of nowhere. And now you're making this whole massive offer and everything. It means big stuff for Mum and me. So I need some time to think it over, ya know."

"Hey, no problem. Of course I get it. Take your time."

He opened the car's back door and held it in place while Brock and I eased ourselves in.

"Well ... you've got my card and all, so just let me know whenever you want to speak again. Goodnight, Evan."

Good night? More like crazy night. The craziest ever. But that didn't sound like a polite thing to say. So, as I pulled the car door towards me, I settled for,

"Goodnight ... Will."

15

Another extremely late wake up the following morning necessitated an immediate visit to the smallest and most important room in the flat. Having successfully carried out that first mission of the day, I was heading straight back to my bedroom in order to establish if I could break the world record for time spent in bed during the course of one 24 hour period, when I almost stepped on the plain white envelope lying on the floor just inside the doorway. I wouldn't have bothered giving it much thought except for the fact that my name was printed in big black letters on the front of it. Was that a letter from North West Secondary School informing me that a terrible mistake had been made and that actually I was welcome to come back to school straight away? Unlikely, mate. Still, as post addressed to yours truly isn't exactly a frequent occurrence, I picked up the envelope and tore it open. A single piece of handwritten notepaper fell out, which I expertly plucked out of the air.

Hey Evan,

I realised that I may have rushed things last night. My bad. So I thought it might be cool to spend some time together and chill a bit in a less pressurised environment. Get to know each other some more without the family or anyone else around. So I know this is a bit radical and sudden, but how about just me and you spending a few days together – on safari in South Africa? I've got a friend who owns a lodge down there and he owes me a couple of favours. And I managed to get us some last minute business class seats on tonight's BA flight, direct to Johannesburg. Then we'll hop on the little private plane that belongs to this mate of mine, meaning we can be at the lodge watching the lions by sunrise the next morning. We'll be back Sunday night. What do you say? Just message me on the number I gave you the other day to confirm and George will pick you up this afternoon at 4 p.m.

Your Father, Will

PS: Don't forget to pack your sunglasses and swimming trunks. It's summer down there and real hot this time of year!

PPS: Perhaps best to just tell your mother you've decided to spend the weekend with friends, or something like that.

There was something else in the envelope. I pulled out a flimsy piece of rectangular paper. And on it were written a few simple words, which also happened to be just about the most exciting words I have ever read:

British Airway 056, 13 February, 2018, 19:00
London, Heathrow – Johannesburg

I glanced at my dog who was lying like – well, like a tired dog – on the end of my bed. Brock still hadn't seemed to have recovered from last night's excitement. You'd have thought he was the one who had been made offers of amends and all, not me. But then something changed in his expression and The Beast stared back at me with *those* eyes. He knew something was up.

"Sorry, super-dog," I said. "But you're gonna have to keep Mum company this weekend all by yourself. Cause ... The Banksky is going on a South African Safari!"

I don't think I'd been swimming since Mum had taken me to the public swimming pool during half-term, back when I was about ten. And I hadn't owned sunglasses since Jez sat on them accidentally last summer, when we were hanging out down by The Corner. Which meant a visit to the nearest Sports Direct was next on my "to do" list. (*"To do" list? Seriously? What was happening to me*?) It was the only store I could think of where you could buy swim gear and shades for under fifteen pounds, and still probably have enough change leftover to get one of those £1.50 football water bottles they always display at the till. I grabbed my hoodie, the lead and my deflated dog and headed for the door ... when it hit me. Another crucial Sherlock moment. *What was I going to tell Mum?* There was only one person I could think of who could help me with a challenge this big.

I knew Tals had a couple of frees around lunchtime on Thursdays and would head straight to the public library at the top of Church Road to study in her spare time, as had become her habit since the beginning of upper 6th. It was one of the reasons we didn't see as much of each other as we used to. So I figured if I legged it, I could catch her just in time. Because once she entered through those big old wooden doors, into that massive tomb of books and silent stares, there was no chance of speaking to her – especially as taking Brock inside that hallowed building would be about as likely as getting tickets for a Spurs-Arsenal match. We raced all the way to the library, The Beast improving his record against me to 474 – 0, and caught up to Tals just as she was stepping off the bus.

"Hey, Tals, wait up!" I shouted.

She turned on hearing my voice, and I could instantly see by the look on her face that she was still annoyed about our interaction inside the school gates the other day.

"Listen," I said quickly, before she had a chance to say anything. "I'm sorry 'bout the other day. I didn't mean to come off as such a plonker. I was just feelin pretty bummed out by the news about the boys and the suspension. I knew it was coming, you know, but I still always kinda figured I could ride these things out. But I guess Porcu-dog had other ideas. Fair enough. Anyhow, I need your advice 'bout something real important, girl. Can we speak?"

There's two types of friends. Those that forgive. And those that don't. Tals is the first type. Top of the list. Always has been; always will be.

"Sure, Ev," she said, breaking into a big smile as my apology floated all over her and landed square inside her heart. "For you – always." Tals steered me to the bench right next to the bus stop. "What's up, little neighbour?"

So I spent a whole lot of time catching up my friend on everything to do with my alleged father: his sudden appearance in the chauffeur-driven E-class; dinner at the palace-like Woodford home; the crazy offer to become a part of their life; his parting remarks about wanting to make things right with me; and finally,

136

this bonkers, last-minute, 5-star safari trip and my huge dilemma. *How could I say no? What do I tell Mum? Do I tell Mum?*

Tals did what she always did so well. She listened. Tucking a loose braid back into place, she cocked her head ever so slightly to the left, fixed her brown eyes on me, and just let me speak, until I was all done.

"Wow, Ev," she said, when I had finally talked myself to a standstill. "That's some serious stuff you got going on there. So let's try and break this down, bit by bit. Where do you want to start?"

That's Tals. The drama isn't for her. She was right. We needed to break the whole thing down – compartmentalise like that PSHE teacher had once said – and try and work this through step by step.

"OK, you're right Tals, like always. So let's start with WJW. I mean, here's the thing: looks like this guy's gotta be my father, right? It sounds crazy to say it, but how else would be know everything about me and Mum and our lives? And why else would he be willing to take a paternity test, make this huge proposal to sort out my life, pay Mum's debt, train me up and hand over his business to me? I mean, that's all mental. It can't be a wind-up. It's gotta be the real deal, no?"

"Agreed," said Tals. "It's all pretty wild, but there isn't any other reasonable explanation. He's your father. Let's go with that. So what do you want to do about it?"

"I dunno. But I tell you one thing: I've never been on a plane in my life. Hell, you know the farthest I've probably ever been is that school trip to Scotland last year. I mean ... safari in South Africa. Lions, tigers, elephants ... I can't say no to that."

"There aren't any tigers in Africa, dummy."

"What?"

"Tigers are from Asia. Not Africa. Go watch The Lonely Planet. But that's beside the point. You're not using your brain here, Ev. Think about it. This guy – I guess we better call him your father – if he really wanted to spend time and get to know you, he wouldn't be going round leaving plane tickets in envelopes under the door and filling your head with all wild ideas and holidays and stuff. He'd be sitting down with you like a normal person and having proper conversations. And he'd be asking you questions about your life – *your* life, Ev – not only telling you about his. What you like. What you don't like. Who your friends are. Who your top player is. What you want to do when you finish school. Those kind of things."

Tals shook her head, her braids swinging back and forth.

"But even more important is this: he'd be speaking to your Mum, the way adults are supposed to. Even though it's hard, he'd be figuring out a way to have that conversation, not hiring private investigators or whatever to know everything about you. Not skiving around in rundown parking lots, having life-changing chats in the back of some flash car while his driver listens in. Not inviting you over for fancy dinners to meet a family that's got nothing to do with you and making offers that will for sure turn your head. Ev, you need to see what's going on here. Making amends is his agenda, his need. Not yours. He's trying to win you over. Splashing the cash and all that. Can't you see that?"

138

I didn't like how Tals was looking at all this. A kernel of anger was beginning to germinate somewhere inside of me.

"Of course I do," I answered. "I may not be Einstein but I'm not a total idiot either, you know. And I *am* thinking about it with my head. This could sort things out for us big-time. For Mum. For me. Can't *you* see that?"

"Maybe Ev, maybe. But why is your father only showing up now? Just cause he's turning fifty and wants to get his life to fit together all nice and perfect by making amends for some pretty big mistakes he's made. I don't know about that. Sounds like he's known about you for a long time. So where's he been while you and your Mum have been struggling and fighting and trying to make it all work? And now he suddenly pitches up and offers you the world? Whether your Mum likes it or not. This will kill her. You're all she's really got; you know that. So what you gonna do – just pick up and leave her all alone in an old, run-down flat, working in that coffee shop, and tell her: 'No worries Mum – everything's all sorted. I'm just going to live with my other family for a while, but don't sress, I'll drop by on Sunday afternoons for a cuppa tea.' Come on."

"I get it, Tals." I said, my voice rising a pitch higher than normal. "That's what's confusing me so much. But you gotta admit, this is gonna help Mum massively. Her life's a mess and it's only going one way. She's probably gonna end up like old lady McLeod down in flat 602B. Drinking gin and babbling away talking nonsense all day, throwing her empties at us. Where does that leave me? I'm getting dragged down by it, by her, when it's really got nothing to do with me. If I take this money, I can finally get out from under this whole big problem. Sort Mum's debt. Sort our lives. Sort my life."

I leaned back against the bench and closed my eyes. There was a pressure building in my head, kind of like a massive overflowing lake pushing all its weight against a dam wall.

"Listen, little neighbour," Tals said in a far gentler voice. "You know I care for you, right? You're my little bro. And we always said we'd be honest with each other, no matter what, right?"

I opened my eyes and faced her. "Yeah, right."

"So I'm gonna tell it to you straight, as I see it, OK? I know this is a big one. The biggest. But you're missing something really important here. You're assuming that a bunch of outside factors – like getting the money to sort out your Mum's problem – is going to make you feel better. But that's a mistake. Because your feelings are always coming from inside of you, from your own mind. So while it looks like something else – like WJW and his cash – can put a feeling inside of you and make you feel good, it just doesn't work that way. Can you can see that?"

But I didn't see it. And I didn't want to hear it. The kernel of anger had finished germinating.

"What you're saying just doesn't make sense, Tals. I haven't even got the money yet, and I *am* feeling better already. Just knowing we can take care of Mum's situation is huge. And what about all the other stuff he's talking about? The safari? The posh house with all my own cool tech stuff? Maybe even a new school, instead of the prison called NWSS? Just thinking about it all *is* making me feel better."

I felt as if my head was about to explode. "And who made you the expert on all this stuff anyhow?" I asked her, an unmistakable edge creeping into my voice. "Just cause you read some stupid book."

"I've read some deep things in that book," Tals answered softly. "Its good stuff, Ev, and I've learnt a lot. I've been trying to understand some important things about life while you've been hanging out all day doing nothing with those wannabe gangsters on the bench. Guys who got nothing good to say about anyone and are just looking to cause trouble. We both know it was only a matter of time before it found them. You're just lucky you weren't around when that whole fight broke out, or I'd be visiting you in prison now too."

"Hey, chill girl," I told her, unable to keep the anger out of my voice any longer. "You're just bitter with Jams because he got a bit rough when you told him you didn't wanna go out with him."

"A *bit* rough? Are you kidding me, Ev? You remember the disgusting things he said to me and the abusive texts he sent after I said 'thanks, but no thanks.' But all of that's beside the point. This isn't about me or those douche-bags on the bench. It's about you and your choices."

I'd had enough.

"Stop it Tals! Those are my bros, you know."

"Those aren't your bros, Ev. I've been wanting to tell you all this for a while, and I'm really sorry if it sounds a bit harsh, especially with everything you got going on right now. But you got to stay away from those boys. Cause when it suits them, they're gonna just use you, and lose you. And I'm tellin you this, cause I worry about you. And I care."

The dam was about to burst. I know that feeling – they call it the red mist out on the pitch – and it was descending now.

"You're out of line Atalia! Actually, I think you're a bit jealous. Yeah, jealous, that's it. No wonder you're giving me such a hard time and ain't happy for me. That I finally caught a break. A big one. But it's OK, you know. Cause I'm gonna get going with my new life, and if you don't want to be part of that, then I'm cool with that."

"Ev, come on," Tals pleaded. Her eyes had gone all red and moist. "I'm just trying to …."

"I know what you're trying to do. You're trying to get all in my head, tellin me that this stuff ain't real, that I'm not going to feel better inside. That it's all some false paradigm, like that weirdo in dreads was tellin me."

"What weirdo in dreads? I don't know what you're talking …"

"Don't matter. Point is: those are my boys. And you stick by your boys. And now I've got a father, who's got cash and wants to give a big load of it to me. So what if I go on a cool holiday? Mum will get over it. And when I get back, I'll decide where to go live and what to do. But I'm pretty sure it won't be around here. I've had enough of this place. And enough of this bull about my feelings."

A tear had escaped Tals' right eye, glistening against her dark skin as it ran down her cheek. But I was beyond caring. The mist had descended and there was no stopping it now.

"Come on Beast. Let's blow this place," I said, roughly grabbing the lead. I stood and began walking back down Church

142

Road, dragging my reluctant dog with me. Then I turned round and fired one last shot. Just because I could.

"You know what, Atalia Mills? It's not cool being jealous of someone else's success. So why don't you stick with your stupid You've Got Everything You Need book, or whatever it's called. That ain't my scene. Never has been. From now on, my scene is getting what *I* want and what I need. And I don't need nobody telling me different."

Turning hard and fast, I started walking again, leaving my oldest friend crying on a cold bench next to a random bus stop, while I went to buy swim gear and shades at Sports Direct. And as I walked, I took out my phone and typed a short message:

Its evan. Send George. will b ready @ 4

Without giving myself another moment to think about it, I pressed SEND.

16

The silence was deafening, the heat suffocating. I could hear the rhythmic sound of a river flowing somewhere not far away, but that was all. I had been ordered not to move a muscle or speak. So I didn't. The urge to cough, to wipe the sweat off my brow, to stretch, to say something – anything – was almost overwhelming. But then I looked at the man in the khaki uniform sitting just in front of me – the one with the powerful-looking rifle spread across his lap – and thought better of it.

No one moved, though I couldn't help but notice the man's fingers flexing and un-flexing almost mechanically around the weapon's trigger. Was that just an anxious habit, or did he really plan to use that thing? I didn't dare ask, so I sat there in the extreme heat and silence, holding my breath ... waiting.

And then ... he appeared. Stepping out of the shadows, he walked directly in front of us. I had never been so close to anything so powerful, so intimidating, so terrifying. If I stretched my arm just slightly, I could almost touch him. Which wouldn't have been a good idea. So I remained perfectly still, holding my breath, one eye always on the man in uniform with his fingers flexing around the rifle's trigger.

He padded forward another giant step or two, and then turned his massive head to look directly at us. I could feel my hands tremble ever so slightly. Those eyes – those incredible pools of yellow and red and black – carried a message as clear as any you might read on a gigantic billboard: *Welcome to my world, where I am the undisputed King of this jungle.* He shook his hulking black mane and gave a belch that must have been heard at least five miles away, before padding down the small incline ahead of us, in the direction of the river. A moment later, the huge male lion, the biggest and most epic of Africa's great cats, disappeared from sight.

WJW turned to me and smiled.

"Now … *that's* a Beast!"

I couldn't disagree with him. Good thing Brock was back in London with Mum, blissfully unaware of the utter humiliation in being compared so unfavourably to a giant pussycat.

Thinking of Mum was hard. I hadn't known how to tell her. What was I going to say: "Hey Mum, just wanted to give you the heads up that I am going to spend the weekend on safari in South Africa with my just-discovered father – the man whose name you have refused to reveal to me for fifteen years – while we discuss potential plans for me to move in with him and his family."

So I did what came far easier. I chickened out. And I lied. Big-time. My hastily drafted WhatsApp read:

Jez just invited me to spend the weekend with him and his cuzins in liverpool. he got last minut tickets for an awesom gig there and we can also use his cuzs tickets for the Spurs game at anfield on sunday. couldnt pass on that. we get an off peak train for much cheaper if we leave @ 4, so just went for it. and its sports day at school tomorrow so figured that would be a good one to miss. will message u. b back Sun nite. Luv u. E. and don't forget to keep an eye out for brock and give him fresh water every day plz.

And because thinking about Mum and my message and my lies was hard, I decided not to.

"Yeah, I agree with you. That's a serious animal. Good thing Jabulani here has that rifle," I said, motioning to the elderly safari ranger all decked out in his lodge uniform, reclining casually in the driver's seat of our specially kitted-out 4-wheel drive Land Rover. I looked around in amazement for what must have been the hundredth time at this strange, raised vehicle we were sitting in. It didn't have any windows and was open on all four sides, like the pictures in one of those National Geographic magazines I had read in the GP's waiting room a year or so back. But this was no photograph. This was the real deal and a 400-pound wild beast had just passed within a few meters of us.

"I still can't believe these wheels don't have windows or anything," I said. "I mean, that lion could have just jumped right into the truck and had us all for an early breakfast!"

We had met our guide before the sun had even come up, as we were about to commence our first foray into the wild in the form of a sunrise safari drive. Staggering towards the Land Rover as I tried to rub the jetlag out of my tired eyes, I was confronted by a large man who hopped out of the truck with a speed that didn't seem compatible with his lined face and thin curls of almost entirely white hair. Extending a huge hand in greeting, he exclaimed,

"Welcome to Mopiri Lodge. I am Jabulani, and I will be your personal safari ranger and guide today as I show you the wonders of this incredible world you have come to visit. My name means 'happiness' in Zulu, my native language. And I am sure you will find happiness here in the beautiful African bush."

146

Now, just a couple of short hours later, Mister Happiness flashed his big white teeth and laughed.

"Nah, don't you worry little boss. I've been doing this for a long time and have never used this gun before. It's just for real emergencies. That big boy isn't interested in us. He's got something much bigger and better on his mind. There's a huge herd of zebra just on the other side of that river over there. That's where he'll be heading now to find his breakfast. Let's go see if we can follow the hunt."

Our guide turned the key in the ignition and the dusty Land Rover roared to life. Moments later, we were careening over the bumpy bushveld, as the locals called it, a world and more away from a school trip to Scotland.

By the time we made it back to the main camp where we were sleeping that night, the sun had dipped beyond the horizon and a deep black darkness was fast descending on the African plains. We had only covered a tiny portion of the vast wilderness, but I found it hard to imagine what else was left to see. We had already encountered immense herds of water buffalo, 300 to 400 of them at a time; whole families of elegant giraffe, the planet's tallest animals; giant turkey-like birds called Ground Hornbills, which Jabulani told us were an endangered species; an enormous troop of vervet monkeys that swung wildly from the massive trees rising on either side of the narrow dirt track, making those nut-case squirrels back in Hendon Park look like rank amateurs; fierce looking pig-like animals with miniature white tusks called warthogs; an entire pride of lions splayed like absolute kings on a sandbank beneath the African sun; and tens – no, hundreds – of massive elephants, the most awesome creatures who it seemed had serious claims to rivalling the lion as the true rulers of the jungle. And yet, as Jabulani reminded us with a terrible excuse for an American accent when we finally disembarked from the purring Land Rover, "You ain't seen nothing yet!"

The first thing WJW and I both did as we scrambled out of the truck was to check our smartphone feeds. No luck. To our dismay, Jabulani informed us that the lodge Wi-Fi – fickle at the best of times here in the bush, according to him – was down. Out here, in the middle of nowhere, where there was no mobile phone reception, that didn't leave us any other options. I would have to wait it out and WhatsApp Mum later, not to mention accept that I wouldn't be getting an update on what was happening with da Ring Gang – assuming there was any. WJW took it worse and went off frowning and grumbling in the direction of his luxurious bungalow. I guess he crashed out with exhaustion – or frustration – not long afterwards, as I didn't see him again until the next morning.

Heading over to the campfire that Jabulani was busy lighting, I reflected on how WJW and I hadn't spoken much during the course of the flight over and the long day out in the bushveld. But the way I saw it, keeping to myself was just fine. I wasn't sure there was much to be said anyhow. From our first conversation in the back of WJW's luxury car, two very different options had emerged: stick with what I had – or more accurately – didn't have; or turn my back on it all and pursue a new, better life. The problem, of course, was Mum. There was no question that I owed her for all she had done, and sacrificed, to bring me up. But there was also no question that she had been going down a path for a while now that looked more and more like the cul-de-sac at the end of our road: a complete dead end. Her drinking had gotten worse lately, her behaviour more unpredictable. How many times could I keep bailing her out, like I did with cousin Jamie at the coffee shop? This was her third – maybe fourth – job in the last year, and there I was cutting a deal to stay in school, just so she'd get another chance. It wasn't a way to live. For either of us.

And then … there was the money she owed Vic, the bookie. This was a big one and I couldn't see a way out. I knew Mum had been visiting that shop for a while, placing bets on Spurs and horses and all kinds of things. But because we never had any money in the first place, I figured she could never lose much. And at least it kept her busy and off the bottle. Yet somehow, she had managed to rack up this huge debt. Mum was right: *what were we going to do?* At this stage, WJW's cash seemed not just the best option, but the only one. And if Mum couldn't see that, well … maybe the chips would have to fall wherever the chips would fall. It didn't seem to me like we had any other choices. Thinking about it, maybe Mum would even thank me one day.

Yet sitting round the just-lit campfire, watching the orange flames dancing in the air, it became clear that there was still one giant problem that none of the above – not even WJW's money – could sort out. *What about that knife?* Every time this question popped into my mind, I pushed it away. Cause every which way I looked at it, there was no good answer. I just wish I had never seen that flash of steel the other day. I wish I had turned around and walked straight out of The Ring, instead of getting down on my knees and sticking my hand in that hollowed-out old log. I wish, I just wish, I had never known about that knife – *that freakin knife*.

But I *did* know. And however much I tried, I couldn't stop thinking about it. Or that guy lying in hospital, all stuffed with bandages so that he didn't bleed out. For the first time, a question

149

that had been hanging around somewhere in the backwaters of my mind, floated to the surface. *Was I really gonna leave that knife to lie in that log forever?*

A high pitched howl filled the silent African night, interrupting my dark thoughts. It was a sound of the wild, unlike any I had ever heard before.

"Hyena," said Jabulani quietly. I had been so caught up in the washing machine of my own thoughts that I hadn't noticed that the big Zulu safari ranger had pulled up a dead tree stump and was sat right next to me, staring into the red and orange glow of the campfire.

"Night animals. Out there now in the bush, calling to each other as they hunt."

"Pretty cool," I said, mainly because it was.

We were quiet for a few more minutes, our eyes fixed on the glowing embers before us.

"Seems like you got a lot on your mind," Jabulani said after a while.

"How can you tell?"

"I've been doing this job for almost 30 years. I've seen people from all over the world come and sit in front of this campfire, after a long day in the wild with the creator's incredible creatures. And I've seen how the silence of the bush always has the same effect. They go quiet. They go into their personal thoughts. And they try to work things out. Most of them don't realise it at first, but I figure that's why they actually come here. Not just to see the Big 5 safari animals from the back of a Land Rover. But to try and find peace in the silence."

The withered guide kept his eyes fixed on the leaping flames. "Can you hear it?" he asked me. "The silence."

It was a strange question – I think at school they call it an oxymoron or something. *How can you hear silence?*

Jabulani seemed to sense my confusion. "Just listen to the sounds of the bush," he gently instructed. "Just listen ... and you'll hear it."

So I listened. In the deep quiet, I heard more distant cries as the hyena called to each other on the hunt. I heard the constant chirping of what sounded like thousands of crickets all around us. I heard the loud, pinging call of a night-bird in the tree just above me.

A strange tingling came over my body. There was nothing out there. And yet there was everything out there. "Yes, I do hear it," I said, "It's ... it's awesome."

"Yes, it *is* awesome," whispered the man whose name meant happiness. "Now ... look up, little man. Look up."

He pointed a long index finger upwards and I found myself gazing at one of the most spectacular sights I had ever seen. Out here, in the middle of absolute nowhere, there was no electric light, no big city pollution. There was just a sky so full of stars that Coldplay's song from a few years back suddenly took on a new, deeper meaning for me. It was a night sky so awesome, so vast, so dark, and yet ... so light.

"That, my friend, is an African sky. I bet you don't see that too often where you come from. What a brilliant universe we are blessed to be part of. Isn't it beautiful?"

No answer was necessary. Instead, for a long while, I did something I couldn't remember doing before: I sat completely still, staring silently at the mesmerising sight above. It was a pretty awesome feeling.

Jabulani's face carried a very chilled expression.

"There is this incredible power that is behind everything you can see right now. And everything you can't see." he said quietly. "I think of it like this super-intelligence, or a superpower, that is bigger and greater than anything we can figure out with our human minds. As I see it, all of nature gets its life from this intelligence. It tells the wildebeest when to migrate in their millions across these African plains. It lets those hyena know how to find each other, out there in the pitch black. It guides the birds from all the way down here in South Africa on their journey across the continents. It tells the seeds how to grow into the massive, ancient mopane tree we are sitting under. Nothing is left out of the embrace of this intelligence, this brilliant wisdom. It covers it all, little man."

He paused then, a small smile spreading over his lined face.

"But listen to me calling you 'little man.' That isn't right. We need to give you a Zulu name, a name that reflects your true essence."

Jabulani sat quietly on his tree stump, gazing at the sky, a thoughtful look on his face.

"I know… how about Dingane?" he said after a while. "It means 'one who is searching.' Yes, that's it – Dingane. Because you *are* the one who is searching. What do you think?"

"Well, um … yeah, it's not bad. I can live with that, I guess."

"Good, now where were we … Dingane? Ah, that's right. The intelligence that covers everything. What makes it tough to talk about is that everyone has a different name for it, a different way of describing it. Some of the guys who work out here in the bush – the biologists and the environmentalists – call it 'the life force.' I've heard that those clever physicists and scientist types call it a 'formless energy.' And then of course, there are the folk, like the people of my tribe, who believe in a higher power. We refer to it as 'God.' In the end though, it doesn't really matter what we call it."

Normally, the kind of thing that Jabulani was going on about would make me run a mile. But for some reason, the way he was describing this superpower, as he called it, sounded kind of cool. Even when he used the "G" word.

"I think I get all that," I said, "But I don't get what's this all got to do with me, with all the stuff that's on my mind?"

"You're right," said Jabulani as he threw a few traditional South African sausages called boerewors (don't even try and pronounce that!) onto the fire. "Well, let's start here by recognising that just as nature has been perfectly designed and just as your body has been perfectly designed, so too has your mind been perfectly designed. This force, this wisdom, is not separate from us – it *is* us. It is a deep knowing of what is true and what is not true. It helps us to learn and to solve problems. It helps us get over hurt and fear and disappointment. It helps us to deal with the scary and the unknown. It helps us to deal with what may look like tough

153

situations and difficult decisions. It is truly incredible. Without it, we would be completely lost. With it, there is nothing else we need. Because we have it all – inside of us. And when you know that – when you *really* know that – everything on your mind looks different and ..."

Another high-pitched howl filled the night air. This one sounded much closer.

"Ah, the hyena can smell the meat on the fire, so they are coming close," said Jabulani, picking up a large stick lying at his side. "But this is our spot. I will go and tell them that they need to hunt somewhere else. There's a whole lot of bush out there, so let me send them on their way."

The big Zulu ranger got up off the tree stump and walked towards the arc of the campfire light, holding the stick in his hand. And then he walked beyond the edge of the light, until the blackness enveloped him. I watched the space where he had been standing for a long while. No more hyena howls.

Then I turned my head upwards, towards the perfect night sky. I considered what we had been talking about, and in that moment, I realised that everything on my mind *did* look different.

And while I thought about that, I did as I had been taught. I listened to the silence. And for the first time, that silence didn't seem separate from me.

17

A completely new face greeted us first thing early the next morning as WJW and I scrambled up the side of the safari truck, clutching onto the rungs of the short step-ladder positioned to assist us.

"Good morning, my name is Roger and I am your ranger today," said a young man wearing an identical uniform to that which our far older guide had worn the day before. "You can call me Ranger Roger," he added, laughing as he did.

WJW and I exchanged a confused glance as we settled bleary-eyed onto the Land Rover's padded bench.

"Where's Jabulani?" I asked.

"Ah, Mister Happiness. To be honest, I have no idea," said Roger. "I got a late night message from the manager telling me that I'm on duty again this morning when I was supposed to be enjoying a day off fishing in the Crocodile River. No mention at all of old Jabulani. But hey, that's cool. So ... I have seen fresh tracks belonging to a leopard and her cubs already this morning; they are probably out hunting. Should we go find them?"

Without waiting for an answer, our talkative new ranger put the 4-wheel drive into gear and off we went, hot on the trail of the family of leopards.

Turning to WJW, I had to raise my voice to be heard above the loud purring of the Land Rover's engine as it negotiated a steep incline up a narrow path.

"I wonder what happened to Jabulani."

"Hmmm, not sure," responded WJW distractedly, his face buried in his brand new iPhone X, while his fingers tapped away agitatedly. It was clear he wasn't in the mood for conversation, so I left him to his device and looked out the open side of the truck, scanning the trees for any sign of a golden spotted leopard and her cubs.

A few hours later, after a brilliant safari drive in the blazing sun, Roger brought the truck to a stop under the shade of a massive thorn tree. He parked just off the track, next to a large lake, the sunlight glistening off its smooth surface like a thousand tiny diamond fragments, and began unloading a big cooler box, pieces of firewood and other items from the back of the Land Rover. While our guide busied himself with getting a big fire going in the middle of a small clearing, we took turns looking through WJW's high powered binoculars at the dozen or so enormous crocodiles, disguised as huge old logs, on the far bank of the lake. In no time at all, the sound of sausages and fried eggs, sliced tomatoes and diced mushrooms, could be heard sizzling away in a large frying pan, accompanied by tantalising smells that promised a bush breakfast of epic proportions.

"I hope you enjoyed those amazing leopards," Roger said in his chatty way that I had already become accustomed to. "Now, after breakfast, Jabulani has arranged a different activity to the normal itinerary – a visit to a special orphanage out here in the bush."

"An orphanage?" I asked, lowering the binoculars from my eyes. I looked over to check on WJW's reaction, but it seemed as if he had dozed off under the tree. "Out here?"

"Absolutely," answered Roger. "I'm sure you have heard how many young children in this part of the world have sadly lost either their mother or father, or both. Sometimes to violence, sometimes to HIV, sometimes to malaria or the many other illnesses and misfortunes that can happen to a person out here in the wilderness."

"Um, not really," I replied, feeling pretty lame as I said the words.

"That's OK," continued Roger good-naturedly. "It's probably not the kind of thing you hear too much about where you come from. Anyhow, it will mean a lot to the kids in the orphanage for us to pay them a visit. They don't have many visitors so they always get very excited to have guests from far away."

A sudden splattering noise coming from the frying pan distracted our ranger.

"Ah, now these eggs and sausages are ready. Let's get your father awake and a delicious, hot bush breakfast inside you both," said Roger.

My father? Was I ever gonna get used to that?

After breakfast, Roger steered the Land Rover south around the lake in a new direction. As we drove, we spotted at least ten massive hippos, half of them sun-tanning on the sandbank and half of them keeping cool in the lake itself. It reminded me a bit of that time Mum and I took a train down to Clacton-on-Sea one bank holiday at the end of August. We spent a long, brilliant day on the beach, splitting our time equally between lying on the baking sand catching some rays and running into the freezing Atlantic ocean to cool down. The memory made me smile. It also made me sad.

157

The bush had become denser and it wasn't long before an elephant would have had to be standing bang in the middle of the track for us to see it. Soon, the dirt path narrowed even more, and then we were heading down a sharp decline which ended suddenly with a rickety wooden gate blocking the way. Ranger Roger (seriously: *Ranger Roger?*) brought the Land Rover to a sharp halt.

"The orphanage," he declared. "Let's go say hello."

We clambered down the step-ladder and walked through the gate that Roger held open for us. Moments later, we were surrounded by a sea of screaming, smiling children.

"Hey, hey, hey ... settle down everyone!" shouted Roger with a big smile and a booming voice in an attempt to be heard above the kids' excited chatter. "Give our special guests some space. And remember your manners."

I looked around – and was shocked by what I saw. There must have been at least thirty children crowding around us, and every single one of them was standing barefoot on the hard, scorching ground.

"Where are their shoes?" I asked our guide.

"They don't own shoes, my friend. These children are very poor. And shoes are a luxury they cannot afford."

"A luxury? But how can they walk on all these thorns and rocks in their bare feet? Especially when the ground is so hot?"

Before Roger could answer, there was a sudden quieting amongst the children. Seconds later, a path opened up in the middle of their ranks. A tall, thin, man dressed simply in matching beige trousers and button down shirt, came walking through it. I instantly noticed his almost regal bearing, as if he were the descendant of a famous African prince or something.

"Good morning gentlemen and welcome to Sizabantwane orphanage. My name is Pastor Joe. Thank you for coming to visit us."

He shook our hands vigorously and I was immediately struck by one of the widest smiles I had ever been greeted with.

"Would you like to sit down and get to know some of our young people here?" he asked. "I am very sorry that I cannot offer you anything to eat or drink – I'm sure you appreciate that we have so little here in terms of food and beverage – but we certainly have a whole lot of extremely curious people who would love to hear all about life on the other side of the big ocean."

I looked over at WJW. It didn't take a genius to read his reluctant body language.

"Um, you know what … I really need to know what's happening with the markets," he said, shifting uncomfortably from one foot to the other. "I'll just wonder over this way towards the gate and see if I can get phone reception over there. Why don't you go on ahead Evan and I'll catch you up in a bit."

"Uh, OK," I said. Cause I didn't know what else to say.

WJW strode back towards the gate, his face buried in his phone again.

"Well, come on then, Mister Evan" declared Pastor Joe, taking me by the arm. He looked down at the children gathered round us. "Who wants to hear all about a little island on the other side of the world called England?" he asked with a big chuckle.

"Me, me, me!" cried a few dozen young voices.

Pastor Joe led the way to a patch of ground, semi-enclosed by four big logs, forming a kind of a makeshift square. It reminded me of The Ring back in Hendon Park. A few of the older kids took up seating space on the logs, while the rest of the children just sat themselves down on the dry, red, baking-hot soil in the middle of the quadrant. Pastor Joe motioned for me to sit on the one remaining log – the sturdiest looking of the lot – that was completely empty, save for an enormous red ant which I brushed away with the back of my hand. The pastor sat down next to me and softly whispered some important information in my ear.

"The oldest of our children is thirteen, the youngest is just six," he began. "It's useful to know that none of them have ever been out of South Africa – actually, only one or two of them have probably ever been to a big city in their lives. They don't have televisions, they don't go to the movies and they don't have smartphones. Many of them don't get to school much. So share with them anything you'd like, because whatever you say will be new and fascinating to them."

I looked out at the group of curious faces assembled before me and suddenly felt very nervous. What did I have to say to a bunch of kids, so different from me, about anything?

"What do I talk about? Where do I start?" I asked Pastor Joe.

To my surprise, he answered my question with another question. "You're a human being, right? And they are human beings, right? So why don't you let them know how life looks as a fellow member of the human race. Tell them what it's like where you come from: your friends, your family, your school, your home. Just tell them about yourself. That's always a good place to start."

I nodded nervously and took a deep breath.

"Um, hi everyone. My name's Evan. I live in a big city called London."

Silence. Once again, I was demonstrating what an ace I was with introductions. Really world-class.

"If you come from England, can you tell us about Manchester United?" one of the older boys called out, breaking the tension I felt building inside my head.

"Manchester United!" I laughed. "Why would anyone want to know about that posh lot? But I can sure tell you something about a great team called Tottenham Hotspur who really do know how to play football. What do you say, Pastor Joe?"

The pastor gave me a big double thumbs up and a heartening smile. That was all the encouragement I needed.

"Well, let me start by telling you what it's like just getting to a game in London. Have any of you ever heard of the Tube? It's like a massive train that goes underneath the whole city ..."

The next hour flew by. There were questions – lots of them. And there was laughter and whistling and all kinds of conversations going on amongst the kids in their own language. They asked me about everything: football (or soccer as they strangely referred to it), the school I attended, tall city buildings, even in Hendon (they absolutely couldn't believe it when I told them I lived in an eleven-storey apartment block!), what it was like to travel on a train, London traffic, London weather ... you name it, they asked it. So I told them everything I could think of. I told them about the caf in the park with the best shakshuka I'd ever had. I told them about Mum and her job at the coffee shop, about Mrs. Dickens' poetry class, about playing basketball with the boys, and about Tals and her university ambitions. I told them all about Brock's obsession with squirrels and about how it was winter now in London so you had to wear warm clothes and thick jackets when we went hunting together. Basically, I did what Pastor Joe had told me to do. I told them all about me. About being human.

And I couldn't believe how excited these kids were to hear about my lame, boring life in England. They couldn't get enough of it. For that matter, neither could I. Which brought the beginning of an idea into my mind. Despite all our differences – skin colour, language, background, education, football clubs – we are not actually that different after all.

Through it all, Pastor Joe sat quietly next to me on the log, his face beaming. Then, just as the questions finally died down, a soft voice from somewhere at the back of the group broke through the momentary silence.

"Excuse me, Mister Evan ... can I ask you something?" came the shy sounding voice of a very small girl standing on the edge of the square. I hadn't noticed her until now. She was definitely one of the younger ones – perhaps eight at the oldest – and as she spoke, she picked at a painful looking scab on her right arm. Like the rest, she had no shoes, but somehow she seemed even worse off than the others. The girl was really thin, her ill-fitting dress completely threadbare, and when I looked more carefully, I noticed she had scabs and sores covering her other arm and legs as well.

"Sure," I said gently. "But first, can you tell me your name?"

"Precious."

Precious. Cool name. I liked that.

162

"OK Precious. What's your question?"

"Do you like living in Heaven?"

"You mean Hendon," I replied instantly, assuming she had mispronounced the word, especially as English was not her first language.

"No. I mean Heaven."

"Uh, I'm not too sure I know what you mean, Precious," I said, suddenly a bit uncomfortable.

"You have food to eat. You have a Mommy. You have teachers. You have a dog. You have friends. You play games. You live in a big tower. You have warm clothes and shoes …"

Precious stopped mid-sentence and suddenly she looked very small and very scared. For a moment, I was worried she was going to turn around and run away into the thick bush. But then, a renewed conviction seemed to come over her and she spoke again, her voice stronger and clearer than before.

"Mister Evan, it sounds to me like you live in Heaven. But I am not so sure you like Heaven. Or … maybe you do?"

It came up on me so quickly that I was caught completely by surprise. That stinging feeling in my eyes and that raw, croaky feeling in my throat. For a long moment, I couldn't speak. I knew – if I tried – the waterworks would flow. Finally, words came out, but they didn't sound like they belonged to me.

"You know what, Precious? It's really great living in Heaven. And one day, I really hope you can come and visit me and …."

"Hey, Evan!" It was WJW, loudly calling me from the other side of the rickety wooden gate. "Listen, it's getting late. And I still can't get reception here. Sorry to break up this whole gathering, but I've asked Roger to take us back to the main camp, pronto. I really need to get online and see what's happening with the markets. So come on, let's get going."

Hold on a second WJW. This was an important moment.

"Well, uh, you know we're kinda just in the middle of something here and …"

"I'm sorry Evan." WJW's tone betrayed his words. It was anything but apologetic. "We need to go. Now."

Before I could say anything else, Pastor Joe stepped in.

"Thank you so much for coming to speak with us, Evan. It's been our great pleasure to host you here at Sizabantwane. We've learned so much about your life back in England. And we also hope you've learned something about our lives here. We really hope you will come back and visit us again soon. Don't we children?"

Amidst the chorus of "yeses" and excited clapping, I scanned the faces of the kids in front of me. I was specifically looking for one of them, because something she had said in her simple, child-like way, had touched my heart very deeply. But in a sea of smiling faces, none belonged to little Precious. She was nowhere to be seen. Then I heard the loud revving of the Land Rover on the other side of the wooden gate and it was time to go.

For a long time on the drive back to camp, WJW and I didn't have much to say to each other. His attitude and tone at the orphanage hadn't gone down well in my book. Mum would never have spoken to me like that – even if she *did* need to leave. But just as I was getting all bent out of shape about it, WJW surprised me:

"Listen, Evan. I'm sorry for being impatient and speaking a bit roughly to you back there at the orphanage. It's just that I'm not used to teenagers, you know. Or boys for that matter. So I hope you can cut me a bit of slack while I learn to figure it out better."

I had to admit: it was a decently sincere apology and all. What was I going to say? *Forget it, mate. You can take your safari, your cash and your big offer and go stuff it!*

So I went down the mature, reasonable route. "That's OK, Will. I get it."

"Cool, Evan. So I got to say, I feel really bad for those kids. They are living in some tough conditions. Perhaps I can make a donation to …"

Just then, two colossal rhinos walked directly in front of the Land Rover, before stopping right in the middle of the path and staring us down, big time. Seriously sick!

It took a good fifteen minutes or so before these massive, prehistoric-looking creatures decided to push on into the bush and give us back our path. Or maybe it was their path? So while we sat quietly in the idling vehicle, waiting for nature's blockage to clear the road, I had a lot of time to reflect. Something had happened at that orphanage. I wasn't quite sure what yet, but it felt kind of like when Jabulani was showing me the stars last night. Deep and powerful and true and mysterious all at the same time. Once the rhinos finally cleared off and the Land Rover began bouncing along the uneven track again, I thought about what a sick little girl had asked me about a place called Heaven. A place that was maybe not as far from Hendon as I thought.

Before sunrise the next morning, we hopped on a small ten-seater plane that took us from the bush to the international airport just outside Johannesburg, South Africa's largest city. But now that the excitement of the trip had worn off and we were headed home, I found myself worrying a lot about Mum. Or more accurately, worrying that Mum was worrying about me. Talk about a vicious worry cycle! My mobile phone plan had no option for making or receiving overseas calls or texts – remember, the farthest I'd ever been until now was Scotland. And without WhatsApp, I couldn't be in touch to perpetuate the lie that all was going smoothly in Liverpool with Jez and his cousins, and I'd be heading home on the train as soon as the game was over. Maybe that was a good thing. Not just having no way of lying to Mum, but also not having virtual connectivity of any form. Somehow, because I no longer had to look constantly at a screen for my connection to people and the world, I found myself settling down. And in that settling down, without even intending to, a lot of clarity about my life was starting to emerge.

My new zen-like peace of mind was immediately shattered when we arrived at the big city airport to catch our return flight to London. We were already pushing things time-wise with the connecting flight, made worse by the long security queues – even using the business class fast-track. Eventually, we made it through passport control and headed directly towards our departure gate. Yet even though boarding had already started, both WJW and I wasted no time in logging on to the airport's 30 minute free internet access. We quickly found seats on opposite ends of a long row of stiff air-lounge chairs right beside the gate and were instantly submersed in the familiar flood of pings and vibrations that enveloped both of our devices. We were connected, again. Sort of.

First came the WhatsApps. Nothing from da Ring Gang. Which made me conclude that either Mo, Jams and D-Von were still behind bars, with no access to phones, or … or I didn't know what to think. On the one hand, that made me concerned. On the other, I felt a weird kind of calm about their whole situation.

Then, surprisingly, there was a short message from Tals. Two days old already, it read, simply:

Ev, I'm sorry if I said things that you felt were hurtful. That was never my intention. You're my best little neighbour ever – and I mean ever! Knocked on your door but your Mum said you had gone to the big game at Anfield with Jez. Lets please make time to speak when you're back. Luv, Tals.

After everything I had said to her, Tals was apologising *to me*? I felt a lump in my throat and that stinging in my eyes again. *What was happening to me?*

And then came the messages from Mum. The first couple just wanted to know how I was doing and if I enjoyed the gig. When I didn't reply, Mum started to get anxious:

Evvy Luv, what's happening? Please call or message and let me know you're fine.

Soon, Mum's WhatsApps became frantic, no doubt made worse by the fact that she couldn't reach me by phone either and that her calls would be going straight to answer message.

167

Your really making me worried. Havent heard from you all of yesterday or today. And I cant reach Jez either. Has something happened to you? Are u ok? Are u in some kind of trouble? Please God, just tell me your ok. Luv u soooo much. *MUM XXXX*

I felt terrible. Here I was, just having come off a 5-star safari eating fresh sausages and eggs for breakfast in the bush, and Mum was freaking out that something bad had happened to me on the streets of Liverpool. But before I had enough time to really feel guilty, a disembodied voice boomed over the airport's speaker system:

"Final call for British Airways flight 057 to London. Will all passengers who have not yet done so proceed to boarding gate 9A immediately."

I grabbed my backpack at the same time as WJW picked up his own hand luggage. We both hurried over to the gate before handing our passports and boarding cards to the stern-looking airline people for scanning. Appearing to be the final passengers to board, we made our way straight down the tunnel of Gate 9A and onto the plane itself. But then I made a crucial, some might say rookie mistake. As we exited the airport's Wi-Fi zone, I glanced at my phone's screen one last time.

Where r u? pleeze call. Dont matter if your in truble. The police have just come to the flat. They want to speak to u something real urgent. Just call.

18

"Excuse me, sir, but you're going to have to turn your device off now. We are about to take off."

I looked up from Mum's message, still frozen on my phone's screen. A petite, youthful-looking woman in a British Airways uniform was standing next to my seat, the smile on her face accompanied by a no-nonsense look in her eyes.

"Uh, sure. Sorry," I mumbled as I powered down my phone and stuffed it in the seat pocket in front of me.

"Thank you," she said. "And don't forget to pull your seat into an upright position and fasten your seatbelt for take-off as well."

The flight attendant lingered for another moment by my seat. "Is everything OK?" she asked. "You look a bit ashen. Perhaps I can get you an airsick bag in case you ..."

"No, I'm feeling fine," I interjected quickly.

But the truth was that I was feeling sick. The police were at our apartment. Talking to Mum. Looking for me. *Why*? Did they know, somehow, that I had been at the park that night? Did they know about that freakin knife?

"Oh, OK," she said. "Well, please let me or any of my colleagues know if you need anything. My name is Linda," she added, pointing to the silver name tag pinned to her left shoulder. "And we're here to help make your journey as comfortable as possible."

"Thanks," I muttered, as she continued making her way down the aisle, checking on passengers and passing on take-off instructions as she went.

"Seems like you made a friend there," said a voice coming from diagonally behind me.

"Yeah, guess so," I responded, swivelling my head to look at WJW sitting in the seat one row back and on the other side of the aisle. I noticed he had two miniature bottles of Johnnie Walker Black Label on the tray-table in front of him, plus a large glass half-filled with cubes of ice. Wasn't that a problem for people in a drug rehab programme?

"I know what you're thinking, but my issue's only ever been with coke, not alcohol," said WJW, in response to my eyeing the expensive whiskey. "Anyhow, might as well take advantage of one of the perks of flying business class, especially as it helps me to sleep and relax on these long-haul flights. You don't get these smooth single malts back there in economy class," he added, motioning with his head to the area behind us that was cordoned off by a ceiling-to-floor thick blue curtain.

"So, what film are you going to watch?" he asked, changing the subject quickly. "The new Marvel movie looks real good. Or maybe the latest *Fast and Furious*? Dwayne Johnson and Vin Diesel are two of my favourite actors. Actually, there's a great interview in here with the two of them," he said, pointing to the inside pages of the in-flight magazine opened on the table in front of him, next to the Johnnie Walkers.

I found it a bit strange that now, right at the end of our trip, he was suddenly interested in making causal conversation.

"Uh, you know, I'm kind of shattered," I said. "The early mornings on the Land Rover and the crack-of-dawn flight have really whacked me. I think I'm just going to close my eyes and see if I can catch up on some sleep."

"Sure thing," replied WJW. "And don't forget how these business-class seats convert into beds once we've taken off. They're more comfortable than they look. Get some rest and enjoy the ride," he said as he inserted his earphones and turned his attention to the screen in front of him.

I leaned back into the seat and closed my eyes, savouring the steady hum of the plane's engines as it idled on the runway. Without meaning to, I found myself thinking – again – about what was hidden away in The Ring. And who had put it there. And why. I knew that this wasn't a Jez or D-Von thing. Smacking a few boys around on a basketball court? Yes. Sticking a blade in someone? No ways. Which left only Mo and Jams. I knew that Mo had bought that knife specifically for dealing with the boys from the other side of the estate "problem", as he called it. So now what? Do I just stay quiet? Play dumb like I had with Tals and Monroe, pretending I know nothing about the whole thing? Or do I finally man up and do something about that knife, that freakin knife? But what? Betray the boys? Seriously?

The confusing thoughts went round and round my head. And so did the feelings of stress, of fear, of treachery. I figured I could spend the next year sitting on this plane and still not see a way out. Which made the idea of watching a movie kinda appealing. But for some reason, I just didn't want to be doing anything that WJW was suggesting at the moment. Anyhow, I *was* genuinely shattered. All the thinking had just made me even more exhausted. The tiredness was everywhere. The darkness came soon afterwards. I didn't even remember the plane taking off.

I woke with a start and a stiff neck. The entire business class cabin of the plane was swathed in darkness. For a moment, I couldn't remember where I was. The remnants of my dream were still with me and I spent a few minutes trying to bridge the gap between the maximum security prison cell in which I had just been incarcerated and the business class bed-seat I was actually reclining in now. I looked back towards WJW and saw him lying on his side, a thin airplane blanket half covering his fully asleep body. Splayed out on the tray-table in front of him were four empty mini-bottles of Johnnie Walker and a half-eaten packet of peanuts.

I needed to pay a visit. So hauling myself out of my seat, I followed the neon toilet signs sending me a couple of rows back, directly opposite the empty galley kitchen. When I eventually emerged from the cubicle – after losing an embarrassingly one-sided wrestling match with the lock on the bathroom door – a uniformed woman with short dark hair was busy pulling something out of a shelf just above her head in the lit up area of the mini-kitchen. It was Linda, my flight attendant friend from earlier.

"Ah, the young man from seat number 17C," she said, turning around as she did. "I heard you having that fight with the bathroom door. Glad you won in the end. Some passengers never make it out."

She laughed. It took me a minute to realise that this was just a form of high altitude banter.

"You look so much better than before we took off," Linda continued without missing a beat. "Now, what can I get you? How about a glass of orange juice? Or a nice hot coffee? I've just finished brewing a pot and was going to start offering them to those passengers still awake. You can be my first customer."

"A coffee would be great." I answered.

"Sure thing," she said. "How do you like it? Black with two sugars?"

"Um, yes. Exactly."

How did she know that?

The flight attendant grabbed a white ceramic mug – another of the business class perks, I had come to discover – off the galley counter and began pouring from the piping hot silver jug she was holding with her other hand. She then opened two sachets of sugar and poured them into the steaming black liquid before handing the cup to me.

"Thanks," I said, grasping the mug with both hands.

"My pleasure. So did you catch up on some sleep?"

"Yeah, I did. But I woke up in the middle of the weirdest dream – actually it was more of a nightmare, I think."

"No surprise there," she said. "Passengers are always telling me about strange and wacky dreams they have up here, in the middle of the skies. Maybe it's got something to do with the altitude." Linda gave a little chuckle and I couldn't tell if she was being serious or not.

"So, do you want to tell me about it?"

"About what?"

"Your dream. Or is it very personal?"

"Oh, no, not too personal." I answered quickly. For some reason, I felt myself blushing. I hoped the air hostess couldn't notice in the dim light. "Basically, I dreamt I was in jail. I don't know why or how I got there, but it was like one of those really scary ones you see on *Prison Break*. Maximum security or whatever they call it. There were huge goons everywhere, with shaved heads and tattoos all over the place. And then some guy pulled a knife and there was a massive fight and prisoners were bleeding and guards were running in with their batons, and I was trying to hide under a table and some nutter was grabbing me by the legs and pulling me out and ..."

I stopped mid-sentence. What was I doing? Telling this lady who I'd never met before all about a weird dream I'd just had was even weirder than the dream itself.

"Hey, I get it," she said, as if reading my thoughts. "Dreams can be pretty scary and weird sometimes. Wait till I tell you about some of the crazy stuff I dream about. But the way I see it, my dreams are just a reflection of a whole load of things going on inside my head when I am awake. And when I fall asleep and my mind relaxes, all that stuff is free to run wild. So my guess is that you've got some pretty hectic things going on inside your head right now."

My instinctive reaction was to run back to my seat, plug my earphones in and escape into the make-believe world of one of the action movies WJW had mentioned earlier. But something kept me standing in the plane's dimly lit galley kitchen. Maybe it was Linda's kind voice, which seemed to offer a whole lot of

174

compassion and no judgment. Maybe it was the fact that for the last three days, since the fight with Tals outside the library, I had bottled up so much inside of me. Maybe it was the simple reality that up here, 34,000 feet in the air in a jumbo jet full of sleeping passengers, things somehow felt different. Whatever the reason, I found myself rooted to the spot, trying to explain what was going on inside my head to a uniformed member of the British Airways cabin crew.

"Yeah, that's right. I do have a whole lot of hectic things going on in my head. And I get, like my sorta mate Monroe says, that my thoughts are creating my feelings and nothing else. That's cool. But here's what I don't get: why can't I just get control of my thoughts? Then I would have better feelings. But that doesn't seem to be working too well, know what I mean?"

"Sure, I know what you mean," replied Linda. "I've asked myself the same question loads of times. But here's the thing: sometimes you can't do anything about your thinking. You can try, but it just seems to have a life of its own. So even though it would be great if we could control our thinking and turn it on and off like this hot water spout over here, it just doesn't work that way. Make sense?"

"Yeah, absolutely. Like I keep trying to *not* think of what's going on with my Mum – how she owes a whole lotta dosh to this dangerous guy and how scary that is – but I can't help it. So I end up thinking about it, whether I want to or not."

"Exactly. So you may not be able to stop thinking – or change your thinking. But as long as you know that thought – and only thought – is creating your feelings, then you're good to go. And you don't need to do anything. Your thoughts will change on their own just as the weather changes on its own."

"Not sure I get what you mean," I said.

"You don't think about controlling the weather, do you?" asked Linda. "So why would you worry about controlling your thinking? You can just stick with thought, cause it's all you got. And that's pretty awesome."

She laughed, obviously quite impressed with her own little banterous poem. Linda was about to say something else when a loud pinging sound suddenly sliced through the otherwise quiet cabin. She glanced at a control panel in front of her.

"Ah, Mr. Derbitsky in seat 14D seems to have lost his pillow again. Let me go find him another one. And then I've got to get on with serving this coffee before it becomes ice cold. I'll catch up with you later, Mister 17C."

While the flight attendant walked down the darkened aisle to attend to her duties, I stayed standing in the galley, cradling my coffee mug. Something had just dawned on me, hitting me straight between the eyes like a bullet. *Thought is all I got.* For the first time in a whirlwind week, I had total clarity. While I had absolutely no idea how we were going to solve Mum's predicament, I knew the answer would come – could only come – from within me. Which meant it would not – it could not – come from WJW and his "offer".

So I hurried back to my seat to tell him exactly that. But I had forgotten what a good job the whiskey had done – he was still completely out on his business-class seat-bed. It was ironic really. For the first time since I'd met the man, it seemed as if he and Mum had something in common.

176

I refocused quickly. Inspired by my conversation with Linda and the clarity it had brought, I dug out my phone and powered it up. Being careful to keep it on airplane mode, I began typing out a couple of WhatsApps that would get sent as soon as I was back in a Wi-Fi zone. I started with one to Tals.

Hey Girl, thanks for the message. I'm totally sorry for behaving like such an idiot lately. U were right about so much at the bus stop the other day. I just couldn't hear it. Have had a lot on my mind. But can't wait to share it with u if you'll have me back ☺

Next came a message for Mum. This one was tough. I hesitated for a long time – and then decided to come clean. And once I made that call, things just kind of flowed out of me. It took a long time to write, even with my fast and furious fingers flying all over the keyboard. But eventually I got there. And by the time I did, there was nothing Mum didn't know about the last week of my life. It was all there: the suspension and the lies; the fight, the knife, the boys in prison; WJW, the trip, his offer; and – perhaps most important of all – my regret at betraying her.

When I finally finished, members of the cabin crew were coming down the aisle instructing passengers to prepare for landing. I looked around for Linda. Our conversation had ended a bit suddenly and there were still some questions I had for her. Strangely, despite the fact that the crew was now out in full force, she was nowhere to be seen. Instead, as I craned my neck to find her, I caught a glimpse of WJW's form beginning to stir. But as we were about to land, it didn't feel like a good time to start an important discussion. So I inserted my earphones, tapped the screen in front of me a few times and dove into the world of Vin Diesel and Dwayne Johnson.

19

My messages went flying through cyberspace as soon as I connected to Heathrow's Wi-Fi. I didn't expect to hear from either Mum or Tals straight away. Mum would still be on shift until seven this evening, her phone probably on silent and resting in her handbag in the coffee shop's cramped little staffroom. And Tals was most likely at the library, where she would have her head so focused on that Othello guy that she may not check her mobile for hours yet. No worries. I would see them both soon enough and do my best to sort things out with them then.

As I was handing over my passport to the uniformed lady at the passport control counter, a message came in on da Ring Gang WhatsApp group. The group had been totally silent for the better part of the past week, but the message from Jams was suddenly full of pent-up noise:

Hey banksky. where u been. would have been rite to cum visit us in the pen, ya know. mo and me been lookin all over 4 u since we got outta there. even went to your house last nite but ure mum says u with jez in liverpool. then jezman says he dont have a clue where u gone. sayin insted somethin bout u going to visit some rich geezer in hamsted. so wats the story bro. sounds like u dun a runner or somthin. that aint cool cause u need 2 stick with da ring gang. so tell us wher u r cause ure bros aint too happy man.

I read the message again but it just left me feeling even more confused inside. These were my boys, my bros, da Ring Gang. But they – or at least Mo and Jams – had also done something seriously vicious, cutting up that boy with the scar. The fact that he and his mates were on our court and all didn't make it right. It was all so screwed up. I wondered if the clarity I had arrived at on the plane extended all the way to the gang. I wasn't sure about that, but in the meantime, without it, I couldn't think of a decent way of responding to Jams' WhatsApp. So I didn't.

Ten minutes later, having easily located our luggage making its way round the carousel, were sat in the back of WJW's E-class. In an impressive move, George, the driver, had been waiting for us in the VIP zone of the parking lot as we exited Terminal 5. He even had two steaming hot Starbucks on tap as we settled into the car. Yet another example – as if I needed a reminder following the luxury trip just gone – of what money could buy.

We sped down the M4 before catching the off-ramp leading us onto the North Circular, which would take us all the way back home. An uncomfortable silence filled the car. Fortunately, the Sunday evening traffic was reasonably light and it wasn't long before the familiar sight of the great Wembley Stadium arch came into view. Realising we would be home soon, I decided it was time to let WJW know where I stood. I may not be clear yet how to handle the whole freakin knife thing, but the dilemma about how to respond to WJW's offer? That one was sorted.

Shuffling my body on the soft leather, I turned to face the man who, less than a week before, had announced himself as my father.

"Um, I wanted to thank you for the trip. It really was something special and I'll never forget it," I began truthfully. "So

179

… I wanted to talk to you about your offer to come live with your family, to work with you and to help Mum and all that."

WJW sat stone-faced, not saying anything. I ploughed ahead.

"You just kind of pitched up out of nowhere, you know, offering to change my life in such a massive way. And I'm grateful for that. Really I am. Cause my life needs a bit of sorting out, no question there."

No reaction from the man – my father – sitting next to me.

"And I think I understand this idea of wanting to make amends. I get that it's important to you, even if it seems a bit messed up to be trying to do that with me, when Mum doesn't want anything to do with it – or you."

Still no reaction. I took a deep breath.

"But here's the thing I've been thinking a lot about. Sorting out my life needs to come from inside me – from the inside-out, if you know what I mean. So the answer can't lie anywhere else. Not even with your generous offer to have me come live with you and everything else. So … thank you Will, but I'm going to stick with Mum and see what we can figure out from there."

I took another deep breath. It felt good to get things off my chest and establish where I stood, once and for all. Hopefully, WJW wouldn't take it the wrong way.

Unfortunately, he did.

"Are you seriously telling me that you'd rather live with your mother in that tiny run-down flat than come and live with us in that house you had dinner in the other night?" His voice had that same harsh tone to it which I had first heard back at the orphanage when

180

he had been so impatient to leave. "And are you seriously telling me you're turning down my offer of financial help to your mother in her time of need?"

"Uh, yeah, I guess I am."

WJW glared at me with a look I hadn't seen – or maybe had chosen not to notice – since I'd first met him. It reminded me a bit of the look I had seen on Jams' face that day down by The Corner when Tals told him "thanks, but no thanks." It struck me that I was giving WJW the exact same response now. It also struck me that this was a man not used to people saying "no" to him.

"Marla warned me this wouldn't work; that you didn't have enough maturity and sense of gratitude to do the right thing and accept my offer. But I didn't want to listen. Well ... now at least I know where we stand. We are clearly just too different, you and me. I mean, I've spent the last fifteen years living on The Bishops Avenue in the Suburb. And you've spent the last fifteen years living on council estates. That pretty much sums it up."

I sat there staring at the man, unable to believe what I was hearing. *Who did this guy think he was? He* was the one who had barged into my life unannounced and uninvited. *He* was the one who had promised me the world. *He* was the one who had told me he would take care of everything – all our problems, all our worries. Not me; him! I felt the red mist descending big-time.

And then ... the clarity I felt deep in my bones came flooding back to me. What mattered was a simple truth: *nobody can put a feeling inside of me.* Not even the man sitting next to me. Only my own thinking could do that. Because thought is all I got. This, I realised, was an insight. I smiled at the realisation.

"What are you laughing at, Evan?" asked WJW in an accusing tone. "You should be more respectful. This is serious."

"You really want to know?"

"Yes, I really want to know."

"OK, fine. You think you can solve all your problems from the outside. You think money and expensive trips and flash cars like this one we're sitting in can sort everything out. You think making amends with people and getting their forgiveness will sort all the bad stuff in your past. You think all this can fill the empty feeling inside of you. But it can't. Ever. Sorry, but it just don't work that way."

Now it looked as if the red mist had descended on WJW. His face had gone all patchy and his eyes looked like they were about to pop out of his head. He reminded me of old Porcu-dog in that moment, and I had to work hard to stifle another smile.

"Listen here, you …"

The car stopped abruptly. Looking out the window, I saw that we had arrived at the big traffic light intersection where the North Circular meets the Main Road. Home turf. Calculating that it was a brisk five minute walk to our flat from here, I made a spontaneous decision right there and then.

"Hey, George," I called out to the driver up front. "Can you pop the boot please so I can grab my bag? I'm going to walk the rest of the way. Thanks mate."

I opened the car door and hopped out before anybody could say anything. WJW just sat there staring at me, eyes blazing, mouth opening and closing, but no words coming out. As I passed the driver's window, it opened a drop and George gave me a quick, almost undetectable wink. WJW didn't see it, but I sure did. I walked round the back of the E-class, heard a faint click and then the boot of the car was rising automatically. Nice one, George. Grabbing my bag out of the boot, I slammed it shut in one smooth movement and started jogging up the street towards home – my home.

I didn't look back.

20

This time, there were only three people present. Plus, in an unusual change from normal proceedings, there was also an older man whose face appeared on the big flat screen, skyped in from somewhere else in the world. The man with the shaved, gleaming head in the loose-fitting dark blue uniform now turned his attention to that face on the screen.

"I understand that the journey went better than anticipated," he began in his gravelly voice. "Is this accurate?"

"Yes, indeed," said the man on the screen, his lined face and wide smile filling most of it. There was the slightest distortion in his voice, no doubt caused by the fact that he was speaking into a device thousands of kilometres away.

"Evan displayed great interest in the understanding of the mind. His capacity to seek out the deeper intelligence responsible for our psychological experience of life was most impressive. It appeared as if this impacted him significantly. Moreover, my associate informs me that the additional experience afforded him with the local young people at the orphanage left a deep impression."

"What about the father?" asked the man in the uniform, moving on quickly. "Did the excursion achieve his intended objectives?"

"This was something I was unable to conclusively ascertain at the point of my disengagement. Perhaps the operative who

accompanied the boy on his journey back is in a better position to make this assessment?"

Having come straight from the airport, the petite woman with dark hair was still in her flight attendant's uniform. Clearing her throat, she launched into her analysis.

"I observed both father and son for a significant portion of their return journey. There appeared to be very little communication of substance between them. However, Evan and I did engage in a spontaneous and meaningful conversation whilst in transit and I can report that he had arrived at quite substantial insight regarding the inside-out paradigm. The effects of even partial immersion in the illusory paradigm appeared to be negligible. My analysis, therefore, is that that the excursion did not achieve the father's intended objectives."

The man in the dark blue uniform sat perfectly still. The throbbing of a small vein on his left temple was the only sign of movement. After some time, he looked up at the flat-screen and spoke again.

"Thank you, Jabulani. We appreciate the contribution of our Southern African colleagues. Please pass on my gratitude to your regional director."

He nodded once, pressed a button on the remote next to him, and then the face disappeared as the screen faded to black. Turning to the woman, he said:

"Your travels have no doubt left you fatigued, Linda. Feel free to leave us now and get some rest."

The lady nodded, stood up and quickly exited the room.

The man in the uniform turned towards the final person remaining in the room – a young girl in the early stages of adolescence. She was dressed modestly in a long white dress that reached to her plain brown shoes and wore a black hijab, the traditional headscarf of Muslim women. This had the effect of covering the top of her head and neck, though not her deep blue eyes or pale features.

"What I am about to share with you is not to be repeated or discussed once you leave this room – not even to other operatives. Is that clear?"

She nodded solemnly.

"You will be aware, no doubt, that a violent crime has occurred recently which we strongly suspect involved known associates of Evan's, meaning the other members of his gang. This has led to extensive deliberations amongst the executive taskforce. The conclusion of those discussions is that we will continue to uphold our critical policy of not intervening in the free choice of the subject, despite the potential dangers involved. In so doing, we have accepted that this may have serious implications. But these are the consequences we are prepared to bear."

He paused and fixed the girl with – if it were possible – an even sterner glare.

"The hypersensitivity of this assignment cannot be overstated enough. I understand that this is your first significant operation and trust you appreciate the great responsibility we have placed in your hands."

The girl stared back at the man in the dark blue .uniform. For a brief moment, she felt her hands shaking uncontrollably, but then she recovered her composure.

"Any questions?"

"One," said the girl.

"Yes?"

"Is his life in danger?"

The man in the dark blue uniform did not answer straight away. In the silence, nothing could be heard other than the faint hum of the sole fluorescent light suspended from the ceiling above his head. Finally, he spoke.

"Yes. It could be."

Then, even though it was only the two of them remaining, he concluded the meeting as he always did.

"And remember. It's an illusion. All of it. Always."

And then, he did something he had never done before. He added three more words.

"Even the fear."

21

The Beast attacked me with such joyful abandon as I walked through the front door that I thought – for a brief moment – he had mistaken me for a giant squirrel on steroids. A wrestling match on the floor followed, as per our combat tradition. Eventually though, I had to bring our emotional reunion to a close; it just wasn't becoming of a dog with a name like The Beast to carry on licking me like that. Anyhow, he'd been alone in the flat for a while and needed to do his thing. So clambering to my feet, I threw my bag on the worn couch, grabbed the lead and – together again – we headed out into the cool night.

Walking down the corridor, I wondered if, by any miracle, the old, creaking lift had been fixed while I was away. The DOWN button was lit up, but as previous experience had bitterly proved, that didn't necessarily mean anything. After a couple of seconds of impatient waiting, it was clear that nothing had changed. So we decided to stuff it and race down the eleven flights of stairs. But just then, a door down the passageway opened and a child I didn't recognise exited an apartment. She crossed the hallway and came to stand next to us by the lift.

"Still not working?" she asked. The girl was quite small and I guessed she was just the wrong side of teenage-hood.

"Uh, no. It never does."

"Oh, that's not good news," the girl said. "We just moved in over the weekend, and I assumed it was a temporary malfunction. My grandfather has a bad hip and is really going to struggle to get up and down all these steps if the lift doesn't work."

"Uh, yeah, that is a problem." I opened the heavy door next to the lift with the word STAIRS stencilled in big green letters on it and said, "OK, let's go Brock."

"Thank you," said the girl, and confidently walked straight under my outstretched arm without ducking and through the doorway. My dog followed at her heels. As she passed by me, I couldn't help but notice her deep blue eyes and very pale face, especially contrasted against the all black hijab wrapped around her head and neck. Up close, I could see how young the girl really was. She couldn't have been older than ten – eleven tops.

I had no choice but to follow The Beast and the girl in the hijab. It was hard to pass on the narrow staircase anyhow, but Brock, behaving completely out of character, seemed to have taken a particular interest in the long white dress she was wearing, which trailed along the floor behind her. He kept sniffing at the hem of it, his short tail wagging back and forth excitedly. Threatening to undermine our hard-earned joint reputation for urgency and speed of movement, my dog slowly and calmly descended in the footsteps of the girl. Strange.

Suddenly, she stopped. I was following so close, I almost knocked her over.

"My name's Aliyah," she offered, turning to face me with a smile. "It's an Arabic name that means 'exalted one'."

"Evan," I replied a little awkwardly, and then, for no reason at all, I added: "I have no idea what it means in English. But a Jewish guy I once played football with told me it means 'rock' in Hebrew."

"Rock," she repeated, and smiled again. "I like that."

She continued descending the stairs, slowly. And we continued following.

"So ... how was your trip?"

"Excuse me."

"Your trip? You must have been away somewhere, because when I looked out the window of my bedroom a few moments ago, I saw you walking into the apartment block carrying a big backpack, the kind you take when you go away on a trip. Did you have a good time?"

"Uh, well, sort of. It's kinda hard to explain."

"I know. When my grandfather took me back to the old country last year to visit all his relatives for the first time, it was also kind of hard to explain. On the one hand, it was so nice to meet the extended family and see where grandfather had grown up and lived for much of his life. But it was all so different from what I was used to. There were lots of things I saw there that I didn't agree with. So it took me a while to settle down again when I came back. Maybe that will be the case for you too."

"Uh, I don't think so. It wasn't that kind of trip."

She started walking down the stairs again, but kept talking to me as she did.

"I know it wasn't. What I meant is that going away sometimes can make you think about things a bit differently. The people you meet and talk to. The things you see and hear. And when you get back, you often find yourself getting clear about a whole lot of stuff that looked pretty confusing before you left."

190

What was this girl on about? And how old was she, *really*? Maybe the whole hijab and long, modest dress look was obscuring things somehow, because though she looked to still be in primary school, she sounded a whole lot smarter than most of my classmates. Then again, on reflection, that wasn't too hard.

I glanced up at the big number '6' stencilled on the wall. Almost halfway. We were both quiet for another couple of floors. Only the sound of her very slightly heeled shoes could be heard as they clicked rhythmically on the stairs. Then she stopped again suddenly and turned to me.

"Do you know that there is a piece of the puzzle missing?"

"S'cuse me?"

"We never know what we are going to think or feel in the future," Aliyah said as she continued her achingly slow descent down the stairs. Couldn't she hurry up? We should have been at the bottom by now. And for that matter, what was up with The Beast? I'd never seen him act like such a sheep, contentedly following this girl at a snail's pace, as if we didn't have squirrels to chase, people to meet and important things to do.

"Now, I don't mean that we don't know what's going to happen in the next moment. That's obvious. Like you had no idea that I'd come walking out of that apartment across the hallway a couple of moments ago. And I had no idea you and your cute dog would be standing there, waiting for a broken lift."

Cute? Nobody had ever called The Beast cute before. I looked down. His tail was wagging back and forth like there was no tomorrow while he gazed up at the girl with what could only be described as puppy-dog eyes. What ever happened to the deadpan

191

stare? The deep pools of black? Who had kidnapped my dog while I was away and replaced him with an imposter?

"I really don't have the foggiest idea what you are talking about," I found myself saying.

"Yeah, I can see that," she said with a smile. "Here's the thing: we all assume we know what we are going to think and feel before something happens. So when we think about the future, we make a mistake by thinking we have a full picture, a finished puzzle. But we don't. Because it's not possible to know what we are going to think in the next moment, never mind the next day or month or year."

She stopped again. This time, I almost tripped over the hem of her dress. Brock looked up at her like a love-struck puppy. Ugh!

"Now, let's say, for argument's sake, that you've got some friends who are in serious trouble. And let's say that you know something which could get them into even more trouble. But they're your friends, right?"

"Right," I answered. *How did she know about friends in serious trouble?*

"Because they are your friends, you assume you will feel bad if you reveal something that gets them into more trouble. It feels like betrayal. But that's only because you think the situation – in this case your friends and how they will respond to the so-called betrayal – can make you feel bad. But they can't. Only thought can do that."

There it was again: that *thought* thing. It was pretty obvious I wasn't going to get away from it, whether on the stairwell of

Sweet Orchard Place, NW4, or in the middle of the African wilderness.

"So ..." I managed to say.

"So ..." continued Aliyah, evidently undeterred by my brainlessness. "Because we don't know what we will think in the future, we for sure don't know what we will feel. So ... there is a big piece of the puzzle missing. Get it now?"

Without waiting for an answer, she turned round and hopped playfully down the final flight of stairs, only stopping when she landed directly opposite the big green '0' on the wall. Brock bounded behind her, yapping excitedly at her heels. Talk about betrayal!

"OK, let me see if I get this clear," I said as I trudged down the last few steps. "You're telling me – completely hypothetically of course – that if I pass on information that could get someone who matters to me into trouble, it doesn't mean I am going to feel bad?"

"That's right. Actually, it *can't* make you feel bad."

I was about to respond by telling Aliyah that was absolutely ridiculous. *Of course it would make me feel bad.* But then I did something extremely unusual for me: I kept quiet and chewed over what this very smart girl had just said.

"Yep, that makes sense," I concluded finally. "There is no situation that has power over me. Nothing on the outside does. Just like it never had any power over Owen, the autistic boy who loves Disney movies. Or that little orphan girl in South Africa who doesn't have any shoes."

"Owen? An orphan girl? I'm not sure who they are, Evan. But it doesn't matter. Because I can hear it makes sense to you now. Which is so cool."

Brock gave a weird little bark just then. If I could understand dog language, I would have guessed he was saying something like: "And you are so cool too, oh Exalted One." I frowned. His behaviour was totally out of order.

Aliyah bent down playfully so that the tip of her hijab was almost touching my dog's wet nose.

"Listen Brock. It's been really good getting to know you. But I've got to go now. And you've got to take care of your boss-man here. We'll hang out again sometime soon."

She stood and looked up at me. I'm not exactly Andre the Giant, but I was suddenly struck by how small she was.

"And as for you, Evan: I think that 'Rock' is the perfect name for you. Like the Rock of Gibraltar. Because you are way more secure than you could ever know. You really *are* a rock."

I didn't know what to say to that, so I said nothing. This was becoming a habit. Maybe even a good one.

"Now, I really need to run and get my grandfather's prescription from the pharmacy before they close," said Aliyah.

Then she turned around quickly and went skipping through the building's concourse and across the parking lot, her long skirt flowing behind her. We watched her go, Brock's tail wagging furiously, while I wondered where that cracking pace been when descending the stairwell.

I stood in the building's entrance for a long moment, reflecting on the conversation that had just gone down. *Nobody and nothing can put a feeling inside of me.* That meant I was free to do whatever seemed the right thing to do.

Suddenly, in a crystal-clear moment – despite all the other voices that had been competing for space in my head over the last six days – I was absolutely certain what that was.

"Come on Beast. We got something real important business to attend to."

We headed straight down Queens Alley in the direction of the park. As we walked, I felt my phone vibrating in my pocket and took it out to read a WhatsApp from Tals.

Hey, just got out the library and got your message. Welcome back! Can't wait to see u and hear all about whats being going on. And been doin some thinkin about how to find the cash your Mum owes that guy. How 'bout a crowdfunding campaign? I googled it and it ain't so hard. We can do this, Ev. Be home in about 20. Speak more then? XXX

I typed a quick reply as we walked.

Luv 2 but gotta sort something first. B back in couple of hours. Catch u then?

Sure. Just knock on my door when your back.

K

I was about to press SEND when a question occurred to me.

Hey, have u met the new Muslim girl who just moved in on our floor? Think maybe flat 1107. The one opposite the lift.

Tals' reply came straight away:

What u talking about? Mrs Shuford has been living in 1107 for 20 years, and will be for another 20. U sure it was our floor?

Strange. I didn't reply straight away. When I did, I simply typed:

K. My mistake. See ya soon. E

We were at the entrance to the park already. Though it was quite late and there was no sign of any customers, the caf was still open. As we walked past the open doorway, an idea hit me.

"Hey Monroe, you here?" I called out.

I heard some plates being stacked somewhere in the bowels of the kitchen.

"Be with you in a minute."

The big Filipino lied. He was with us in half a minute. Ledge.

"Hey Evan," he said, wiping his huge hands on a dirty checked dishtowel hanging out the front of his apron. All OK?"

"All good Monroe," I replied. "Sorry, in a bit of a rush right now but can I ask you a quick favour?"

"Sure. What you need?"

"Uh, a bit weird, I know, but can I borrow one of those empty pizza boxes?" I asked, pointing to the high stack of square cardboard boxes with the words *HOT PIZZA* emblazoned across the top and sides in big red and blue letters.

Monroe laughed. "Usually customers ask for a pizza *in* a box – not an empty box. But of course you can have one. We got dozens of them, as you can see."

He reached past the counter behind him and used one of those enormous arms to pull a box out of the stacked pile.

"Thanks Monroe," I said as I took the box from him. "I owe you one."

"Well, you may owe me one, Evan, but certainly not for a pizza box. Not sure why you need it, but no worries at all. Now, I got to get back to that dishwasher before I can close up for the night. Catch you later."

"Cool." I turned quickly and gently tugged on the lead. "Let's go, Beast."

I was so on mission as I exited the caf that I almost ran straight into D-Von. He had his back to me so didn't see me coming until I was just about on top of him.

"Hey, D-Man. What's happening, bro?" I asked, real surprised to see him out here on his own at this time of night.

My mate didn't respond. He was standing on the elevated concrete patio of the caf, which overlooked the empty basketball court. The yellow police tape had been removed, though a couple of stray leftover pieces were still stuck to the fence, fluttering aimlessly in the wind. D-Von was stood staring at that court, like he had seen a ghost or something.

"D. You hearin me, bro?"

My friend turned slowly round to face me. He looked far gone. His black baseball hat was all skew – neither back to front nor front to back. His eyes were bloodshot, his zits out of control all over his face, and his unshaven look was – well, it wasn't working.

"Hey, Ev-bro," he finally said. A fist-bump greeting didn't seem quite right at this moment in time. "Got yourself a nice big pizza there," he added, motioning with his bloodshot eyes to the box tucked under my arm.

"Good to see you bro, outta lock-up and all," I said, completely ignoring his pizza observation. "Must've been rough."

"Yeah … rough."

D-Von was so baked, I realised, that I could probably get stoned just looking at him. Which also made me realise that this conversation wasn't going anywhere fast.

"Listen, mate. I gotta run this pizza home to Mum before it gets cold. I'll message you later. But I wanna catch up and hear the whole story, K?"

"Yeah … whole story."

I turned to go, planning on pretending to head back home, before doubling back behind the caf without D-Von seeing me.

"Ev," he called out suddenly.

"Yeah, bro?

"We screwed up, man. We really screwed up. Ain't right that we screwed up so much."

Then, without waiting for a response, D-Von turned back towards the court, resuming his trance-like vibe.

I watched him for a long moment. Whatever planet he was on, it definitely wasn't planet earth. Tucking the pizza box under my arm, I held it tight as if it really *did* contain Mum's supper. Then I circled round the far side of the caf heading in the direction of The Corner, taking care to keep my eye on D-Von to make sure he wasn't taking care to have eyes on me. But I needn't have worried. He was staring at that court like one of those deer I had seen just the day before in the African bush, unmoving and unblinking under the bright spotlights of the Land Rover. It was all a little disturbing, to be honest. But I had other things to worry about right now. D-Von, stoned and all, would have to fend for himself.

Brock knew exactly where we were headed and got to the deserted benches a few moments ahead of me. While he raised his leg and did his thing, I kept going, stomping through the thorns and doing my best to avoid smashing into random waist-high tree stumps that could cause a man serious harm in places you don't want to get harmed, if you know what I mean. When I got to The Ring, it was completely enveloped in darkness – none of the light from the park lamps or the caf had extended this far into the thick bushes. Flicking on my phone's torch and using its narrow beam as a guide, I walked straight up to the log with the secret hiding place. Dropping to my knees, I placed the pizza box on the ground while slipping my gloves over my hands. I would need them for what I was going to do next. Then I thrust my right arm as far back as I could. Even with my gloved hand, I could feel the cold steel on my fingertips through the thin material. Gaining purchase on the thick handle, I pulled the knife out and shined the torch on its gleaming blade. The faint streaks of red were still visible on its surface. But I didn't want to look at it. I wanted to remove it. Opening the pizza box, I placed the knife carefully inside. Then I closed the lid, tightly securing the cardboard flaps on its sides so that there was no chance of the blade slipping out. I straightened up, brushed the dirt off my knees, and pointing the phone's torch ahead of us, The Beast and I headed out of The Ring.

Perhaps for the last time.

22

I was so focused on my next destination that it didn't even occur to me to leave The Beast behind. If those German Shepherds down at the police station didn't like it, that was their problem. Not ours. Hugging the pizza box and its precious cargo close to my chest, we hopped onto the 183 and made our way quickly through the quiet Sunday evening streets, hoping off at the Aerodrome Road stop just as I had done almost a week earlier. But unlike then, I wasn't coming to check on my mates and their wellbeing. This time, there was a different purpose to my visit altogether.

We strode resolutely through the automatic doors and right up to the glass partition where my old friend, PC Judy Patel, was sitting in the same position as she had been on my previous visit to the police station. Her face was once again buried in a computer screen while her right hand manipulated a wireless mouse with very slow, deliberate movements. I briefly wondered if she was playing an online version of Solitaire, the card game popular with people born before the Second World War, but then realised that this was simply not possible. No game, even one called Solitaire, could possibly be played this slow. For her part, PC Patel demonstrated not the slightest interest in acknowledging my presence in the demilitarised zone. So, embarrassing as it is to admit, I resorted to a tactic I had seen Porcu-dog use on multiple occasions when bringing order to a school assembly: I uttered a loud, throat-clearing noise. To my surprise, this did not generate any reaction. I wondered if, since my last visit, the bulletproof partition been made soundproof as well? Fortunately, Brock came to my rescue, uttering a loud bark at that moment, which generated the desired effect. PC Patel turned her head – very slowly – in our general direction.

"Excuse me, Ma'am, but I was wondering if I might speak to DS Manning please?"

It took her a moment to recognise me, but when she did, PC Patel's entire demeanour underwent a radical and instant transformation. I briefly wondered if the wider Colindale area had been hit by a minor earthquake.

"Mr. Banksky!" she declared, jumping out of her desk chair while her mouse went clattering to the floor. "We've been looking for you!" she shouted through the bulletproof glass. "Where have you been?"

"Umm, well, yeah, you know, basically … it's kind of a long story."

I couldn't have been less articulate if I had a basketball lodged in my mouth. Brock, sensing my communication limitations, barked again, louder and more urgently than before. I got the drift of what he was barking. *Focus, Banksky.*

PC Patel frowned. "Dogs are not usually allowed in here. They disturb the sensitivities of our professionally trained German Shepherds out back."

I held my ground. The Beast was staying with me.

She went quiet for a moment, presumably sensing that something bigger was at stake here than the emotional wellbeing of her stuck-up police dogs.

"But as we have been urgently trying to get hold of you, and as you're here now, we'll make an exception in this case. I am just

202

going to fetch DS Manning. Stay right here. And don't go anywhere," she added, a bit too forcefully for my liking.

Patel disappeared into the warren. I looked down at The Beast.

"What?" I asked him.

Deadpan eyes. His meaning was clear. *Don't blow this, Banksy.*

The constable's miraculous transformation was complete when she returned, at full pace, within 60 seconds. A spot in the Great Britain Olympic relay team clearly beckoned.

"Come through," she ordered, opening the door to her lair. Though not an expert linguist, I couldn't help but notice that the word "please" seemed to have disappeared entirely from PC Patel's vocabulary since my last visit to the station. "And throw that pizza box in the bin over there," she instructed, motioning with her eyes to a small grey office bin in the corner of the room. "Food is not allowed in the interrogation ... I mean, in the interview rooms."

"Uh, sorry, but no can do. This isn't food. It's evidence. Or at least I think it might be."

The constable looked at me as if I had just suggested that Simon Cowell should start buttoning his top button. In response, I clutched the box tighter to my chest. Brock gave a low growl. His meaning was clear. *Back off police lady. We ain't playing around here.*

She seemed to get the message. "Whatever. Let's get going. The Detective Sergeant is already waiting for you in Room 3."

PC Patel led the way. When she opened the door to the interrogation – I mean interview – room, DS Manning was standing and typing something on his phone. He turned to face me as I entered, frowning as he saw Brock following at my heels. He frowned again when his eyes settled on the cardboard box I was holding out in front of me, as if I was presenting an ancient emperor with a gift of precious jewels brought from far across the oceans.

"Evan Banksky. What a surprise," the Detective Sergeant began in a tone that definitely couldn't be described as welcoming. "Now, before we go any further, do you understand – unlike previously – that as you have come to speak with us of your own accord, this is a purely voluntarily conversation and there is no need for you to be accompanied by an adult at this moment in time."

Of course I understand, I wanted to reply. *Cause as the man coming forward with the key evidence – even taking into account that it's about to be presented in a pizza delivery box – it's a no-brainer that I have just become the game-changer! So of course it's voluntary, Mister big-shot copper.*

"Yeah, cool," I said instead.

"Good. So … We've been looking for you, Evan. Where have you been for the last 24 hours?"

Though I sensed that he had toned down his psycho stare somewhat since we had last spoken, there was a definite edge to Manning's voice. It was clear he wasn't interested in small talk. Good. Neither was I. So rather than answering him, I simply took a big step forward and placed the pizza box down on top of the same rectangular table we had sat around last week. I quickly lifted the lid off the flat cardboard box before he had the chance to ask when I had got a job as a Domino's delivery dude. Under the strong

204

overhead LED lighting, the silver blade shone like a samurai sword. Nobody said anything for a long minute. We all just stood there staring at the knife. And at the faint streaks of red on its broad, six-inch surface.

Finally, the Sergeant spoke. "Where did you get this? And who does it belong to?"

I could feel The Beast bristling by my side. "I can answer your first question. I can't answer your second one."

Manning gave me the kind of look that could have made Sherlock Holmes himself reconsider his profession.

"Well, you better start answering what you can then," he ordered in a stern voice.

And so I did. I told him about The Corner, I told him about The Ring and I told him that was where we always messed about, the five of us. I told him how I had seen a glint of steel in the sunlight the other day in that very spot. I told him about the secret hiding place inside the old log. I told him what I had found inside it six days ago. I told him how I had left it where I had found it. I told him how I had felt really guilty about that decision ever since. And I told him how I went back there less than thirty minutes ago. Which was why there was a six-inch knife with red streaks lying on the table in front of him now. I told him everything. Until there was nothing left to tell. Almost.

Detective Sergeant Manning listened patiently, letting me speak myself to a standstill. When I finally finished, he calmly asked me, "Evan, have you touched this knife with your bare hands?"

"No. I know all about fingerprints and stuff," I explained. "I watch *Line of Duty* you know." I pulled my thin gloves out of my jacket pocket. "So I wore these," I added, holding them up above my head like I was lifting the FA Cup. Mister Articulate, maybe not. But Sherlock Holmes – you better believe it, mate!

"You did well, Evan."

The Sergeant offered a semblance of a smile. He hadn't exactly transformed into a cuddly teddy bear, but I could definitely sense a softening in his attitude towards me. So did The Beast: the hair on the back of his neck had started to come down.

"Now, do you have any idea who this knife belongs to?"

"Uh … well … uh …"

"Evan, let me ask like this: Do you remember any of your mates – any of Jamal, Maurice, D-Von or Jeremy – ever talking about buying or getting hold of a knife?"

This was the moment of truth; this was why I was here. To tell the truth, the whole truth and nothing but the truth. I steadied myself with a quick talking to. *What happened to that boy on the basketball court was wrong. And neither my boys, nor anyone else, can make me feel bad about telling the truth. Only my mind can do that. And I'm not prepared to go there.*

"Yeah, about a month or so ago, we were just kinda messing around in The Ring, ya know. Talking smack and stuff. And then Mo says something about buying a knife. For protection. Especially cause things were starting to hot up with those others boys across the estate."

"Did he say where he got it?"

206

"The hardware store on the high street, just round the corner from the estate."

"And that's all he said?"

"Yeah, that's all. We started talking about something else then. And we never talked about no knife again after that."

Manning went quiet for a moment, and then, almost to himself but just loud enough so I could hear, he said, "That corroborates something we heard from Jeremy."

"What does that mean?"

"It means that your friend Jez was co-operative during his interview. He told us that just before the fight went down the other night, he saw Mo, as you call him, with a knife in his hand."

Well, that helped explain why Jez had got out of lock-up early. Something kinda important he had forgotten to tell me, obviously.

"And it means," continued Manning, "That we have two separate witnesses independently informing us that a knife was most likely in the possession of one of the members of your 'gang.' So our next task is to establish accuracy. In other words, we need to ascertain whether the knife used in the recent incident in Hendon Park is indeed the knife sitting before us on this table right now. And then we need to determine if that is the same knife purchased by Maurice at the hardware store. That's our job and we'll do it swiftly. But you bringing it here has moved our investigation forward significantly. Well done, son. You should be proud of yourself."

The Detective Sergeant smiled again and placed a long arm on my shoulder. That didn't go down well with Brock, standing guard by my side. The Beast let out a long, low growl. Manning got the message. He removed his arm from my shoulder and gave my dog an approving look. The Beast acknowledged it with his black deadpan pools. Mutual respect established.

Now that the Sergeant had stopped treating me like a terrorist in Guantanamo Bay, I couldn't hold back any longer.

"Look, I'm real sorry, but there's one other thing I should have told you earlier."

"Yes?"

"I was there that night. In the park."

"OK," said Manning slowly. "When was that and what did you see?"

"Well … like I told you before, I was with Mum that night trying to fix her up. But what I never told you was that I *did* eventually make it to the park. I just was running late and all. So I got there like just after that guy got jacked, ya know. Actually, I didn't even know he'd been jacked until the next day. I really didn't see nuthin and just had a major panic and ran to hide in the underpass on the other side of the courts until everything had settled down. And then I crept back home before anyone could ask me any questions and get me into any trouble. Anyhow, that's the whole truth, I promise."

I paused, not sure if I had just said something that may land me in a cell with the other boys.

"Am I in trouble cause of all that?"

DS Manning was looking at me far different than before. Definitely not psycho.

"No, you're not in trouble, Evan. You hadn't given us a formal statement previously anyhow, so there are no legal contradictions we need to be concerned about. You're just an eyewitness to events that occurred after the actual crime had been committed and who hadn't come forward until now. And at the time of initially coming across the knife, you had no reason to know it had been used in a crime. You should have brought it to us then, but I can understand why you didn't. So don't worry about it. We'll get it all down in your official statement."

"Cool. That's sick."

"Yeah … sick," repeated Manning, though it definitely didn't sound cool *or* sick coming out of his mouth.

"So … is there anything else you need to tell us?" Manning asked. The half-smile was back. "Any other surprises you'd like to share?"

"Naw, nuthin. That's it." I was suddenly feeling really tired. "Listen, I haven't seen my Mum in a couple of days. She's been worried sick about me. And that really is the truth. Can I go now?"

"Yes, Evan. You can go now. Like I said, you've done real good stepping forward like this. I know it can't have been easy. It was the right thing to do."

"Uh, thanks."

"There's just one thing we need to tell you." Manning paused and another look came over his face that I couldn't read. But somehow, it made me feel uneasy.

"What's that?"

"Jez has already been released, as you know. And so has D-Von. We can hold suspects to a serious crime for up to 96 hours max, which is what we did in this case. But without sufficient evidence to make a formal arrest, we were forced to release the other two boys at the beginning of the weekend. Of course, with the discovery of this weapon, that all changes now. It goes without saying that had we known about this knife earlier, we would not have released them, especially not Maurice. But no worries, our team will go to work as quickly as it can. We will have this sent to the lab straight away for fingerprints, blood sampling and other tests. As soon as we have sufficient evidence, appropriate action will be taken."

I wasn't sure what to say. So I said nothing. Meanwhile, the look on Manning's face had become easier to read. Concern.

"Evan, this case is suddenly moving fast. And being completely honest, I am somewhat concerned for your wellbeing now that the boys have been released. Do you have any reason to think that they would know you may have discovered this weapon?"

I thought about that for a minute. "Uh, no. Why would they?"

"Because it appears as if this knife was specifically hidden away in the location you are describing, perhaps after it was used in a crime. And very few people knew about this so-called 'secret hiding place'."

The Detective Sergeant made quotation marks with his fingers as he said the final three words, as if he needed to emphasise the point.

"What are you saying? That one of my boys would hurt me?"

"I'm not sure, Evan. I'm really not. But just to be on the safe side, is there any place you could go and stay for a couple of days while we sort things out at our end. Extended family perhaps? Somewhere safe, where nobody really knows you?"

"Are you serious?" I replied, stifling a big yawn. "I ain't got anywhere to go. It's just me and my Mum and Brock here. And speaking of Mum, she's going to be finishing her shift real soon and will be getting worried about me. So I've really got to get going."

"OK, I understand," Manning said. "But here's what we're going to do. First, we are going to give you a ride home. We won't drop you right outside your building – don't want to attract too much attention – but we'll get you near enough. Think of it as a special service of your local police force. Second, I am going to ask two of our best community officers to conduct regular checks of your council estate, and especially your apartment building. Just to keep an extra eye on you. Third, I am going to personally call your Headteacher, Mr. Porterfield, first thing in the morning so that he knows what's been going on and cuts you some slack when you go back to school tomorrow. And finally, in the event that anyone bothers you, absolutely anyone, then I want you to call me straight away."

Manning reached inside his uniformed coat and pulled out a rectangular business card, which he handed to me. Brock let the exchange go without a growl. He was clearly warming to Mister big-shot police sergeant. Perhaps he could even get a job here one day, doing what those mean-looking German Shepherds did.

211

"I mean it, Evan. You can call me on this number here any time of day or night if you need to. OK?"

"Uh, OK."

"Good. Now, let's get you home."

The Detective Sergeant grabbed the phone resting on the table and barked a command into the handset for a squad car and driver to meet us out front immediately. Then he led us back down the passageway, through PC Patel's lair and into the parking lot at the front of the station. An official police car – all yellow and blue with real lights on top – was already waiting for us. As Manning opened the back door, I turned to him and asked the question that I had been dreading to ask.

"The boy who got stabbed. How's he doing? Will he make it?"

"He pulled through, Evan. It was touch and go for a while; he'd lost a lot of blood. But he's on the mend now. He'll make it."

I didn't know what to say to that. So I just nodded, gave Brock a little nudge onto the back seat of the police car, and followed him in. The Detective Sergeant closed the door firmly and gave a thump on the vehicle's roof to indicate it was time to go. And as we made our way down Aerodrome Road, sitting in the back of a copper's car for the first – and I sincerely hope – last time in my life, I reflected on my ridiculous recent turn of fortune. And all because I had delivered a six-inch knife in a pizza box to the police.

Taking out my phone, I messaged Tals and asked her to meet me on the corner of the high street nearest to our building – I couldn't wait to see her reaction when she realised the latest mode of transport we were using. Then I put my arm around the world's coolest dog, and together we looked out the window from the back seat, both of us deep in thought. I wasn't sure what was on Brock's mind, but I couldn't stop thinking how this ride home sure beat bus number 183.

23

Mum had finally seen my WhatsApp and had replied with hysterical, over-the-top joy.

Thank God youre alright!!!! Thats all that matters. SOOO excited to c u. Have to stay late to lock up shop. Jamie had an emergency with one of his kids. Will u come and meet me here at 9 and we can walk home 2gether? Don't worry. We'll figure everything out. Luv u more than u know. XXXX

I glanced at the time in the top right corner of my screen: 8:25 p.m. Enough time to catch up and make good with Tals quickly before meeting Mum at the coffee shop. And as I had hoped, my friend was waiting on the corner where I had asked her to meet me as we rolled up. The look on Tals' face was priceless when it hit her that it was The Beast and me exiting the copper's car.

"Look at you," she called out. "Mister Sherlock Holmes himself. And I presume that makes you Watson," laughed Tals, looking at my dog. The Beast humbly bowed his head in acknowledgement of his new status as one of the world's great crime-solvers, before bounding over to greet her.

I slammed the police car door shut, shouted a friendly "thanks for the ride" and gave a thump on the roof for good measure. Just like I had seen the Detective Sergeant do. And just because I could.

When I turned round, Brock and Tals were in the middle of an embarrassingly intimate embrace. At least embarrassing for a canine of The Beast's reputation and standing in the community. But then Tals extricated herself from my dog's slobbering, stood up and came over to where I was standing on the side of the road, looking me straight in the eyes as she did. I could see that hers were moist.

"It's so good to see you, little neighbour. You have no idea how much I've missed ..." Her voice caught in her throat just then. She couldn't say more. She didn't need to.

"This is kinda awkward," I said awkwardly. Which just made it more awkward. "So ... how long we gonna stand here on the side of the road, getting all soft while Brock makes a fool of himself in public? We got a lot to catch up on. First, why don't you tell me more about this scheme you're cooking up to help sort Mum's dues. Didn't quite catch your message but did you say loudfunding or something?"

"Crowdfunding, not loudfunding, you moron!"

"Whatever. So what's the story with that, girl?"

"Simple. You get a whole lot of people to give little bits of cash for something important you're raising money for."

"Yeah, think I heard of that somewhere. But how do we do that?"

"We set up a GoFundMe page. Then we post messages on Instagram, Snapchat, WhatsApp – all our platforms – to every single person we know. And we drive everyone crazy until they cough up."

"Sounds like a sick idea. But why would anyone wanna give cash to us, especially for getting Mum out of a bind that was her making in the first place?"

"Leave that to me, little neighbour. I just covered marketing in my Economics A-level, which has given me a whole load of good ideas. But just to give you a taster: I'm gonna message the entire WhatsApp group of Sweet Orchard Place. That's like at least two hundred people. So even if they each just give a fiver, we're well on our way."

"Man Tals, you're good. You've always been the brains behind this operation."

"Yeah, well, brains or no brains, I never scored a ride in a coppers car. So you gonna explain that or do I need to figure it out all by myself as well?"

"Keep it together, I'm getting there," I laughed. "But listen, I gotta meet Mum at the coffee shop soon. Should we walk and talk while we make our way there?"

"Sure. Let's go," said Tals.

We began heading in the direction of Mum's work, crossing the street and making our way down the dark, grim alley scattered with used cigarette butts, empty beer cans and other gross stuff you would prefer not to see. Badly scrawled graffiti covered much of the high concrete walls, adding to the inner-city feel of the narrow space. But this was our turf and we knew it well. It was good to be back on it – together. Meanwhile, freed of the cramped confines of the police car, Brock bounded ahead, intent on letting every single lamppost – most of which weren't working – know who the real boss around here was. Then, a big ginger tomcat made the rookie mistake of choosing the wrong time to cross the alley. The Beast let out a bark of delight and set off in hot pursuit down the rubbish-strewn path. We both watched him go and laughed.

"Good to see The Beast hasn't lost his will to hunt," laughed Tals. "Now … are you gonna explain how you scored that ride or not?"

"So … there's this sergeant guy who I went to speak to down at the police station. He started off being a bit of a hard-case, but turns out he's a pretty chilled guy. After we was finished speaking, he told one of his coppers to give me a lift home in an official car."

"You serious?"

"Yep, way serious. Here, if you don't believe me, check this out." I dug into my pocket and handed Tals the business card DS Manning had given me. "Look, it's even got his mobile number on …"

"Hey, Banksky!"

I turned round. Two muscular figures were jogging down the poorly lit alleyway in our direction. Even under the weak light of the half-working streetlamps, I recognised the massive snake tattoos from a distance before it became obvious that it was Jams and Mo heading our way. As they drew nearer, I noticed something long and silver in Mo's hand. It looked a bit like a screwdriver. Or a bicycle spoke, maybe. What was that all about?

"Hey guys," I said. My voice seemed to be a pitch higher than normal and I had a real weird feeling in the pit of my stomach. It felt weirder when Tals grabbed my arm.

They stopped right in front of us. I wasn't sure what to say or do. So, nervously, I offered my right hand in a fist bump manoeuvre. Neither of them offered a fist back.

"Where you been, man?" asked Mo. His voice was cold. Tals' grip tightened on my arm.

"Uh … nowhere important. Just been sorting some stuff, that's all."

"Funny that," sneered Jams. He moved a step forward, right up in my face. I could smell the foul mix of vodka and smokes on his breath. I knew that smell well. "Why would someone who was nowhere important be getting out of a copper's car?"

If it was meant to sound like a question, it didn't. More like an accusation. Now I could feel Tals' fingers digging into my skin, even beneath the material of my jacket. Before I had a chance to think of a clever answer, Jams continued, his tone going from sneering to full-on aggro.

"Me and Mo was just crossing the road when we saw that copper's car pull up on the corner. So I turns to Mo and says, 'Wonder what them pigs want from us now? They just let us go and now they back for us already?' But then we see that it's one of our bros getting out the pig car. Acting all friendly and polite and stuff. So I says to Mo, 'Isn't that Banksky? The one who didn't pitch up for the ballgame last week. The one who ain't replying to his WhatsApps. The one who don't seem to wanna be part of da Ring Gang no more. The one who used to hang around but didn't come to see us or do nuthin for us while we been down in lock-up.'"

That wasn't fair and I needed to let him know it.

"Hey Jams, I tried to come see you boys at the police station the other day but ..."

Jams acted as if I hadn't uttered a word.

"So I says to Mo, 'What's that all about?' And Mo says to me, 'I dunno. But sure looks suspicious that one of our boys is in with the pigs while the rest of us are just starting to breathe air again after spending four days in lock-up.'"

Then Mo himself jumped in. "Yeah, and one other thing we can't figure out. Jams and me were down by The Ring the other day, and had a look for something real important we'd stashed in the log back before the pigs got us. But it ain't there. Which is outta order, cause ain't no-one got a scooby about that hidin spot except for da Ring Gang boys. So ... whaddaya say to all that, Banksky boy?"

I couldn't think of anything to say to that. But Tals could.

"Listen guys, we're just on our way to go see Ev's Mum. Sounds like you've both had a hectic few days, so why don't you just go chill a bit."

Mo turned towards her, a mean sneer on his face.

"We ain't talkin to you, you big cow. So why don't you keep your fat mouth shut and sod off ..."

Suddenly, I found my voice. "Hey, easy there Mo. That ain't no way to talk to anyone, specially not ..."

"Shut up!" shouted Jams. "Now, you gonna explain what you was doin in that pig's car or do I need to beat it out of you?"

Tals wasn't having none of it. "Back off, you big bully."

219

Without warning, Mo reached out and grabbed her roughly by the arm. Tals' grip on me fell away as she stumbled to the ground.

"Hey, let go of her..."

Out of the corner of my eye, I glimpsed something coming towards the side of my face. I tried to duck. Too late. Something hard and heavy thudded into my head. Something else – was it a boot? – seemed to fill my entire stomach. I staggered, gasping for air. But I couldn't take any in. My lungs were on fire. My head felt like it was in a blender. A clubbing blow landed on the back of my neck. Sparks of red light filled my vision. Then a flash of steel. A sharp pain. And more red. But this time, it seemed to be pouring out of me. I heard someone scream. Was it Tals' voice? But why did it seem so far away, like it was coming from a tunnel under the water? My legs began to give way and then I was falling. What was that noise coming from the underwater tunnel somewhere down the alleyway? Was Brock OK? More violent sounds: a dog snarling, clothes tearing, people shouting, ferocious barking. And more screaming. Was it someone else's voice? Or was it my own? Then I heard footsteps running.

And then the darkness came. And I heard nothing.

24

The cramped, underground room was full, the air stifling. Everyone had been summoned. No-one spoke. Until one man did.

"The situation is most concerning," began the man in the loose-fitting dark blue uniform, his tone even more solemn than usual. "Evan is in a critical condition. He is being attended to by an excellent medical team. There is nothing more that can be done from a physical perspective other than to wait."

The occupants of the room remained silent. Not only was there nothing to be done. There was nothing to be said.

"In the interim, we have elected to expand the scope of our mission to take into account the unexpected circumstances. Specifically, I will personally remain in close proximity at all times in the event that he regains consciousness."

A murmur of surprise ran through the assembled group. They had never heard of the man in the uniform taking such a hands-on operational role. Ignoring the reaction, he nodded his perfectly shaved gleaming head.

"If he needs assistance, I will be there."

The dark brown eyes behind the wire-rimmed glasses seemed darker than ever. He used them to scan each individual seated in front of him.

"Whatever happens, this group can rest assured that they have done everything expected of them. All protocols were correctly followed." His bald head shook back and forth ever so

slightly before continuing. "This was simply a case of outside events taking hold and running their course."

The room was perfectly still. Then the sound of a chair being pushed back punctuated the silence and the youngest person present stood up.

"Sir, is it possible that perhaps we did not take all necessary precautions?" asked the Muslim girl in a soft voice. Before waiting for a reply, she continued, more loudly. "Is it possible that we are, to some degree at least, responsible for this situation?" Her voice faltered then, but she bravely asked one further question. "Is it possible that we put Evan's life in danger?"

If the silence had been loud before, it was positively deafening now. It was one thing to be courageous, but the girl's outburst bordered on insubordination. Even youthful naiveté would surely not save her a rebuke now, perhaps even dismissal from the entire programme?

But then the man in the dark blue uniform did something that he very rarely did. He smiled, ever so faintly.

"Your concern and sense of responsibility are noted, Aliyah." He looked directly at the young girl, an expression of genuine empathy settling on his lined face. "We all feel saddened by this turn of events. And it is understandable that we may appear affected by them. As a matter of fact, it is to be expected. We are human ... after all. And part of the human condition, as we all know, is that we experience feelings and emotions."

A slight tremor in the man's voice could be heard above the low hum of the room's sole fluorescent lightbulb.

"I am sure I speak for us all when I say that what has transpired is not what any of us would have wished. Moreover, I anticipated this information might be difficult for some of us to absorb. So I took the unusual step of consulting the Chair. And this is what she asked me to communicate to all of you."

He paused for a long moment. There was nothing but stillness in the cramped room.

"The outside-in can be very subtle. It is, by definition, most deceptive. This is why – as she explained – it is called an illusion."

He paused again and looked into the eyes of each of the men and women seated before him. When he reached the young girl with the hijab wrapped around her head and neck, his eyes lingered. Despite the unmistakeable moistness in her dark blue eyes, she bravely held his gaze. They both nodded at each other.

"As always, our task is to bring understanding; to offer perspective; to provide an explanation. This is why we do what we do. And we will continue to do it, whatever happens. We will do it for Evan Bansky. *Because our mission is truth."*

Those assembled remained completely silent. They all knew that the man in the dark blue uniform was indeed speaking the truth. It was why they were all here, dedicating themselves to this work. But it didn't mean that it didn't hurt. That they weren't hurting. As he himself had said ... we are all human.

After a long pause, the man brought the meeting to a close, in the same manner that he always did.

"And let's remember. It's an illusion. All of it. Always."

And then, to their great surprise, he added not one, but two more sentences.

"Even the pain. Even our pain."

25

The first time, even before I opened my eyes, the fire in my gut was all that I felt. It was the most intense, searing pain I had ever experienced. So I lay there – wherever there was – eyes closed, teeth clenched, not thinking about anything but the pain. Until I drifted away...

The next time, I actually opened my eyes. Progress. The incredible pain was still there, but maybe just a little less. I tried to lift my head, to see more than the plain white ceiling and bright spotlights above me, but that didn't go well. Neither did trying to speak. There was something lodged in my mouth, so that wasn't going to work. I drifted off again...

When I next opened my eyes, it was all dark. I tried to make sense of what had happened to me. Fragments of events floated into my mind like shards of broken glass that didn't quite fit together: banging on the roof of a police car, Brock chasing a ginger tomcat down a rubbish-strewn alley, passing a rectangular card to Tals, a snake tattoo getting in my face, someone falling, a flash of steel, shouts and screams and barking and blood ...

In the pitch dark, it was all quiet. Too quiet. I panicked. Where was I? Had I been kidnapped? Taken somewhere dark and evil to lie and rot .... I tried to shout for help, but all that came out was a muffled noise. There was something still in my throat. What was it? Why were they silencing me? I heard a noise and panicked more. Who was there? What did they want from me?

I felt someone touch my hand. It was soft and cool. And then ... the sweetest, most beautiful sound I had ever heard.

"Shhhh, Evvy. Shhhh. I'm here. Mum's here. You're safe. You're going to be OK."

In the dark, I couldn't see Mum's face. But I could hear her voice. And it's all I needed to hear. I closed my eyes again and held on to that precious hand...

The pain in my side was still there, but it wasn't my enemy anymore. The room was bright now. I lifted my head. Painful, but I could do it. No sign of Mum. But swivelling my head just a little, I saw someone else I recognised. Standing by a window. Looking out. Eyes red. And swollen.

I opened my mouth. Whatever had been lodged there before was gone now. I could speak. Hallelujah!

"Hey ..." I managed to gasp. My throat was parched. Dry as a desert. "What's up girl?"

"Ev!" cried Tals. "Thank God you're awake. I've been so ..."

And then the tears came. Buckets of them. It was as if she had drained the River Thames of all its water and stored it in her eyes until this moment. Finally, the deluge ended. A long period of sniffling followed. When it was all over, I couldn't resist a quick joke at Tals' expense.

"I thought you'd be happy to see me. So why you acting like you're at my funeral?"

I started to laugh, but a massive spasm of pain went surging through my body. My grin became a groan faster than an Anthony Joshua left hook. A look of concern spread across Tals' features, mixing with her tear-stained face. But then, as my attempted banter slowly registered, she broke into a wide, beaming smile. It was the smile of a friend. A best friend.

"Welcome back, little neighbour. We've been waiting a long time for you to come round."

I scanned the room with my eyes. Even lying on my back, I could see that there were three identical beds besides mine. From what I could gather, they were all occupied by patients who looked as if they could have been around at the time of World War I. Which is a nice way of saying we were not likely to be swapping Dr. Dre downloads as a way of getting to know each other. Glancing at my more immediate surroundings, I noticed that I was hooked up to a long drip pumping some kind of clear liquid into my body plus a couple of other machines that were making soft beeping noises.

"Looks like we're in a hospital," I observed. Whatever had happened to my body, the good news was that my mind had clearly retained its razor-sharp qualities. A Rocky-level comeback was definitely on the cards.

"That's right, genius." Tals sat down on the edge of the bed I was lying in. "Now let me go call someone to come check on you straight away and give you something for the pain. And then I'll call your Mum and let her know you're awake. Though I hope her phone is off and she's getting some sleep."

"In a minute," I said, though I could definitely have done with some pain-meds real urgent. "First, I need you to tell me how I got here. And where's Mum? Why would she be sleeping in the middle of the day? Is everything OK with her? And finally … why are you such a wreck?"

I paused. The torrent of words left my throat sore, my side aching and my head pounding. But I had a lot of questions and I needed answers. So I ploughed ahead, doing my best to ignore the pain.

"And while you're at it, can you explain why my head feels like a herd of elephants just played a football match using it as the ball and my belly as the pitch? And why my throat feels like someone poured petrol down it?"

Tals laughed. "And there I was thinking that you being out cold for the last three days would chill you out. It's good to have you back, Ev." Her voice got more serious then. "Listen, don't worry about your Mum. She virtually hadn't moved from that chair over there for the past 72 hours, but I finally managed to persuade her to go home about an hour ago to get some proper sleep. But she only agreed if I promised not to leave the room until she got back. She didn't want you waking up alone."

I nodded. There's only one Mum. Despite all her struggles, all her disappointments, all the messing up – hers and mine – Mum had been there for me. Always had been. Always would be. That, I realised, is love. Nothing could have been clearer to me in that stark moment.

Then, suddenly, a terrifying thought occurred to me.

"Brock! What happened to him? Is he OK?"

"He's good, he's cool Ev," Tals said quickly. "And I've been walking him a couple of times a day while you've been lazing around here getting this free accommodation and all. So don't worry, we got you covered, little neighbour."

I breathed a major sigh of relief. There's only one Tals too.

228

"So how badly am I banged up?" I asked after a while. "Give me the lowdown."

Tals' eyes started to mist over again, but then she steadied herself.

"You got beat up pretty bad, Ev. Those jerks took you out with a bicycle spoke which sliced you up inside. You lost a ton of blood and were in surgery for a good few hours; the docs had to take out your spleen cause it was cut up so bad. But don't worry, you can live just fine without it."

Tals took a deep breath while her eyes flickered across my face. I was having a tough time taking it all in, but I didn't want her to know that.

"Go on," I said. "What else?"

"Well, you've got a golf-ball size bump on the back of your head from getting sucker-punched there. Bad concussion. So that explains why you feel you got stuck in the middle of a game of elephant football. And the reason your throat is killing you is that until a few hours ago, you had a long tube stuck way down it to help you breathe. They call it 'intubation.' But as you were starting to do better earlier this morning, the doc took it out."

"Right," I said. I raised a hand to my throat, feeling a thick bandage where the tube must have been not long before. I didn't have anything banterous to say. What Tals was telling me was no laughing matter.

"OK, enough medical stuff," Tals said, ending that part of the conversation quickly. "Let me go find a nurse now."

"Yeah, OK. But listen, I really don't remember much of what happened. So before you do, just tell me what actually went down in that alley."

Tals sighed. "OK, let's do this quick. Where should we start?"

It took longer than she had planned, but Tals got the whole story out eventually. Starting with the moment my boys – let me rephrase that – my ex-boys, Mo and Jams, had decided to see how a twelve-inch razor sharp bicycle spoke would fit in my stomach. That was the flash of steel I had glimpsed, nanoseconds before it was thrust into my abdomen. In the end, I was lucky, Tals explained. Another couple of inches to the right and they probably would have punctured a lung. And that would have been it. Done for. Game over. No extra time. But I'd still bled buckets, Tals said. And most likely it *would* have been game over if not for two critical factors.

First, Brock. A split second after she had screamed, Tals described how The Beast came charging up that alley at a speed that she had never before seen – not even when taking on his squirrel chasing super-dog park persona. I was already on the ground by then, but just as Mo was swinging a huge boot at my head, the Beast leapt through the air and took him down like he was a soft little squirrel. And when Jams tried to pull Brock off, he almost bit his hand off.

"Actually, it was pretty much close to his whole arm," said Tals. "I'd never seen Brock like that. Those fools didn't have a chance. Brock really was super-dog. He saved your life, Ev."

The one-time rescue dog had become my rescuer. Just thinking about what The Beast had done for me was starting to choke me up.

"You said two things," I croaked, moving on fast. I tried to turn on my side but a sharp stab of pain in my stomach forced me to remain still on my back. I held my breath and counted quietly to five, waiting for the agony to subside.

"What was the other?" I asked finally.

"The card you had given me, not ten seconds earlier," explained Tals. "It had fallen on the ground in all the commotion. But as soon as Brock had chased those savages off, I saw it right there next to you, soaking in your blood. I guess I should have called 999 but I remembered what you had just said about that DS Manning guy and kind of went with that and called him. My hands were shaking so much I could barely thumb the numbers in. He answered straight away and when I screamed that you were bleeding all over the ground, he told me to find something to use as a tourniquet to stop the bleeding. I saw Brock's lead next to you which he told me to wrap round your stomach, just above the wound, and to pull it as tight as possible. It wasn't easy, especially with all the blood pouring out. At the same time, I could hear him shouting to someone to send an ambulance immediately. I was crying and shaking all over, but the whole time he was talking calmly to me, telling me exactly what to do. And it couldn't have been more than three minutes before I heard the sounds of a siren. Then there were police and paramedics all over the alley, sorting you out..."

The door to the hospital room swung open suddenly. "Well, well. Look who's woken up. I thought I heard talking coming from this room."

A short, thick-set woman in a loose-fitting dark blue nurse's uniform came striding into the room.

"Hello Evan," she said in what sounded like the same accent as those West Indian cricketers who I'd heard interviewed on *Talksport*. "My name is Jan and I am one of the nurses on the ward who has been looking after you."

She nodded at Tals in a familiar way. It was clear the two of them had got to know each other over the past few days.

"Seems like you two have already been doing some serious catching up. But I'm going to have to interrupt now so I can run some tests, give you medication and see how you're getting on. Miss Mills, would you mind giving us a bit of space?"

"Of course," said Tals, getting off the bed and moving towards the door. "Anyhow, I want to message Ev's Mum and tell her that he's up and doing OK. Hopefully it'll be the first thing she sees when she wakes up. She'll be so happy to hear the news."

Jan began pulling the curtain along the rail that surrounded the hospital bed, separating me from my WWI roommates.

"I'll let you get to work," said Tals, "And go easy on him," she added with a cheeky best-friend smile. "He's a bit soft, you know."

26

Tals reappeared not long after the nurse had finally finished inspecting me, an inspection that didn't go too well. I felt like a car that was about to fail its MOT. The good news was that the meds were already starting to do their thing, the pain slightly more bearable.

"Still couldn't reach your Mum, but am sure she'll get the message soon," Tals said as she walked into the hospital room.

The look of concern on my face must have been easy to read.

"Hey, don't worry, Ev. Your Mum's cool. I don't think she's touched any booze or pills since you've been in here. Must have been tough on her, but she's been real brave, from what I can see."

The relief flooded over me. "That's good to know. Thanks, Tals."

We were both quiet for a long moment.

"Listen, Tals, I've been a massive jerk and I'm real sorry ..."

"Yo, Ev. Don't sweat, I get it. It's cool. We are all living in our own separate realities, so that explains why me and you haven't always been on the same page lately. Know what I mean?"

"No, I don't know, Tals," I said. "What's this separate realities thing you're talkin about?"

"You really wanna know?"

"Yeah, I really wanna know."

"OK, well, here's something else I learnt from that clever book of mine, the one I lent you and still haven't got back," she said with a smile.

I definitely deserved that one. "Go on," I said.

"I see and feel my thinking. And you see and feel yours."

"Come again."

"I'll put it in words that even a knucklehead like you can understand," she said, laughing. "Basically, we all see and feel life through our own eyeballs. That's just an expression which means that we experience life through our own thoughts. And that means – whether you like it or not – we are living in separate realities."

"So?"

"So ... it means that we can never expect other people to see the world the way we do. As they think it, so they will see it."

Tals knew that look of confusion on my face better than anyone.

"OK, Einstein. I can see you're gonna need an example here. So ... let's take that time last week when we disagreed about the idea of you going to live with your so-called father. You remember that?"

"Course I do. I was so vicious to you 'bout all that. Man, I really regret that now."

"Hey, it's cool. That's not why I'm bringing up. I'm just trying to give you a case of when we both saw the same thing completely different."

"How does that work then?" I was getting there, but it was taking time. Fortunately, the golf ball on the back of my head gave me a good excuse.

"Like I said, Ev. You are just seeing that issue through your own eyeballs, through your own mind. And so am I. So that creates two completely different realities for us both."

"Well, isn't that a problem, then?" I asked. "Surely we should both see things the same way, specially as we are friends and all?"

"No ways. It's only a problem if you don't see that it's your thinking which is creating that view of things," explained Tals. "Because then you're likely to decide that your view is the only one that matters. But when we see that we are just having an experience of something in our own minds – whether it's another person, or idea or whatever – then we also understand that others won't see things the same way as us. They won't because they don't think like us. Actually, like I was saying before, they can't. It's just not possible."

"Keep going," I urged Tals, "This is making a lot of sense."

"So here's what often happens: when other people don't think the same way we do, we usually make out as if there is something wrong with them. Then we end up feeling all hurt, angry, peed off, judged, etcetera, etcetera. Before you know it, there are all these barriers between people. Like what happened between us the other day at the bus stop outside the library. It was just a whole lot of misunderstanding and bad feeling."

Then it hit me. "I get it. What you're saying is that even when we think different, it doesn't mean we have to end up fighting with each other. We can just know that we are both 'seeing our thinking through our own eyeballs', just like you said, Tals."

"You got it, little neighbour. Actually, contrary to popular opinion, that kick to the head hasn't entirely dislodged your brain," Tals joked.

She was about to throw a playful punch in the direction of my shoulder then, but she must have realised that in my current condition, it would likely lead to some kind of emergency response from the critical care team. So I had to settle for her tickling my big left toe instead. Talk about cutting a man down to size!

When Mum finally got the message from Tals, she made a beeline straight for the hospital. She came rushing into the room so fast she almost ran straight into an orderly who was arriving with the dinner cart at that exact moment. It was an emotional reunion, to say the least – with me, not the orderly. After a period of crying, kissing and gentle hugging (my spleenless stomach couldn't have tolerated her usual hold-on-tight hugs), Mum pulled up a chair close to my bed and gripped my hand tight, not saying anything for the longest time. It occurred to me that this may well have been the exact same thing she had been doing for most of the last three days.

It was a good silence, the kind you can only have with the people you know completely and really love. In other words – despite all our problems – it was the kind of silence I could only have with Mum.

Just then, an important looking lady in a long white coat came strolling into the room, with Nurse Jan at her side.

"Hello. My name is Dr. Casey," she announced, nodding at Mum in a friendly but professional kind of way. "It's time to see how you're getting on, Evan."

The doctor and nurse gave me a thorough once-over, making it clear that they weren't taking any prisoners. The news was a mixed bag: on the one hand, Doc Casey explained that now that I had come out of the coma, the worst had clearly passed. On the other, she warned me that I had lost a whole lot of blood and needed to go real easy as a result. Meanwhile, Nurse Jan cautioned that the biggest risk after major surgery was that of infection. So basically, the instruction was to chill, which to me, was another way of saying that I had a long, uninterrupted game of Fortnite ahead of me.

They couldn't, however, refuse a visit on the first afternoon of my return to consciousness from Detective Sergeant Robin Manning. He came to take an official statement of what I recalled had occurred in the alleyway. But as there was nothing I could remember once that first blow had landed on my head, that part of our conversation didn't last long. It didn't really matter though, cause Tals was the real witness here. She'd seen it all up close and hadn't held back in her own interview down at the police station on the night of the attack. Apparently, something like half the Metropolitan Police had been put on alert to find Mo and Jams, which resulted in them being caught at Kings Cross station trying to catch the last train out of London late Sunday night. They were snookered by the discovery of some of my blood found on items of clothing they were both wearing at the time. And for good measure, they both had serious bite marks on their arms and legs where The Beast had shown his mettle in his finest hour. DS Manning also told me that the knife I had brought to the station on Sunday night had indeed turned out to be the crucial missing piece of evidence that the police had been waiting for. Not only did the blood on the blade match that of the boy who had been stabbed on the basketball court, but fingerprints on the handle belonged to both Mo and Jams.

"Our theory," Manning explained, "Is that Maurice – Mo – probably committed the actual stabbing in the midst of the fight, while Jams was the one who tried to hide the weapon in that secret log of yours. That's why we caught him on the night of the fight trying to scale the fence on the far side of the park, behind the thick bushes surrounding that area. It's down to the Crown Prosecution Service now, but based on all this evidence, you can be pretty damm sure those two boys are going away for a long time."

I said nothing in response. Knowing that the boys were going down for taking me out, as well as that boy on the basketball court, didn't make me feel any better. It just made me feel sad – for them, for us, for everyone caught up in this mess.

While I had half-expected Manning coming to see me, I got a major surprise with some of the other visitors who pitched up out of the blue. There was my English teacher, Mrs. Dicken, and, even more surprisingly, my Headteacher himself, whose arrival presented a specific challenge: in my weakened and post-concussion state, I had to make sure not to slip up and call him Mr. Porcu-dog. Fortunately, the big bump to the back of my head hadn't mushed my brain that badly! He was actually pretty cool and even said that the whole threat of exclusion thing would now be permanently dropped. Good man.

Then there was Monroe and Keith, chef and owner of the park caf respectively. Monroe came strolling in with a suspicious look on his big, friendly face. I burst out laughing – and holding my side in pain – when he produced a packet of cold chilli chips from somewhere inside his massive jacket. Keith told me, in a conspiratorial whisper so that the nurses wouldn't hear, that Monroe had been waiting to give these to me for the past three days. Ledge. Then came cuz Jamie and Sandra from the coffee shop. Like Monroe, Sandra had smuggled in some contraband – a batch of fresh blueberry muffins – while Jamie informed me that Mum could have as much time off as she needed while I was recovering. There were also guest appearances from good old DC Chipman and Mrs. Shuford of Sweet Orchard Place fame, plus the entire Under 16 football squad of North West Secondary School, including subs. And then, to my huge surprise, Jez and D-Von arrived outta nowhere during one of the few moments when I was left alone. After they had both shuffled sheepishly into the room, we faced one of those awkward moments when no-one knew where to start or what to say. But as a man who prides himself on the quality of his banter, it felt right that I take the lead.

"So, heard you guys have been having some pretty rough basketball games lately."

They laughed, I laughed and the ice was broken. Jez explained that the charges against him and D-Von had been completely dropped. They had admitted to the police their role in the initial punch-up on the court, but it was clear they knew nothing about a knife other than what Jez had already told them. I was also well pleased that D-Von looked a fair bit better than when I had seen him outside the caf on the night of the attack. Unlike then, his eyes were clear and his hat was on straight – back to front of course. So I was real happy to see how they both seemed to be doing OK, and even happier when they told me they had been let off by the police with a caution – I knew they were not the problem here. But two other guys were. To my surprise though, it was Jez who wanted to go there quicker than me.

"You were right when we spoke in the park last week, Ev," he began.

"Right about what?"

"Right about what had been happening with the gang. Right that Jams and Mo had been getting more and more hostile, and right that things had got more and more outta hand with all the drink and weed and stuff."

I nodded, while D-Von just kept looking down at the floor. Jez pushed on. His voice was a slightly higher pitch than normal, a sure sign, I had learned over the years, that he was feeling upset about something.

"I feel like such a loser for not speaking up that day down by The Corner when Jams came on to Tals like such a slimy reptile. Tals didn't deserve that, but we all just sat there like a bunch of chickens and said nuthin …"

His voice trailed off. There wasn't anything any of us could say. We had let Tals down, massively, and we all knew it. After a while, I spoke up.

"Listen, boys. That was just one of the warning signs. There were others, like when Mo and Jams began starting up with those other boys from across the estate for no reason. I guess we all missed the signs. Or maybe we just didn't care then. Anyhow, it's all about that separate realities thing, ya know?"

No, they didn't know.

So when Nurse Jan appeared and told the boys that visiting hours were up and they needed to head out, they both seemed pretty relieved to get going. D-Von made his way out of the room straight away, but just as he reached the door, Jez turned around and said,

"Hey, Ev, listen man, I'm real sorry 'bout everything that's gone down." There was an even higher pitch to his voice now, but he pushed ahead. "You've always been the best of us lot. And even though you're the youngest by some way, I've always respected you the most. So you take care of yourself, bro. Cause I got a feelin that you're the one most likely to do some good in this messed up world we live in."

I said nothing for a long moment. Somehow, I think we both knew that even when I got out of this place, we were unlikely to be hanging around together again by The Corner. Although just two weeks in the past, those days already seemed a long way away. Finally, I replied,

"Thanks bro. That means a lot."

And then he left. And I was alone again.

27

I turned my head to look at the luminous bedside hospital clock. 3:47 am. It was the fourth night since I had regained consciousness, the seventh since the whole thing in the alley had gone down. The doctors had told me earlier that it wouldn't be long before I was ready to go home. And after another couple of weeks of resting up, my body would be pretty much back to normal. That was the good news. But the bad news, which I didn't choose to share with anyone, was that my mind felt like a complete mess.

During the hours I had spent tossing and turning in the uncomfortable hospital bed, my thoughts had become as dark as the pitch black room I was lying in. They filled my mind endlessly, not giving me a moment's rest. The initial feelings of gratitude for having survived the alleyway assault had slowly ebbed away. In their place came a whole lot of doubts and confusion. Why had this happened to me? Would I ever find normal friends, the kind who didn't go around stabbing people for fun? Besides my dog and a girl-best-friend who was a couple of months from completing school, who did I really have in my life that I could count on? Not to mention Mum's issues with booze. She seemed OK now, but we'd been through temporary lulls before and look where that had got us. Why would this time be any different?

All alone in the dark room, the questions kept popping into my head at a speed that would make Donald Trump's tweeting look tortoise-like slow. What about my injuries? Would I ever be able to play footie again? To work out hardcore in the gym? To race The Beast across the park?

And then the big question, the one that needed an answer more than any other: what were we going to do about the money Mum owed Vic the bookie? Last she told me, Tals' crowdfunding idea wasn't exactly about to make us millionaires, certainly not before the end of the month, which was only a few days away. So we still had a major-league problem on our hands and a huge monkey on our backs. Sure, it was nice of Monroe and Keith, Sandra and Jamie, and even Mrs. Dicken and old Porcu-dog, to come and visit me in the hospital. But none of them were offering anything more than cold chilli chips, blueberry muffins and lifted suspensions. Time was running out to find a serious load of cash. And to make matters worse, every time I raised it with Mum during her visits, she just brushed me off, insisting I not worry about such things while I was lying in a hospital bed.

I thought about that list I had written back in our flat, the one when I divided the page into two columns and wrote down everything I knew about my life. It was when everything seemed to be going wrong at once: my suspension, the stabbing, Mum's problems … And I remembered what I had written at the end of that page: *my life is a complete mess … and there is nothing I can do about it!* After everything that had gone down over the past two weeks, I realised that what I had written then was as true as ever right now. In that moment, it wasn't the ache in my side or my missing spleen that I was scared of. It was the despair that had reached all the way inside of me and wouldn't let go.

I tried to resist my thoughts but that didn't work. The next thing I knew I was thinking all about WJW and his flash promises. Maybe the so-called clarity I had arrived at on the plane after speaking to the BA flight attendant was all just one big illusion? Had I made a mistake, been too impulsive when I hightailed it out of his car on the way home from the airport? He had been a bit out of order, sure, but maybe I needed to go back to WJW with my tail between my legs and see if he was still willing to help us out? Now that Mum knew all about him, maybe there was nothing to lose? After all, surely grovelling at WJW's feet was a lot better than trying to get that Vic guy to cut us some slack? So it didn't take long before I began composing the mother of all WhatsApp apologies in my mind to send him:

Sorry I was so reactive the other day, Will. I was just real tired after the long trip. Maybe we can work out some kind of compromise, like I spend two or three nights a week with your family and the rest of the time with Mum...

My mind was whirling faster than that wild ride I had once ridden at the fun fair. I needed a distraction. Relief. Anything. But lying in a dark hospital room with three roommates whose average age must have been about 89, I wasn't getting any.

"Arggghhh," I groaned. For the first time in almost a week, it wasn't from the physical pain.

A slither of light cut across my line of vision. The door to the room opened and a shadowy figure cut across the illuminated path for the briefest of moments before becoming encased in darkness again. I heard the sound of soft, padded footsteps heading towards my bed. My heart skipped a beat. Who was there? What did they want? I fumbled for the switch of the small reading light located just above my head. After a second, I found it and flicked it on.

A middle-aged man was illuminated by the light. I knew he was a nurse because he was wearing the same, loose-fitting dark blue uniform I had seen the other nurses wearing over the last few days. The light seemed to add an extra shine to a completely shaven head that included two piercing brown eyes behind wire-rimmed glasses, the real old fashioned looking kind. As my heartbeat returned to normal, it occurred to me that this must be a new nurse, as I hadn't seen him before.

"I heard you groaning while I was busy with my night rounds, so I came to check on you," said the man in a deep, gravelly voice. "Is everything OK?"

"Yeah, fine," I whispered. Though I needn't have bothered. None of my companions had their hearing aids in, so there was no chance of waking them.

"You sure I can't get you anything? Some water maybe?"

"No, I'm cool."

"OK. My name's Jack, by the way. I'm the night nurse for the trauma recovery ward and I've been keeping an eye out for you most nights this past week while you've been sleeping."

"Evan," I said.

Introductions over, I was hoping the nurse would go away then and leave me alone in the dark room to stew in my even darker thoughts. But he just stood there at my bedside, looking down at me a little strangely, the arc of the reading lamp radiating off his shining skull.

"That was a pretty loud noise you uttered a moment ago. So I want to make sure there's nothing you need before I move on with my rounds," said Jack. He seemed to consider something for a second, before adding: "I've been doing this job for a long time, and I've come to know the difference between a groan coming from pain in the body and a groan coming from pain in the soul."

Pain in the soul? That sounded like some kind of new punk rock band.

"I just can't sleep, that's all," I said, deciding to keep my opinions about punk rock bands to myself. "These stitches are really itchy. And it doesn't help when I've got so much else on my mind."

Nurse Jack gave me a sympathetic look. "Yeah, well, that's a normal reaction following on from significant physical trauma. The body often heals quicker than the mind, though in the end, they both get there eventually. So if it helps, I'd be happy to talk a bit about all the stuff that's going on in your head; the stuff that's making it hard to sleep. Many of my patients have found that helpful over the years. Especially when the dark thoughts come to them at four in the morning. What do you say?"

I wasn't too keen on Jack's suggestion. But then again, he's the nurse and I'm the patient. He must have some idea what he's doing, right?

"Uh, OK. So, where should we start?" I asked.

"Well, how about you cast your mind back to before this whole incident occurred which landed you here in the first place. It may help if you close your eyes."

I did.

"Now ... once you've done that, I suggest you reflect on some of the – should we call them 'unusual' – interactions you had last week, before you arrived in the hospital."

"I'm not sure what you mean," I said.

"Ah, I think you do. But let me give you a hand. I'm referring to the chat you had with that tall man who's got the long dreadlocks and the over-excited Staffie. Or the talk you had with the homeless lady who wears the funny hat and walks around carrying all those bags. Or the exchange you had with that old man down by the police station; he of the huge, wild beard. And those are just some of the conversations I'm referring to."

I opened my eyes as wide as I could. *How did he know about all of that? Was this nurse some kind of mind-reader?*

"I'm not a mind-reader," continued Jack, acting just like a mind-reader. "But I know all of this because ... because we're *with* you, Evan."

"What do you mean, 'with me'?" I squeaked. My voiced sounded like it belonged to an eight-year-old girl.

"I mean we've been with you the whole time. Since you got suspended from school. Since your so-called mates landed themselves in jail. Since the man claiming to be your father appeared on the scene. And even ... even since those boys decided to use your head as a football and your stomach as a bicycle wheel."

I was stunned. "Who *are* you ... really?" I croaked.

But instead of answering my question, Jack did something strange. He picked up the clipboard hanging off the end of the hospital bed and studied it intently for a moment.

"Evan ... Banksky," he read aloud. Jack glanced up from the board. "I knew a Banksky once," he said quietly. "Ann Banksky."

My blood went cold. At the same time, a sweat broke out across my forehead.

"That's my mother's name," I said, my voice barely audible.

The nurse put the clipboard down very slowly on the end of the bed.

"I know."

My head was whirring. The Royal Free night nurse knowing my mother? This was *way* too big a coincidence. Actually, maybe it was just a mistake. Maybe there were two Ann Bankskys?

"Are you sure we're talking about the same person?" I asked Jack.

"Your mother would be in her mid-thirties now. She has – or at least had – blonde hair. Like you, she's a huge Spurs fan. And she has a son who would be about to turn sixteen right now. A son who looks a lot like her. Am I right about all that?"

I didn't answer. We both knew my silence meant nothing less than a firm 'yes'.

"I don't get it," I said finally. "How did you know my mother?"

At that moment, the pre-dawn quiet was punctuated by the painful sound of a series of wheezing coughs coming from one of my elderly roommates in a bed opposite. Jack quickly hurried over to the man's bedside and spent the next few minutes fussing over him until the coughing subsided. All the time, I heard the nurse talking to his patient in a soft, gentle, comforting voice. And in no time at all, the rhythmic sound of the man's light snoring had returned to normal.

Making his way back to my bed, Jack said nothing for a long time. I'd never met the man until ten minutes ago, but somehow I

248

sensed there was something he needed to say, and didn't quite know how to say it. That was fine by me – I wasn't going anywhere, at least not for the next few hours. Finally, Jack pulled up the stiff chair resting next to my bed, sat down slowly in it, and cleared his throat.

"Evan," he began, his brown eyes fixing on mine. "Do you know you had a sister?"

Instantly, my world went spinning on its axis. The nurse had just raised the one thing – maybe the only thing besides who my father was – that Mum and I never talked about. Ever. Except for that one time, when I was maybe eight or nine, tops …

It was in the middle of that long, boiling summer and our little flat on the eleventh floor was stifling in the suffocating heat. Mum was sat on the edge of her bed, her back turned away from me. So she didn't see me come tiptoeing silently into her room, long after she had put me to bed.

"Mummy," I called out. "It's too hot. I can't sleep …"

She slowly turned to face me. I was shocked by what I saw. Because it was the first time I had ever seen Mum crying, really crying. The tears were rolling silently down her cheeks. Her eyes were so red and swollen that I thought, for a moment, she was real sick. And then I saw what she held in her hands: a bottle of red liquid in one; a photo in the other.

"Mummy ... what's the matter? What's in that bottle? And why are you looking at a picture of a little baby?"

"Evan," she began. Even though I was young, I couldn't help but notice that she seemed to be slurring her words. "This is not just any baby. It's your sister. Isabel."

"Mummy, I don't have a sister."

"You don't now. But you did once," she explained, putting the bottle down on the little table next to her bed.

"So where is she now, Mummy?"

Mum didn't say anything. She just stared at that photo of the baby for what seemed like ages. Finally, she looked up and said,

"She died. She just went and died, Evan. But if she hadn't just died, your sister would have been six-years-old today."

A sister? Isabel? Who just went and died. I tried to make sense of what Mum was saying.

"But Mummy, why didn't you ever ..."

There was something on her face that stopped me right there, mid-sentence. Without saying another word, Mum opened the drawer of her bedside table, turned the photo upside down, and closed the drawer. Then she got off the bed, took me by the hand, and led me back to my stifling bedroom. Opening the small window above my bed as wide as she could, Mum turned to me and said, in a voice I had never her use before:

"Don't ever ask me about your sister again, Evan."

I never did.

"Yes," I answered Jack, the night nurse, very slowly. "I know I had a sister." Then my tone turned suspicious. "What's it to you?"

"Because ..."

Jack took off his glasses, pinched the bridge of his nose and wiped his eyes with the back of his hand.

"Because ... because your sister ... Isabel, was ... my daughter."

28

The silence between us lasted a long time. Other than the distant sounds of a hospital starting to come to life as a new day dawned, the rhythmic snoring of my fellow patients was the only noise to be heard. The quiet gave me time to think about the earth-shattering revelation Jack had just shared with me.

"That's ridiculous," I said, eventually. "How could you possibly be my sister's father?"

"If you let me, I'll explain."

"Go on," I said. I was surprised at how strained my voice sounded.

I was a junior nurse here in the Royal Free when you were born. I first met your Mum the very next day. She was trying to get to the nursery to feed you and she made a wrong turn down one of the hospital corridors – landed up in Imaging and X-Ray. I was sat behind the nurse's station doing some paperwork when she rapped on the desk to get my attention.

"Sorry, but I'm a bit lost. Which way is the newborn nursery please?"

I looked up into the eyes of the prettiest women I had ever laid eyes on.

"Uh ... well, it's a bit complicated to find from here. Why don't I show you?" I offered as I came round from the other side of the nurse's station. "Looks like congratulations are in order."

"Yes, thank you. I had a beautiful little boy yesterday."

And that was all it took. My heart was stolen from that moment, so I knew that I couldn't let her leave that hospital without getting her phone number. Which I made sure I did.

Jack paused. It seemed as if he weighing up how much more to share with me. I decided to make it easier for him.

"You've come this far, so why don't you just tell me the whole story?"

The nurse nodded slowly.

Your Mum was full-on busy with you so we didn't see each other much straight away. But once you were sleeping through the night and things had settled down for her, we started dating properly. It was brilliant. We never ran out of things to talk about. We loved doing the same things. And you were such an easy baby. We'd take you on long walks in your buggy and you loved it. We even took you to the zoo once. I remember how you just sat staring with your big blue eyes at those crazy monkeys swinging all round their cage. Then, as things had got real serious between us, I invited you both to move into my little studio in

Kilburn with me. It wasn't much, but we were all so happy. I was completely in love with your Mum. And she felt the same way about me. She was so young, and though she'd been burned by your father already, we had something different, something special. So we decided to have a baby together. And sure enough, less than a year later, we had a beautiful baby girl. Isabel. I loved that little girl. And I loved you, even though you weren't mine. It didn't matter to me. It was all going so well, until … until the night we all went out together to see the Christmas lights in town. Your Mum wanted to take the tube, but I wanted to drive, insisting that you would see the lights better from your car-seat. We got into a real stupid fight about that, and I refused to back down. I just took little Isabel and strapped her into the baby-seat behind me and told your Mum to put you in yours. I didn't give her a choice.

And then … and then, we were arguing so much that I missed a light coming down Finchley Road. I saw that lorry a split second too late; it ploughed right into the side of our little Skoda. I woke up in the hospital four days later. Bad concussion and a broken pelvis. Miraculously, besides some scratches and bruises, they told me you and your Mum were completely fine.

And then they told me what had happened to little Isabel. She was thrown straight through the back windscreen. Her car-seat hadn't been strapped in properly and she died the minute her tiny head hit the pavement.

Jack's eyes glistened with tears but he did nothing to wipe them away. Meanwhile, my head felt as if it was going to explode. The blows kept coming, leaving me silent and stunned. I guessed Jack sensed that, because he just kept on talking.

I was devastated. That little girl was everything to me. But at least I still had your Mum and you. Or so I thought. I was wrong. She didn't come to see me in the hospital. She didn't answer my calls or texts. After three operations, I was finally able to walk out of there on my own. But when I got home, she wasn't there. Just a note saying she had taken you – and everything that was hers – and left. Forever.

Of course I tried so hard to find her. But no one knew where she had gone. And this was the days before social media was so common. It became clear that she didn't want me to find her ... so I never did. I realised that your Mum couldn't forgive me; she held me accountable for Isabel's death. I understood that, because so did I – for a long time. I hated myself for what happened. I had lost everything: my baby daughter, my girlfriend, you. My heart was broken. And my body. I was racked with physical pain, so it started with prescription drugs that I stole from the hospital supply room when no-one was looking. From there it was a slippery slope which I fell down real fast. Before I knew it, I was a prescription pills addict. It was a long, lonely, painful road after that. And I never saw or spoke to your mother again. But that doesn't mean I had given up hope of one day finding her. Or you.

Jack leaned back into the chair, into the shadow of the dark room. But if he was done, I definitely wasn't.

"So let me get this right," I began, in a tone I hadn't used much recently. "You ran a red. You didn't strap my baby sister in properly. She died. And then Mum fell apart. And ever since then, she's been a wreck. Drink, gambling … it's all your fault!"

Red mist time. I glared at Jack. The nurse met my gaze and returned it, but said nothing. Suddenly, I was so fed up. Enough!

"Leave me alone!" I shouted with the last ounce of strength I could muster. "Just get out and leave."

My nurse – the father of my dead sister – looked at me for a long time. Then he turned silently away from my bedside and exited the room.

I woke with a start. The hospital room was filled with light. Two nurses were busy attending to one of my fellow patients on the other side of the room. I'd been sleeping for hours. As fragments of the pre-dawn conversation with Jack swam to the surface of my mind, I began to wonder if the whole thing had been one ridiculously realistic dream. Maybe the nurse in the dark blue uniform with the shaven head and old-fashioned glasses was merely a figment of my imagination? But then, looking across the room at the elderly patient lying peacefully in the bed opposite me,

I remembered Jack's expert care when the man's chest had filled with rasping coughs. There was no doubt that Nurse Jack really existed. And equally no doubt that all we had discussed in the very early hours of the morning had gone down just as I remembered it had.

My thoughts were interrupted when Dr. Casey came striding into the room accompanied by Jan, my daytime nurse.

"Good morning, Evan," Doc Casey pronounced. "Or should I say, 'good afternoon'. We've been waiting a long time for you to wake up."

The Doc picked up the clipboard at the end of my bed and spent some time turning pages and reading notes, doing the kind of thing that I guess doctors are meant to do.

"I think you're about ready to go home. According to Nurse Jack's night notes, all seems in order from a recovery perspective. So I'll book you in to see the rehab people down on the 5th floor later this afternoon. That will take up a bit of time, but assuming they are satisfied, you should be good to go first thing tomorrow morning."

"Sick. Thanks Doc."

"I'm not sure 'sick' is the right word to use in a hospital, but I get what you mean. Now, I'll leave you in the very capable hands of Nurse Jan. She's got some final tests to run and will also go through instructions for post-recovery with you."

Doctor Casey moved swiftly out of the room, leaving me and my daytime nurse to run through everything – and that means a lot of things – I needed to know about taking care of myself in the days and weeks after a major, life-threatening injury. When she was finally finished, I thought I probably knew enough to skip the first four years of medical school and jump straight into a surgical rotation.

A message from Tals followed came pinging in soon after Nurse Jan had done with me:

Ev, I almost forgot. Remember u asked me 'bout some new girl who moved in on our floor with her grandfather. Well, dunno how I missed it. Must have been cause my heads been down busy with the crowdfunding and exams and stuff. But I did see some new people coming outta 1106 the other day – not Mrs Shufords place but the one next to it. It was an old man with a young girl. She was wearing a long hijab so couldn't miss her. My bad on getting that wrong first time round. XXXX

So that explained it. We *did* have new neighbours: an old man and his granddaughter who went by the name of Aliyah.

After that revelation, the rest of the afternoon dragged by. Mum had missed me when I was sleeping earlier, while Tals had an A-level Biology mock which was gonna keep her busy till visiting hours were long over. And I couldn't get the mobile version of Fortnite to work properly on my phone. So the highlight of my day ended up being two hours spent practising various physical exercises down in the rehab department. Fun.

The lack of visitors and meaningful action left me a lot of time – too much – to think about the previous night's wild conversation with Jack. And the more I thought about it, the angrier I became. As I continued to connect the dots, the picture became

258

increasingly clear. This man had screwed up, big-time. Mum had trusted him – she'd had a baby with him for crying out loud – and he had let her down. And while he ended up going downhill with his whole prescription pills addiction thing, poor Mum had obviously been trying to keep it together, bringing me up and all. But taking into account what had gone down for the most of the past ten or so years of her life – her ongoing battles with depression, drink and gambling – it had obviously not gone too well. She had been trying to keep her head above water, but half the time Mum must have felt as if she was drowning. And it was all that flippin nurse's fault! I could never – would never – forgive him for completely stuffing up our lives.

I tried to distract myself by watching some TV, but it was all cooking programmes and that slimy Jeremy Kyle guy making fun of all those people having a tough time of it. Dr. Dre and Kanye West didn't do me no good either. Nor did the lame games I had on my phone. Supper looked so disgusting that I ended up just giving the whole thing a miss. Sleep ended up being the least boring thing to do.

29

"Go ahead, Evan. Say anything you need to say."

It took a minute to get my bearings in the dark room. Jack was back sitting in the stiff chair next to my bed, staring straight at me through those old school glasses. I wasn't sure how long I'd been asleep, but looking over at my slumbering roommates, and taking into account the otherwise quiet hospital, it was obvious we were somewhere in the middle of Jack's night-shift. As I was leaving this place first thing in the morning, it was not the time to hold back.

"You screwed up," I declared.

"Yes. I did. And I've been sorry every day of my life since."

"I totally understand why Mum left you."

"I do too."

"I could never forgive you."

"I understand that."

"So … why did tell me all this?"

"Because I wanted you to understand."

"Understand what?"

"That your mother had to face something so painful, beyond what almost anyone can fathom. Something so tough that she didn't know how to deal with the pain inside her heart. Or even how to speak about it. Which explains a lot of what happened after. And a lot of what is still happening for her now. I wanted you to know all that."

"Why … why do you care?"

Jack said nothing for a long moment. Then, he simply shook his head sadly and said,

"I never stopped caring, Evan."

I didn't know what to say to that. And my anger was starting to run out of steam. Which meant a change of direction was probably the best strategy.

"Tell me something. All those people – the dude in dreads, the stewardess, Aliyah … who are that lot? Really."

"They are just ordinary people," Jack answered. "People who have got regular lives and regular jobs. Except for Aliyah, who's still in school, and Elsie of course, the homeless lady. She doesn't have a job. But that's her choice. Anyhow, that's beside the point. The point is that they are all involved in the same project. I've just got more operational responsibility, that's all."

"So what is this project, then? Some kind of secret agency or something?" I smirked.

"Yeah, something like that," Jack answered, dead serious. "Most people don't know about us. We keep a low profile. I know it's hard to believe in this day and age, but we've got no website and no social media presence. Our aim is to work in the shadows; to find people who need our help and to make it available to them until they are able to stand on their own feet and don't need us anymore."

"Come on, man. No website. No Twitter or Instagram page. That's too wild for me to believe," I said with a snort.

"Yeah, we're used to that response," replied Jack without missing a beat. "So let me explain a bit more. The woman who started the project is a most remarkable lady. We refer to her as the Chair – short for Chairman. She's very old now and has had a real tough life. Her only child was stabbed to death in a gang fight that took place outside a football stadium when he was right about your age. Her husband had died a few years before that. She had no-one left. So she knows what it's like to suffer, to experience massive loss, to feel completely alone, to have completely given up."

Jack paused and looked out the single darkened window of the quiet hospital room.

"The Chair understands what it's like to live in the shadows without hope. Yet, despite all that suffering, she truly has a huge heart. She cares about people, really cares. She wants to alleviate as much psychological suffering as she can, as quietly as she can. Because she knows that people who are suffering in that way spend much of their time in those same shadows. So that is where she operates; where she has asked us all to operate."

I considered that explanation. It wasn't what I had expected to hear, but it kinda stacked up. I wanted to stay angry with the nurse, but I was finding it harder and harder. Anyhow, I had to tread carefully here. I needed answers and the only person who could provide them was sitting right in front of me.

"So, how did she go about setting up this weird kind of secret agency thing?" I asked, despite myself.

"That's a bit of a long story, but I'll do my best to keep it short," Jack began. "A tribunal concluded that the football club was guilty of gross negligence regarding its safety procedures. The club was ordered to make a massive financial pay-out – tens of millions – to the family of the victim. But The Chair didn't want any of the money for herself. What she wanted was to bring an end to the kind of conflict and misunderstanding that had brought about the death of her son in the first place. So she used all the funds awarded to her to set up Project Illusion. She developed and placed operatives all across the country – and beyond. Like any good leader, she had a plan and she executed it."

It was all a bit much to take in. So I tried to break it down, to compartmentalise, just like Tals had done with me the other day.

"Why Project Illusion?" I asked. "I don't even know what that means properly."

"Illusion is a word which reminds us of something very important," explained Jack.

"Reminds us of what?"

"That the assumption that the outside world has power over us is one hundred percent an illusion. It's an innocent mistake we all make, this assumption, but it's an illusion nonetheless."

I thought about that for a moment. It made sense. But there were still a couple of things bothering me that didn't.

"So what has this project got to do with me? Why have you been 'with me', as you called it last night? Spying on me. For that matter, how did you even know about me?"

Just asking the questions was getting me all worked up again.

"All good questions," responded Jack calmly. "The short answer is that our North London branch had been looking into the increased gang activity in your area recently. Your little 'crew' had already attracted a fair amount of attention, even before the stabbing in the park. So the surveillance team were running down profiles of you all, when one name came across my desk that caught my attention. *Banksky*. Not exactly a common name. So I investigated – discreetly – and discovered it was indeed that same boy who I'd taken to the zoo in his pushchair thirteen years before. Whose mother was the woman I had loved so deeply. Well, as you can guess, I couldn't let that go. Not after everything that had gone down all those years ago. So ... I used my authority to do something beyond our normal remit: I ordered the team to keep an extra special eye out for you."

Jack paused then and looked at me hard.

"Which means, Evan, that we haven't been spying on you. Actually, though you didn't know it, we have being trying to help you."

I didn't like the sound of where this was heading.

"Let me get this clear. You people were meant to be like some kind of guardian angels, looking out for me this whole time?"

Before Jack could answer, I ploughed ahead, an acid taste rising in my mouth.

"So why *didn't* you help? You know how tough it's been: Mum hitting the bottle, the money we owe this bookie, my newly minted father making too good to refuse offers. Where has your special help been all this time, *Mister Caring*?"

I gazed straight at Jack, a whole lot of hostility in my eyes. He didn't flinch.

"This may be difficult for you to understand, Evan, but we have one rule we stick to no matter what: we respect people's choices. Really, we do. If they want our help, we will do our best to give it. We will educate and explain and support as best we can and as much as people wish to hear. That is the role of our operatives. But it's not for us to interfere in the free will of others. People are doing the best they can with the thinking they have. Our job is to help them to understand that thinking and the feelings that come with it. This is the mission of Project Illusion. The rest is out of our hands."

I opened my mouth to object, to counter with a verbal jab, to say something else, anything else. But then it hit me. Jack was right. We are all doing the best we can with the thinking we have at any moment. I could certainly relate to that.

The realisation left me feeling like a tyre that had just got a massive puncture. I could almost hear the air hissing out of me.

"OK, I think I get it now," I said quietly.

I was running out of energy, but I still had questions that needed answers.

"So … what happened to *you*, Jack? You were in such a bad place, with Mum leaving you, and your grief, and the drugs and everything. So how did you land up OK?"

"Now that really *is* a long story, mate. And I've got to get on with my rounds or I'm gonna get fired here. But I'll just tell you this: I was one of those people who got helped by The Chair in the early days. And what she taught me didn't just help me. It saved my life."

Jack closed his eyes then. I had the feeling that whatever he was about to say next wasn't going to be easy for him.

"I want you to know, Evan, that nothing would make me happier than reconnecting with your mother. Just being able to speak with her, to share what I have learned which has helped me so much in my own life. But however hard it is, I have to respect that isn't what she wants. At least not then, and, I guess, not now. But who knows ... maybe one day?"

A long silence filled the quiet hospital room. Only the humming of the medical machines supporting my roommates could be heard. Finally, Jack spoke again.

"But that didn't mean – it doesn't mean – that I couldn't reconnect with you. Or at least give you the opportunity, now that you are almost sixteen-years-old, to say 'no' to our help."

I didn't quite know what to make of that. Jack *had* been doing his best to look out for me, while sticking to the principles of Project Illusion at the same time. But I still couldn't get out of my head the idea that he had been responsible, in a major way, for so much of my messed up life in the first place.

All these confusing thoughts and feelings – the whole conversation actually – had left me completely exhausted. But I still had one final question that needed to be asked.

"I get that you learned some important stuff and started to do better, Jack. But how did you land up doing what you're doing now, like all the others?"

"You're questions keep on coming," said Jack. "That's why Jabulani called you 'the one who is searching'. Wise man, that Jabulani. Well, here's the real short version cause I really do have to go check on my patients, Evan. Bottom line is that once I was back on my own two feet, I wanted to give something back to those who had helped me. And I guess The Chair figured I had something to offer, because she put me in charge of the whole of the South East. And it's also why you and I are speaking right now."

"What does that mean?"

"It means that The Chair authorised this conversation"

"The Chair?" I asked in surprise. "She knows about me?"

"She absolutely does, Evan. But it's not for me to explain how or why. I'll leave that to her when – if – the time is ever right."

"What do you mean, 'If the time is ever right'? When will that be? Who is she? How will I even know where to find her?"

For the first time since I'd met him, Jack smiled. "Don't worry," he said with a strange look in his eyes. "You'll know when you need to know."

He glanced at the clock next to my bed.

"Now … you've got to get some sleep and I've got to look after my other patients," said Jack as he eased himself out of the chair and turned towards the door. "So … good night, Evan Banksky."

"Wait," I called out as he reached the threshold of the room, my voice trembling. "I still don't know if I can forgive you."

"I know, Evan. I wish you would. I really do. But that's your choice. And if you can't, I understand. And it's OK. Because I don't need your forgiveness to feel whole inside. I would like it. But that doesn't mean I need it."

And with that, Jack pushed the door open and walked quickly through it, leaving my anger, my confusion – and my forgiveness – hanging in the thick, stale air of a dark hospital room.

30

The man in the loose-fitting dark blue uniform stepped out of the ward and headed quickly down the corridor. A door on his right appeared, with the words HOSPITAL STAFF ONLY *written across its middle in big black letters. He pushed the door open and ducked into the small, empty room.*

Taking out his phone, he hesitated for a brief moment. Though he knew she went to bed very late, he decided a text message was preferable to a phone call at this time of night.

His message was short, yet still he typed it slowly and deliberately.

We have spoken – at length. As anticipated, Evan appears uncertain whether he can forgive me. I told him that is completely understandable. But my assessment is that he is ready see beyond. He is ready to finally escape the illusion. And he is ready to meet you. The rest I leave in your hands. Jack.

He pressed SEND. Then he leaned wearily against the inside of the door, blew out a deep breath and rubbed the fatigue – and the pain – from his eyes. It had been hard at times, as it so often is. Extra hard because of whom he loved – loves.

That's the way it is with illusions.

But at least his mission here was complete. For now.

31

Even though I was super-keen to finally blow this place, I overslept and woke up real late again. Casting my eyes along the tray attached to the hospital bed, I noticed a very poor excuse for a meal: a soggy bowl of greenish porridge that could have been called "fresh vomit flavour" and a couple of pieces of squidgy looking fruit. Pears, maybe? I couldn't say I was sorry I'd slept right through breakfast. My only regret, having spent a full week subsisting on hospital food – supplemented by the occasional smuggled blueberry muffin – was that I hadn't managed to sleep through lunch as well.

The trauma of my breakfast tray behind me, my mind turned to the second consecutive late-night conversation with Jack. But those angry thoughts were quickly interrupted when my daytime nurse came hurrying into the room wearing an alarmed expression on her face.

"Quick, Evan, you've got to get up and get dressed!" Jan gasped breathlessly.

"Why? What's up? What's the matter?"

"No time for questions. Someone heard that you were on this floor and has insisted on coming to see you, not taking 'no' for an answer. And he is coming our way, now!"

The nurse was frantically trying to pull a shirt out of the small chest of drawers next to my bed.

"So quick, up with you," she shrieked, the alarm in her voice palpable. "We need to get you out of that gown, get some clothes on and ..."

Jan didn't manage to finish her sentence. Because just then, the door swung open and a tank-like, intense-looking dude in a dark suit came striding into the room. He looked around slowly and deliberately. A wave of terror surged through me. Had Vic the bookie decided to send one of his thugs to rough me up a bit and send a warning to Mum? Pay up or your son will be the one who pays instead. My panic intensified when the Tank turned towards the open doorway and beckoned whoever was standing there into the room. Was it Vic himself?

Out of the corner of my eye, I saw Jan start to tremble. Across the room, two of my fellow patients went wide-eyed in shock. At the same time, there was a dramatic gasp from the man in the bed to my right, nearest the doorway. I panicked, sure I was a dead man. But before I had a chance to pull the red emergency chord hanging above my bed and sound the alarm, the person strode purposefully into the room. And to my shock, it *was* a familiar face – kind of. But it wasn't Vic.

"M... Mm ... Mister," stammered Jan, before finally finding her proud West Indian voice. "Mr. Beckham. Welcome to the trauma recovery ward of the Royal Free Hospital. May I introduce you to Evan Banksky, survivor of a recent violent knife assault, serious crime-solver and ... our local hero."

The most famous footballing celebrity in the world stepped forward as I almost toppled out of bed.

271

"Please don't get up," said David Beckham, holding his right hand out to shake mine. "May I just say, Evan, what an honour it is to meet you."

According to Nurse Jan's later account, the shocked silence lasted less than ten seconds. From my perspective, it was about the same amount of time since Spurs had last won the league title. In other words, a very, very long time. Fortunately, David seemed to have been in this kind of situation before and handled it as cool as you imagine a guy with *those* kinds of tattoos would.

"I'm so sorry for barging in on you like this," he began by way of explanation. "But I was busy with some official visiting duties on behalf of the charity I am an ambassador for, when I heard from one of the staff that there was a young man lying in a hospital bed on the ninth floor who is a real hero."

"Uh, no worries. It's not like I got too much else to do, ya know?"

David laughed. I laughed. Nurse Jan laughed. The Tank laughed. The roommates laughed. In other words: a lot of people laughed.

"So ... how are you getting on since the attack?" he asked casually, as if we had just bumped into each other on the tube and were having a quick catch-up on our way home from a big game.

"Um ... well ... basically ... um ... yeah, not too bad, ya know ..."

In the moment of truth, I had proved something that few people on this planet can ever have proven so definitively: that my brain and tongue had no meaningful relationship to each other.

"That's awesome to hear," said David, clearly not bothered that I was speaking as if English was not my first language, possibly not even my second. "Listen, they have a busy schedule planned for the rest of my visit to the hospital, but I was wondering if we could have, you know, like a quiet word."

"Uh, yeah, that would be sick."

"Brilliant," he said, before glancing at his bodyguard, "Michael, would you mind if I have a moment alone with Evan?" Then, turning to Jan, he asked, "Would that be OK with you, nurse?"

The two of them nodded simultaneously and exited the room faster than it takes for Donald Trump to fire a member of his cabinet. Which is real fast. That just left the two of us (well, five I guess, if you count my three elderly roommates, aka my "new boys"). Then David Beckham leaned in very close to the bed and for the briefest of moments, I wondered if he intended to adjust the pillows around my head and take my temperature. He did neither. But he did whisper the following:

"Sometimes you see it. And sometimes you don't."

"Uh... excuse me, Mr. Beckham. I didn't quite catch that."

"Please, Evan. Call me Becks. Anyhow, here's what I think happens to so many of us," he continued with the kind of focus I had seen countless times on the TV when lining up one of those famous free kicks. "Sometimes, we innocently and mistakenly believe that our feelings come from something other than thought."

David Beckham stopped there and focused that gaze on me, the same one that had done many a keeper over the year.

"And sometimes we don't."

"Umm, yeah ... I get that ... Becks."

Did I really just say that?

"Cool," said Becks, in a way that really *did* sound cool. "And don't worry, because everyone gets tricked by this. All of us. Even Posh and I," he added.

"Uh, OK. That's good to know."

"Yeah, it is," he continued. "And because we all forget how it works at times, it just doesn't make sense to judge ourselves or others. Because it's not as if we forget on purpose. It's just that it's really hard to see sometimes. And when that happens, it sure can seem as if the situation we are thinking about has the power to cause our feelings. But just remember Evan, it does not."

I couldn't believe my ears. David Beckham, one of the most famous people in the world, talking to me about getting tricked by feelings and thought. Just like Tals and Monroe. And just like all the others. *What? How? Why?*

"How ... how ... how do you know all that?" I stammered.

"Sorry, Evan. But can't give away all my secrets at once. Otherwise, next thing you know, everyone will think they can bend it like Beckham. Which could ruin my rep. Now listen mate, gotta run. It's been a pleasure."

And then David Beckham, OBE – that's right, you heard me – Becks, Golden Balls, DB 7, former captain of the England Men's football team, turned around and, with the Tank in tow, walked casually out of my hospital room. What a ledge!

274

32

The inhabitants of the room took a while to regain their composure. A heated argument had broken out amongst the over 80s regarding the most influential England player of all time: Matthews, Charlton or Beckham? Jan was cursing softly to herself because she hadn't asked our visitor to sign the back of her nurse's uniform or a piece of bog roll or something – anything really. I, meanwhile, was busy wondering what kind of airhead fails to take a video – or at least a picture on his phone – when being visited by one of the most famous people in the world. I sensed that the inability to adequately answer this question would plague me for the rest of my life.

It was Nurse Jan who managed to pull herself together first.

"Right then, Evan. Seeing that all the excitement is over, I'll just pull this curtain to give you some privacy so that you can get yourself dressed and ready to go," she said, before adding with a cheeky smile, "Because now that you're mixing it up with the rich and famous, we really need to get you out of that hospital gown once and for all."

Thanks Jan.

With the curtain in place, I managed to untangle the shirt which my nurse had been flailing at moments earlier. Carefully pulling it over my still spleenless stomach, I flicked on my mobile. A bunch of messages came pinging in straight away. Glancing at the clock on the screen, I saw it was almost lunch time, which meant that they'd be coming round with the hospital meal any minute. Which also meant I needed to get out of here – fast! But then the first message, a voice WhatsApp from Tals, caught my attention.

Hey Ev. Just heard from your Mum that they're letting you out real soon. Brill! Am out walking Brock in the park now, but will make sure he's all dressed, ready and waiting when u arrive back. And here's the other awesome news: we've just passed the 10k mark. You hear that? We're halfway to hitting the crowdfunding target! Contributions been coming from all over the place. The Sweet Orchard WhatsApp group came up with almost a grand in total. Keith at the caf gave 100 quid; a bunch of girls in my class pulled together for another 100. Your cuzin Jamie said he'd chip in the wages your mum had walked out on a couple of weeks back. And get this: old lady McLeod just told me as she was stepping out the lift, that she was good for 200! Can u believe that? I know we're running outta time, but we can do this Ev.

Wow! When she'd first suggested the whole crowdfunding thing, I thought Tals was off her rocker. But somehow, that amazing girl had started to make it happen. We still had a long way to go to raise the full twenty grand, and there was only a few days left until Vic's deadline for repayment ran out, but who knew ...?

Another message from Tals about something completely different followed soon after:

Hey, haven't forgotten its your birthday on Wednesday. 16 has gotta be worth a little celebration, no? But I have a feeling you're not into anything too

*wild right now. So how about a quiet lunch at the caf?
Just you, me and Brock. Will ask Monroe to get those
chilli chips ready. My little birthday treat for my little
neighbour man. Whaddaya say?*

Birthday lunch with The Beast and my best friend? A thumbs-up emoji was the only reply necessary. And things just got even better when I listened to the voice WhatsApp from one Detective Sergeant Robin Manning.

*Evan, DS Manning here. I heard you're heading
home later today. That's great news. Anyhow, I just
wanted to give you a heads up about something I
didn't mention earlier because I didn't want to raise
your hopes unnecessarily. An award was put up
regarding the Hendon Park case. Normally, these
rewards are not available to minors, but you
bringing the knife to us was the crucial piece of
evidence that enabled us to solve the crime. So I've
just spoken to my commanding officer, and taking
all the extenuating circumstances into account,
she's agreed to make an exception and allocate the
reward to your mother to accept on your behalf. So
you can tell your mum to expect ten thousand
pounds to arrive in her bank account in the next few
days. Make sure you both go out for a big meal to
celebrate. Because you deserve it, Evan. As I said
before, you did good, real good. Cheers, mate.*

I played the message over three more times, making sure I heard it all just right. *So let me get this straight*, I said to myself. *I have just been awarded ten thousand pounds for providing the evidence that helped solve the case. Which means, along with the ten grand already raised through Tals' campaign, we were there – we had smashed the 20k target and could pay Mum's debt to the bookie! Sick! Sick! Sick!*

If hadn't been standing in my boxers at that moment, I would have whipped that hospital curtain open and given Nurse Jan a huge high-five, and possibly lifted her above my head as well, stitches and everything.

"Hey, what's taking you so long?" came Nurse Jan's voice from the other side of the great curtain divide. "You need some help in there, Evan?"

I looked down at myself in my boxers. Not a pretty sight.

"No thanks, I'm cool. Just gimme a sec."

Focus Banksky. It's time to get moving.

While I pulled my jeans on, I quickly read the next message. This one was from Mum.

Hi Hon. The hospital just called to say they are discharging you around lunchtime, so I've asked Jamie for the rest of the afternoon off. And old DC offered to lend me one of his used cars to come and pick you up. So will message you when I'm 5 minutes away and then you can come down and meet me outside the main entrance. Can't wait to have you home. Luv MUM XXXX

I typed a quick response:

Cant wait 2 b home.

I flung open the curtain, wincing from the tug on my stitches as I did. Maybe I needed to slow it down a bit. But then I heard the familiar rumbling of the lunch trolley, coming ever swiftly closer. Amongst my roommates, the rumour was rife that it was Mac 'n' Cheese day – again. Based on last Thursday's experience, that could mean spending the majority of the afternoon in a very small room with a single toilet bowl and no-one else for company. It was simply not a risk I was prepared to take at this stage of my recovery.

"Hey, Nurse Jan, I gotta get going," I said, trying to keep the panic out of my voice. "Mum is meeting me downstairs in five," I said, glancing nervously in the direction of the doorway.

"You sure, Evan?" she replied with an unmistakably evil grin. "It's Mac 'n' Cheese day."

"I'm sure," I replied instantly. "I'm still young and have a long and productive life ahead of me, you know."

I quickly stuffed the few clothes and personal items I had stored next to the bed into my old backpack. Last to go was a book I had first started reading on a bus ride to Colindale Police Station, just two weeks previously. It seemed like a lifetime ago. I glanced at the title again: *What If We Have Everything We Need Inside Us?* Despite my rush to get ahead of the lunch trolley, I paused for a moment. I hadn't quite finished reading the book – to be completely honest, I'd only read a few bits here and there (don't tell Tals!) – but suddenly I knew with crystal clarity the answer to the question on the book's cover:

We are OK, no matter what. Because if we have everything we need inside us, then we have everything. So we are OK, sorted, good to go. Simple as that.

"Right you are," said Jan, interrupting my private Nobel Prize for Literature winning moment. "Let's get you out of this place, once and for all."

And with that, I pulled my bag gingerly over my shoulder and followed Nurse Jan out of the room which had been my home for the last week, waving goodbye to my new boys as I did, and wishing them all the luck in the world in surviving the lunch-time meal.

Mum's five minute warning came pinging in just as we entered the hospital corridor. I couldn't wait to tell her the awesome news about the reward and Tals' crowdfunding campaign. Could this finally be the break she had been waiting for?

Jan had walked me to the elevator and – obviously concerned about the risk of over-exertion – pushed the DOWN button on my behalf. A moment later, the loud beeping of the lift announced its arrival, masking the sounds of torture coming from trauma room 8C down the hall where a grown man in hospital pyjamas had just been forced into taking his first bite of Royal Free Mac 'n' Cheese.

"You take care of yourself, Evan," said Jan, "It's been a real honour being your nurse."

Suddenly, she swept me into her arms and gave me a hug so tight I feared, momentarily, that her intention was to send me straight to the X-ray department with a suspected dislocated rib. But just as I was starting to lose consciousness, Jan let go. And then, her eyes a weird kind of puffy, she turned away quickly and headed back to my former hospital room to check in on the rest of her boys.

280

I stepped into the lift and glanced at the final unread message on my phone. It was a long one from WJW. And as I began reading it, my heart sank just as fast as the rapidly descending lift.

Evan, I've been waiting to hear from you for over a week. I figured you would have the good grace to come to your senses and apologise for your words and actions on the way home from the airport. But then, and thanks to Marla's input, I realised that wouldn't be fair. You're still young and relatively immature and it would be unreasonable to have those expectations of you. So I have decided to let it go. But I cannot let go of my responsibility to you. If anything, seeing how those orphan kids in South Africa were living, I decided I can't let the same happen to you.

I glanced up from the screen at the panel indicating the lift's progress. Still five floors to go. I felt a sweat break out across my forehead, while my stomach heaved. But it was not from the downward descent of the steel cage I was trapped in at this moment.

I have come to see, Evan, that sometimes making amends and doing the right thing involves taking tough decisions. My lawyer tells me that legally, as you are still a minor, you really have no rights here. He also tells me that with your mother's ongoing problems and all, not to mention the financial inability to support herself, never mind you, she's really got no chance in a custody hearing. And it's not like I've been avoiding making payments or not taking responsibility for you. Actually, she is the one who will have to explain in front of a judge why she has been keeping you from me all these years. To tell the truth, my lawyer advised me right back when I first found out about you to apply for custody straight away. But I told him to wait – wait until you and I had finally met, had a chance to get to know each other and see if there was another way. Which, as you may have realised, was my very genuine offer. But as you've decided to reject that alternative way, I am left with no choice here. So, I wanted to let you know that as of this morning, after lengthy consideration, I have filed for unrestricted custody. I am sorry if this is not what you would have wished for or the way for it to unfold, but I am certain I am doing the right thing. I know this will be hard on you – and your mother – but I honestly believe you will thank me one day.

Your Father, Will.

The lift hit the ground floor with a slight shudder. Which was nothing compared to the pounding in my head and my heart. I limped through the automatic doors and made my way out the main hospital exit, straight into the No Parking pick-up/drop-off area. I spotted Mum sat in a borrowed car right by the doors, staring straight ahead with a faraway look on her face. Staggering over, I opened the passenger door and gingerly lowered myself into the car. Mum said nothing. She simply placed her phone in my hand. And then, she began to sob, leaving me to look down at an already opened email.

Dear Ms. Banksky

Acting on behalf of my client, Mr. William J Woodford, I hereby notify you of his immediate intention to apply for full and unrestricted custody of his son, the minor, Evan Banksky. Mr. Woodford wishes to settle this matter without having to resort to a court order. However, in the event that his paternal custodial rights are contested, he will be engaging the legal services of our firm to ensure that ....

I read a few more lines but they were just filled with legal jargon and posh words that I didn't really understand. But the email's first couple of sentences were simple to comprehend, even to a minor like me. WJW had indeed chosen the nuclear option. With all his money and his lawyers and his desire to make amends and take responsibility, he was coming for us.

For me.

33

The tears streaming down Mum's pale face told a story of desperation and fear that I knew well. Because it was those same feelings that had wrapped their long tentacles around me too in this moment – and wouldn't let go. Seeing the look of absolute devastation on Mum's face, my heart shattered into a thousand tiny fragments. In that moment, I realised, more than ever, how losing me simply wasn't an option for her – no matter what.

For a long while, we both sat completely still in that borrowed car, each of us consumed by the wild and terrifying thoughts running through our minds. Suddenly, there was a sharp rap on the passenger window. I almost jumped out of my seat. The face of one of those people in a parking attendant's uniform filled the glass.

"You can't park here. It's a drop-off zone, five minutes max. Move on please."

I managed to give the dude a thumbs up. But it's a good thing the window was closed, because any attempt at speaking would have been impossible. The stinging feeling at the back of my eyes was stronger than ever. I closed them, knowing that was the only way to prevent what would surely come next.

And then, in that moment, in the blackness, when it was as dark as it had ever been, dark enough to see the stars ... the understanding came.

I am living in the feeling of my thinking. And so is Mum. From the inside-out. It's how we work. Always has been. Always will be.

That is the superpower of our minds – the perfect way our systems have been designed. Which means, however bad things look, that we are going to be OK. We are good to go.

I opened my eyes. Mum had stopped crying, but her red eyes were frozen on an invisible spot on the windscreen. I reached over and took her cold, limp hand in mine. She didn't move.

"Mum," I said. "We're going to figure this out. Just like we've figured it all out until now. No matter what happens, no matter where or who I end up living with, we will be OK."

I squeezed that hand – the one that had held mine so tightly only a few days before in a dark hospital room – a bit tighter. Finally, she turned her gaze away from the windscreen and looked at me through her sad, red eyes.

"You know why, Mum?" I asked.

She didn't answer. She didn't need to. I had this one covered.

"Because we have everything we need inside us."

We sat silently in the car for a long while, gripping each other's hands, not daring to let go. Then I saw the parking attendant dude heading back our way, a scary-looking scowl on his face and a yellow parking ticket poking out of his front pocket.

"Come on, Mum," I said. "Let's go home."

Epilogue

The end of the story ... for now

The old woman tucked a stray strand of long grey hair into her ponytail. Huddled over the steaming plate of food, she pushed its contents back and forth with a fork. Normally she tucked into the shakshuka with gusto, especially when made to perfection by the friendly Filipino chef in this small, quiet café on the edge of the park.

But today wasn't a normal day.

The pain, always so close to the surface, had broken through today. But she was good with that. Deeply respectful, in fact. The pain was not something to be afraid of. Nor something to avoid. So she let it wash over her. Because that was what needed to occur. Especially today.

With her free hand, the old woman picked up her phone and looked at the photo which filled the screen. The picture of her son.

She knew every line, every contour, every detail of the boy's face in that photo; a face so young. Sixteen-years-old to be precise. She wondered, as she often did, how he would look all these years later, a fully grown man, most likely with children of his own by now. But try as she may, she had never been able to conjure up an accurate image of the boy as a man.

And today was no different. His face remained frozen in time. Frozen in the moment, sixteen years ago today, when that

286

knife had plunged into his heart; when he had collapsed, never to rise again, on that filthy ramp outside the teeming football stadium.

A single tear escaped her eye, dropping onto the table in front of her. She did not wipe it away. It was a tear of deep sadness. But also a tear of healing, a tear of the soul. It belonged. Especially today.

On this same day, all those years ago, her sorrow had known no bounds. Her despair had reached a crescendo. When hope was a word that had no meaning. When the tears had threatened to drown her beneath their immense weight. When the pain had her clamped in its terrifying grip and would not let go. When there appeared to be no escaping the illusion.

It was the day when she had lost him. Her son. Forever.

But that was before the healing. It was before the understanding. It was before the truth.

And so today, the very same day as all those years ago when he had been taken from her, the illusion no longer frightened her. Even in the moments when it did.

For it was also the same day that another perfect soul, a beautiful baby boy, entered the world. Born to a young mother who was also very much alone, struggling with the whole weight of this mysterious world. Sixteen years ago, today. Sixteen-years-old, today.

A gust of cold air blew through the doorway as it suddenly opened. A young woman, tall and full of confidence, walked into the café, followed closely by a dog of brown, black and grey. And then, limping slightly, a boy – a young man, really. The one Jack had finally found. Instantly she was reminded of her own. The pain and sadness flooded over her. And so did the pride and joy.

"I'm telling you, Ev," the young woman was saying, "WJW made a mistake taking you to South Africa and it could cost him big when it comes to the custody hearing. I asked Mr. Pettitger, you know the guy who used to be a lawyer before he started teaching Politics A-levels, and he said that taking a minor out of the country without the mother's knowledge is a real no-go. So, how's that gonna look in front of the judge, hey?"

"I dunno, Tals, but sounds like you could be on to something there. It's def worth bringing it up at the hearing, cause we need all the ammo we can to keep WJW from takin me away from Mum."

The sound of a chair scraping against the caf's floor caught their attention. An old woman was standing slowly, clutching hold of her cane for support. She shuffled slowly over to where they were standing by the counter. It took a moment, but then he recognised her.

"Hello Atalia. Hello Brock," the old lady said with a smile of such care, such warmth, such humanity. She turned then, facing the boy directly.

"You don't know me, not yet at least. But you may have heard someone – a certain nurse perhaps – refer to me as The Chair."

And then the old lady with the long grey ponytail and the black walking stick – the same lady who had been sat in this very cafe the last three times he had been here – flashed another smile that told a thousand tales of love, of forgiveness, of wisdom, of understanding.

"Happy Birthday, Evan," she whispered. "I have been waiting here a very long while to meet you, but the time never seemed quite right – until now. Come, we have much to talk about. And many illusions to reveal together …"

What Next?

As you no doubt realised, Evan Banksky is not a real person. But the issues and challenges facing himself, his friends and his family, absolutely are. Violence, conflict, anger, relationship troubles, addictions, social media pressures, stress, destructive behaviour, self-harm, mental health issues, low self-esteem, confusion and misunderstanding – these are all part of the real world in which we all live.

In discovering the thinking which is the source of his destructive behaviour, Evan taps into the incredible superpower of his mind and uncovers the innate potential we all possess. **IHEART** – a non-profit organisation educating young people about their built-in resilience and natural mental health – was set up to give teenagers an opportunity to find out what Evan himself learned.

If any of that sounds relevant or helpful, check out **www.iheartprinciples.com** to see how you can get involved. Or just drop us an email: **info@iheartprinciples.com**

And if you are interested in finding out what happens next to Evan, Tals, Brock and the future of Project Illusion, then keep an eye out for the next book in the ILLUSION series ...

A Massive Thank You ...

Writing a book involves the contributions of a whole load of people, even more so when the author's knowledge about many of the subjects covered is extremely limited. Many friends and professionals generously offered their time and crucial input which richly informed the different parts of Evan's story, ranging from police booking procedures to gaming to school suspensions to surgery to "street" language to a single mother's decisions. So a huge thank you to: Dr. Anthony Kessel, Dan S, Meir Dove, Kim Miller, Simone Krok, Tali Ross, the helpful members of the Metropolitan Police, the brilliant baristas at Costa Coffee, and the many others who provided input and advice along the way. Eli R, Kelly Conway and Mary Mann all stepped forward at crucial stages to trawl through the manuscript, point out mistakes and suggest important changes. I listened more than I made out. Noga Applebaum and Rich Ryan both played vitally important roles in guiding me with excellent and critical feedback. Joanna Gilbert did a brilliant job with the cover. Thank you also Brian B for getting us going. Steve Emecz: you are one very supportive and patient publisher.

Many teachers and guides have shared great understanding and wisdom with me over the years, none more so than Valda Monroe and Keith Blevens. Their incredibly deep understanding of the superpower of the mind is the foundation for this book.

My sincere thanks goes to IHEART's small but growing core of supporters, trustees and Advisory Council members, all of whom are very generous in offering their support, time and expertise. And my deepest gratitude to those who have generously contributed by sponsoring chapters of this book.

I am privileged to work with an outstanding team of passionate, dedicated and talented colleagues at IHEART/Innate Health. Each one of Alex, Dana, Debbie, Gray, Jez, Jo, John, Kat, Raiut, Ruth, Shosh, Stacey, Terry, Zia and all our facilitators and practitioners are fulfilling a paradigm-shifting role in bringing about a transformation in how our young people are educated about their innate mental health and resilience.

When I am writing, the family generally sees less of me (not necessarily a bad thing, they claim) or, at the least, a more distracted version. For that and a multitude of other reasons, my six extraordinary boys deserve my heartfelt appreciation. More importantly – and especially as this is a story about a young man who uncovers his own innate resilience and superpower – they deserve my love.

And then, of course, there is Terry – an extraordinary wife and my greatest teacher.

Who are the Authors?

Brian and Terry Rubenstein have co-authored two previous books (well, Brian was sort of the ghost-writer for them). The Amazom.com best-seller, *EXQUISITE MIND – How a New Paradigm Transformed My Life and Is Sweeping the World,* tells the true story of Terry's journey from years of suffering to mental wellness. It's a good one. *The Peach Who Thought She Had to Become a Coconut,* is a series of essays on the power of thought and innate resilience. It's also a good one.

Terry is the founder and Head of Education for IHEART and the London-based Innate Health Centre. She is also the co-author of the innovative IHEART curriculum for young people and is widely recognised as a leading thinker, educator and speaker in the field of mental health and resilience. For over a decade, she has taught and impacted countless people through her uplifting training seminars, writings and online talks.

Brian, CEO of IHEART, is widely recognised as Terry's husband.

They are the joint parents of six wonderful sons, ranging in age from 6 – 22. And in case you were wondering, even their Cavalier King Charles Spaniel is a male!

What is IHEART?

A while back, Terry, Brian and the team set up a non-profit organisation called **IHEART – Innate Health Education and Resilience Training** – to address the crisis facing our youth.

The vision: a step-change in how young people perceive their wellbeing and mental health, creating resilient adults and contributing members of society.

The programme is brought to life through the dynamic IHEART curriculum which empowers the discovery of the built-in knowledge and confidence to manage the challenges that are a part of almost every teenager's life, such as: social media, anger & conflict, difference & prejudice, relationships, self-image, anxiety & stress, addictions, and bullying.

And as parents and teachers also have such an important role to play, IHEART runs Facilitator Training for teachers and organisational leaders as well as Parent & Teenager courses.

Partnering with schools, organisations and across families, the IHEART programme has already led to a significant increase in the resilience and wellbeing of many young people.

So go to **www.iheartprinciples.com** to get more information about this revolutionary project and to see how you can bring IHEART to your school, community or family.

Sponsors

The following very generous supporters have partnered with IHEART in empowering our young people to develop greater resilience, wellbeing and hope:

Andrea Dennis and Family

Roots and Journeys

This book has been generously sponsored in loving memory of:

Edith and Wally Stimler

Fabian Garcia Miller

Dr JSR

Anonymous